GROWING HOME

Growing Home

A NOVEL BY

Dori Stone

Stone, Dori, 1983- author.
     Growing home : a novel / by Dori Stone. -- Third
edition.
     pages cm
     SUMMARY: A homeless girl and her mother find solace
in a diverse local community garden and join the
struggle to preserve it.
     Audience: Grades 5-7.
     LCCN 2016908845
     ISBN 978-0-9976434-0-4
     ISBN 978-0-615-76651-5

     1. Homeless persons--Juvenile fiction. 2. Community
gardens--Juvenile fiction. 3. Mental health--Juvenile
fiction. [1. Homeless persons--Fiction. 2. Community
gardens--Fiction. 3. Mental health--Fiction.]
     I. Title.

PZ7.S87625Gro 2016   [Fic]
                    QBI16-600091

Cover design by Matt Stone and Ian Adair
Interior and cover illustrations © Jay Bonestell
www.bonestellstudios.com

This is a work of fiction. Names, characters, places, and incidents are
products of the author's imagination or are used fictitiously.

Dedicated to Morgan Cisar,
who planted the first seeds
of inspiration for this book

Acknowledgments

I would like to express gratitude to my parents, Ilona and Barry Stone, for nurturing the young writer in me from the beginning.

Many thanks to all who read the original manuscript and offered editing suggestions: Eric Greening, Lori Sievers, Quill Chase, Venus Powell, Nancy Koren, Jean Stafford, Bill Ingalls, Nancy Cohn, Stephenie Wilson, Gloria Wilson, Ann Bonestell, and my family. Your keen insights and feedback have been very helpful.

Thank you also to Agrarian Effort Co-op, for opening doors to the world of gardening and community; to Ted Zerger, for showing me your Peace Garden in Salina, Kansas; and to the South Central Farmers of L.A., for perseverance in a struggle that moved me deeply to begin this novel. Also to Bob Metz, for what you teach about the balance of wisdom and compassion, and to Tory Blue, for inspiring those pivotal lines about speaking from the heart.

Finally, words cannot express my appreciation to the Chase family for the bounty you've brought into my life these past few years— not only in gardens and vegetables, but in friendship, support, love, and the gift of a place to call home during the writing of this book.

1

WHEN WE FIRST moved to El Chorro the summer I was ten years old, I knew it wouldn't be for long.

"Just until we get back on our feet," Mom said. "This is a brand-new beginning for us, Tal."

Soon we'd have enough money to head up to Washington, where housing was cheaper, and get our very own place. "By the time school starts, we'll be all settled in," she told me.

I leaned my forehead against the tinted bus window, watching the blurred patterns of fields stretching into the distance, and smiled. *All settled in.* Just the two of us.

We'd been living at Uncle Jim's apartment in L.A. almost as long as I could remember, but lately he and Mom had begun to argue. He kept calling her a "grown woman" who should support herself, even though he knew she'd been looking everywhere for a new job. They argued about it every day, until finally Uncle Jim told us to leave. I remember that night, how I sat with my ear pressed to the bedroom door, trying to catch each word.

"You've had three years to get your life together, Nora," he said. "And you're no farther than the day you moved in!"

"Jim, don't you know I'm trying—" she began, but he wouldn't listen.

"What kind of example is this for your daughter? It's time to grow up, and staying here isn't helping!"

In the silence, I could imagine her clear blue eyes filling with tears. Uncle Jim wanted us to leave. There was no point arguing anymore.

So after school let out for summer, we packed our stuff and boarded the Greyhound bus to a place called El Chorro. Mom showed me where it was on a map, right in the middle of California, nothing around it but empty fields.

It was hot inside the bus, and the ride was taking forever. I sighed and pressed my face against the cool glass, trying to stop thinking about my friends back home and the way our lives were getting farther apart with every mile.

The bus arrived in the middle of the night, after I'd fallen asleep with my head propped against the seat's armrest.

"We're here," Mom whispered, giving my shoulder a gentle tug. "Come on."

We collected our bags and shuffled clumsily down the narrow aisle and out into the warm night air. Mom and I were the only passengers getting off in El Chorro, and the driver hastily yanked our suitcases from the luggage compartment and dumped them on the curb before climbing back aboard. The bus roared to life and pulled away with a belch of exhaust, leaving us suddenly alone in the empty parking lot beneath the dim glow of a street lamp.

Mom and I looked at each other. Then, without speaking, we picked up our stuff and headed toward the small depot with a CLOSED sign on the door. I watched anxiously as Mom traced her finger over a sign in the window.

"Well…" she said at last, "the bus here doesn't run at night. We'll have to walk."

We rearranged our things so they'd be easier to carry, cramming smaller bags into backpacks and tying jackets to the handles of suitcases, then set off down the dark sidewalk to look for a motel. We stopped at the first one we saw: a long, squat building with peeling paint and a flickering green vacancy sign.

Sighing with relief, I dragged our biggest suitcase into the front office and flopped down on top while Mom paid for a room. Morning seemed like weeks ago. I lay across our bags and squinted my eyes at the ceiling to make the lights melt into dancing, blurry circles. Maybe this was a dream, I told myself, and any minute we'd wake up back at the apartment: no more arguing, everything back to normal.

But Mom's words from earlier on the bus kept repeating through my head. *Just a couple months. By the time school starts, we'll be all settled in.*

I wanted to believe her. So there in the motel office on our first night in El Chorro, listening to the steady drone of cars on the freeway outside, I closed my eyes and told myself, again and again, that it wouldn't be for long.

2

W HEN I WOKE UP the next morning, Mom was sitting on the edge of our bed, flipping through a phone book and scribbling numbers. She leaned down to kiss my cheek.

"Did you sleep okay, Sweetheart?"

I stretched and nodded, looking around the small room with its TV set, chest of drawers, and yellow drapes. *Almost like a real house*, I thought to myself. Back at the apartment, Mom and I slept on a fold-out couch in the living room and kept our stuff in Uncle Jim's hallway closet, but this almost felt like a real bedroom in our very own place.

Later that morning, we checked out at the motel office and carried our suitcases down the street to the nearest bus stop. It was still early, but the sun felt hot as we trudged past gas stations and shops with signs in Spanish.

We were going to see Mom's old friend Hattie, who owned a big hotel where she and Mom worked a long time ago. I'd heard stories about fun, mischievous Hattie with fiery orange hair, who was Mom's best friend in high school but lost touch after Mom moved away. Now Hattie might be able to help us get back on our feet; she was the reason we'd come to El Chorro.

"I'm sure she'll be so excited to see me again, after all these years!" Mom said, grinning. "And to meet you, Tal."

After two bus rides and another long walk, we finally arrived at the Plaza Inn and entered an air-conditioned lobby with a shiny floor, chandeliers, and gold-rimmed mirrors. The woman at the front desk was busy talking to a group of men with briefcases, so Mom and I sat down on a stiff leather couch, luggage piled around us, and waited. The woman at the desk kept squinting in our direction, and when the businessmen left, she squinted again and asked, "May I help you?"

"Yes!" Mom practically leapt from the couch. "Thank you! Is this hotel still owned by Hattie Johnson? She's an old friend of mine, and I just got back in town so—"

"I'm sorry ma'am, but Ms. Johnson is not in right now. Did you… want to make a reservation?"

"Oh, no thanks. We're just passing by and thought we'd try to catch her. Would it be okay if we waited for a while?"

The woman glanced at our things again, a random assortment of scuffed suitcases, backpacks, and old shopping bags that seemed embarrassingly out of place in the shiny hotel lobby. She frowned. "I'm sorry, ma'am, but this lobby is reserved for our guests and their visitors. You're welcome to stop by later this afternoon to speak with Ms. Johnson."

The phone started ringing, and she slid a business card across the desk before returning to her computer.

Mom looked at me and sighed. "Alright… let's go."

We picked up our luggage and stepped back into the dizzying heat outside. Wavy lines rose from the asphalt, and our bags felt three times heavier than before. But we set off anyway, pausing several times to wipe sweat from our foreheads. By the time we reached a small park down the street, where Mom and Hattie used to take their lunch breaks, my ears were pounding and my neck felt drippy with sweat. Mom must have been uncomfortable too, because she dropped our two suitcases with a thud, sank onto the grass beneath a tree, and closed her eyes.

"What if Hattie doesn't remember you?" I asked after a while, leaning back against the tree trunk and tilting my head upward to look at the leaves.

Mom shook her head and smiled. "Nah, that's impossible. I can't wait to see the look on her face! We were always best friends, Hattie and I."

"Then how come she never came to visit?"

Mom pulled a blade of grass and twisted it between her fingers. "Oh, I don't know... we had some misunderstandings back then... just went our separate ways, you know?" She tossed the grass into the air and watched it fall lightly back down. "But that was a long time ago. Once friends, *always* friends! I'm sure she'll be so glad to see us."

She lay back on the grass with a carefree laugh, and I couldn't help laughing a bit too. Mom's happiness had always seemed the most contagious thing in the world.

I ran over to the playground, to dig tunnels through the moist gravel beneath all the hot, white sand. For a while, I even forgot we were in El Chorro, with nowhere to stay and all our belongings piled under a tree a few yards away. All I knew was the rusty squeaking of a swing set as I sailed back and forth in the hot breeze.

When we got hungry, Mom bought sandwiches from a gas station across the street, and we had a little picnic together on the grass. Later, after she'd returned to the gas station twice to use a pay phone, we gathered our bags and trekked back down the sidewalk to the hotel. The woman at the desk said Hattie would be with us soon, so we returned to the big leather couch and waited. Mom sat up taller now, blue eyes glittering, like a kid about to open birthday presents.

After a few minutes, a door beside the front desk opened and a tall blond woman in a silky suit that swished around her ankles came toward us, high heels clicking on the marble floor.

Mom rose to her feet, clutching her purse in both hands. "Hattie...? Is it really you?"

The woman smiled thinly, lips barely curved, like someone posing for an old-fashioned photograph. "Nora, my goodness, it's been so long."

But instead of laughing and throwing their arms around each other like I'd imagined, they both just stood there. The soft background music in the lobby seemed to get louder, and I could hear a clock ticking on the wall behind us.

"Hattie, this is my daughter Talia." Mom turned and put her arm out to me.

I rose from the couch, sweaty thighs peeling away from the leather, and put out a dirt-stained hand to shake Hattie's pale, manicured one. Was this really the red headed, fun-loving Hattie in all of Mom's stories?

"Well, what a surprise," she said, letting go of my hand. "It's nice to meet you, Talia."

Mom was unable to contain herself a moment longer. "I can't believe it's *you!*" she blurted, throwing her arms around her old friend. Hattie returned the hug with a few light pats and smiled, but it wasn't the kind of smile I'd expected.

"So, are you two just... traveling?" she asked, eyeing our luggage piled around the couch.

"Actually, we're sort of moving right now," Mom told her. "I got laid off a few months ago and haven't had luck finding work, so it's been pretty hard... but we're heading up to Washington. I hear everything's more affordable up there."

"Oh, so you're just passing through!" Hattie exclaimed, seeming a bit friendlier. "How long will you be here in town? Maybe we can go for coffee or something."

Mom shifted from one foot to the other. "Well, I'm guessing we'll be here a little while... a couple months anyway. Getting all the way up north is a bit out of my price range right now."

She didn't mention everything we'd sold just to buy our bus tickets to El Chorro.

"Well, that'll be nice, spending a bit of time in your old stomping grounds!" Hattie replied with a stiff, high-pitched laugh. "So where are you staying?"

Mom shifted again. "Actually, we don't really have anything lined up right now, and I was hoping maybe—"

"Nora, perhaps we'd better talk in my office," Hattie broke in, glancing at me.

Mom's smile had faded, her forehead creased, and I could see the vein in the side of her neck that always popped out when she felt upset. "Sweetheart, will you stay here with our bags for a minute?"

I nodded, disappointed, and sank back onto the couch as Hattie led Mom through a door by the front desk. At first the lobby was quiet again, but then Mom and Hattie must have begun talking louder, because bits of their conversation floated out from behind the desk.

"No, we *can't* just hire you back... our manager let you go for a reason, Nora... I already gave you a chance... we gave you a million chances!"

A door clicked shut and it was quiet again. I sat waiting for what seemed like forever, picking at a scab on my knee and feeling sorry for Mom, until finally she reappeared from behind the front desk, alone this time, face flushed and red.

"Come on, Tal, let's go."

Without a word, we picked up our bags and walked out the glass doors of the lobby into the blazing afternoon sun, lugging everything back down the sidewalk for the fourth time that day.

"Why doesn't Hattie want to help us?" I asked cautiously, once we'd reached the bus stop and were sitting together on the narrow metal bench.

Mom looked down at her lap and shook her head silently for a long time. "She's still angry about things that happened a long time ago. When we worked together, she loaned me some money... it's complicated, Tal."

"Oh." I hated when grown-ups said that things were too complicated.

"Just promise me," she said after a minute, voice wavering, "that you'll always give people a second chance. 'Kay? Everybody deserves a chance to start over."

I leaned my head on Mom's shoulder and let out a long sigh. Why didn't Hattie want to give us a chance? Couldn't she see Mom just needed a fresh start, to do everything right this time?

I didn't ask more questions. We sat there waiting for the bus, the heat and silence like heavy blankets draped around us. Mom gripped the suitcase handles so hard her knuckles turned white, and neither of us said another word until we were back at the little motel with peeling brown paint and a blinking vacancy sign.

∾

Our new room looked identical to the first one.

"Tal, how can people change so much?" she asked through tears, sinking onto the bed and burying her face in her hands. "I just don't understand how someone..." But the sentence got lost in sobs.

There was a lump in my own throat too, but I swallowed hard and held it there. The last thing she needed was *both* of us crying. If Mom's happiness was the most contagious thing in the world, then so was her sadness. It was like a big river that overflowed its banks and flooded everything, until the whole world was underwater.

I sat down on the bed and put my arm around her shoulder. "Maybe after she thinks about it more, she'll change her mind," I said hopefully.

"She's just a completely different person," Mom whispered. "I don't even know her anymore. Did you see the way she looked at us Tal? Like we were just bums on the street! Did it even cross her mind to offer an extra room, or loan us a little something to get back on our feet, or..."

She was crying too hard to continue. I sat there rubbing her back in silence, not knowing what else to do. Mom had just lost her only hope of a friend, and now we really had nowhere to go.

She reached for the tissue box on the nightstand, blew her nose a few times, and took a shaky breath. I rubbed her back some more, and we sat like that forever and ever.

∽

"I'm sorry Tal," she said after a while, wiping her eyes. "You shouldn't have to see this."

I gave her another hug and said not to worry. "You still have the number of that lady who needs a housecleaner, right? Maybe you can work for her."

Even though Hattie didn't personally offer to help, she had given Mom the business card of someone looking for a new housekeeper.

Mom didn't respond, and I got up from the bed stiffly, legs asleep from sitting so long. My hands and hair felt gritty with sand from the playground earlier that day.

"I'm going to take a bath," I announced.

Still no response, so I walked into our tiny bathroom and turned the tub faucet as high as it would go, then stared at my own solemn face in the mirror until steam fogged the glass.

I looked like a smaller, scrawnier version of Mom: a splash of freckles across the nose, the sparkle gone from her crystal blue eyes. Strands of limp brown hair hung in tangles around my face, and my neck was smudged with dirt where I'd wiped away the sweat that afternoon. I wondered if Hattie thought I looked untidy, and if that made things worse.

Sinking into the warm bathwater and gazing up at cracks in the ceiling, I could hear Mom starting to cry again in the other room. I lay there listening to her sobs and the drip-drip of water leaking from the faucet, thinking about how much could change in just a single day. I wondered why Hattie had acted the way she did, and why Mom seemed to feel things a hundred times stronger than anyone else.

Mostly, I wondered how many nights we'd stay at this motel, and where we'd go next. I stayed in the bathtub until the water was getting cold, my skin had wrinkled like raisins, and the room was finally quiet.

3

I N THE MORNING, Mom lay in bed staring at the wall for a long time. I kept suggesting that she hurry and call the lady's number on the business card, but she just said "I know" and kept lying there. Beginning to feel exasperated, I ventured to the motel office and brought a newspaper back to our room, found the employment page, and began reading through ads.

"Mom, look, you could work at the front desk of this car place!"

She shrugged.

"And there's a thrift store looking for cashiers. Here, I'll circle these for you."

I scanned the columns for good sounding jobs, paying close attention to the hours and salaries. Maybe it would be easier to find work in El Chorro than back home, where she spent weeks going for interviews without any luck.

"Here's a lady who needs a caregiver. She pays a lot, you should call her first." I drew a big star in the margin. "Mom, you should get up and start calling…"

"I know, Tal. I will."

But the morning dragged on, and she seemed unable to move. "Just give me some time," she said. "I don't want to sound upset on the phone."

So I waited, filling in black-and-white newspaper photos with my crayons. After a while, Mom sent me to the office to pay for another night at the motel and get her some coffee. I was worried. *Didn't the motel cost too much?*

Even after propping herself up in bed to drink the coffee, Mom still didn't get up or make any calls. After I'd finished re-reading my copy of *Charlotte's Web* for the fourth time, flipped through every TV channel, read the entire comics section of the paper, bought us lunch from a vending machine in the hall, and counted all the ceiling panels in our room, it was too much to bear. We couldn't just sit here all day!

"I'm going for a walk," I announced, crossing my fingers that she'd be too sad about her own problems to say no.

Mom nodded and mumbled to be careful, not go too far, and not talk to strangers.

Relieved to be free at last, I ran out the door and flung it shut behind me, skipping through the parking lot and twirling in circles around a few lamp poles on the way. The sun was already hot, but I didn't care. It just felt good to be outside, away from the motel room and Mom's sadness.

Eager to explore, I headed in the opposite direction from the bus stop where we'd gone before. At the corner stood a square white building with a sagging porch, surrounded by picnic tables. It looked almost like a one-room schoolhouse from the old days, I thought, but a wooden sign near the entrance read *El Chorro Buddhist Church*.

I crossed the street and continued through a neighborhood of small houses, all painted different colors—yellow, pink, turquoise—with front yards of patchy grass or bare dirt strewn with kids' toys, bicycles, and little plastic swimming pools. Some of the yards had clotheslines draped with laundry, and dogs who ran to the fence barking loudly as I passed.

Two younger kids stared at me from the other side of the street, then ran away yelling something in Spanish. The aromas of food cooking and faint sounds of television wafted into the street from open windows, and I ran my hand along the fence posts and imagined me and Mom living in a house like one of these someday, with our own yard and maybe even a dog.

The neighborhood ended at a wider, pot-holed road called Ito Street, lined with big trucks and vacant lots of weeds, junk piles, and old rusty cars. This was probably what Mom meant by not going too far, but something down the street had caught my eye.

Too curious to turn back, I crossed the road and headed down the sidewalk beside a tall chain-link fence, keeping my eyes straight ahead and ignoring the din of machinery and clanging metal. Up ahead was a long strip of brilliant yellow and green, much too bright for such a dusty, loud place. Was it a mural, or some kind of billboard?

I continued beyond the chain-link fence, where the sidewalk became narrower and crowded with prickly, dry weeds, then past a brick building with boarded-up windows. Boards and pieces of metal lay scattered in the dry grass.

Suddenly, it was right in front of me. A wall of *giant flowers*, towering above my head on stems as thick as poles, with fan-like leaves fluttering in the breeze. They were more like trees than flowers, I thought, like a whole forest of fire-fighter yellow, or a sky with a hundred glowing suns. I felt dizzy looking up at them. Bees whirled overhead, buzzing and landing on the flowers' wide gray centers. It was like something from *Alice in Wonderland*, or from a dream.

The ground at my feet was dusted with powder the color of egg yolks, filling cracks in the sidewalk and collecting around clumps of dry weeds. I craned my head up toward the flower tops for a long time. *Who would plant such beautiful things here? Why?* Filled with curiosity, I began walking again.

Just beyond the wall of flowers was a rusty gate with a small sign reading *Nihonmachi Community Garden.** On the other side of the gate, a winding dirt path disappeared into a thick, sprawling jungle of plants.

I suddenly noticed an old man with a wide straw hat, crouched on the ground near the gate, his hands in the soil. As I came nearer he looked up, tipped back the brim of his hat, and called out "Good afternoon!"

Mom had warned not to talk to strangers, but this man seemed so friendly that I hoped she wouldn't mind. He had a thin, wrinkled face, narrow eyes with deep smile creases, a small white beard, and a gentle smile.

"Is this your garden?" I asked timidly.

"No, no. It is for everyone." The man spoke with a faint accent, his voice so quiet I found myself leaning over the gate to hear.

"This is your first time coming here?" he asked.

I nodded.

"Ah, welcome. This is our community garden, where anybody can have a place to grow plants."

"Did you grow those big flowers?" I asked, pointing.

"Oh no," he replied, shaking his head and laughing a little. "They plant themselves! A long time ago, somebody planted flowers there. They made seeds, which fell to the ground and sprouted the next year… and this continues."

"Like kids growing up and having their own kids?"

"Yes, exactly like that."

"Cool!"

The old man's smile grew, revealing a chipped front tooth and more wrinkles than the lines on a roadmap. I watched as he lifted a tiny plant from a bucket beside him and pushed it

---

* For translation of non-English words, see glossary at end of book.

into the ground, scooping the soil into a bowl-shape around it with muddy hands.

"What are you planting?"

"This is *senburi*," he replied in the same soft voice. "In Japan, where I am from, it is a very important medicine."

"A medicine?" I repeated, confused.

The man nodded, lifting three more plants from his bucket. "Yes. *Senburi* is wonderful for stomach ache, poor appetite, any problem of digestion."

He gently pushed another plant into the ground and shaped a bowl of soil around it, then rose and came over to the gate. I was surprised to see how small he was for a grown-up, even shorter than Mom, with a long button-down shirt and drawstring pants that swung loosely over his thin frame. He must have been old, I thought, to have so many wrinkles and such white hair, but his movements were easy and smooth like a boy's. Beside the gate, he turned on a faucet and filled his bucket, then returned to pour water around each plant.

"Would you like to come inside and see the garden?" he asked when he had finished.

I hesitated. I was curious what lay down the path, inside that big jungle of green... but Mom might be getting worried.

"I have to go now," I told him. "But can I come back later?"

"Of course," he replied. "You are welcome here. You could even have a space to grow some plants, if you like."

I stood silently for a moment, wanting to tell him how we were actually moving to Washington and having a fresh start, until Mom got too sad to keep going. But instead, I just thanked the old man and turned to run back down the sidewalk. I ran as fast as I could, past the wall of giant sunflowers and the truck yards of clanging metal, through the colorful neighborhood, all the way back to the little brown peeling-paint motel.

❧

I arrived breathless, throwing open the door of our small room. Mom had finally gotten out of bed and was sitting on a chair by the window, writing something. Her eyes were red from crying.

"I started writing her a letter," she muttered, crumpling the pages. "But what's the use."

"Did you make any calls yet?"

She sighed. "No, Sweetheart. Not yet. This has been such a blow... I just need some time to feel better, 'kay?"

We don't have time! I wanted to shout. But instead, I began telling her about the garden with the giant flowers.

"It's just a few blocks away," I said, stretching the truth a little. "Can I go back later?"

She frowned. "You said you were talking to a man there?"

"Yeah, but he's really nice. He's from Japan, and he was planting a Japanese plant that's like medicine for bellyaches, and he says that's a place where *lots* of people grow things!"

She thought for a long moment, then sighed again. "Just be careful, okay? I know it's safer here than L.A... but still. Come back if anything seems weird."

I nodded with excitement and began counting the hours until I'd be free to explore again.

Finally, later that evening when it was a bit cooler outside, I headed back to the garden with the wall of sunflowers that had planted themselves. The old man was nowhere to be seen, but he *had* said I was welcome anytime... I paused for a moment, then carefully unlatched the gate and headed down the little dirt path.

I could hardly believe my eyes. From inside, the garden felt like another world, a whole neighborhood of yards with no houses, each surrounded by fences of wire, boards, woven branches, and shipping pallets. Most of the yards had gates with painted signs saying things like *Bienvenidos* or *Familia Santos*, decorated with strings of colorful flags or hanging bundles of dried plants.

This was the 'jungle' I'd seen from the sidewalk: a whole world of plants in more shades of green than I'd known existed. There were plants spilling from barrels, boxes, and kitchen pots, plants growing in tidy rows along the ground, plants sprawling in unruly patches that climbed up fences and twisted their way into the tree branches overhead. Huge, spiny cacti rose into the sky beside giant flowering bushes, with what seemed like a hundred dragonflies swooping through the air above it all. Smaller pathways branched off the main path like narrow alleyways, and I moved slowly through the bright green maze, staring in awe.

Some of the little yards were filled entirely with plants, but some also had space for tables, barbecues, and small sheds. Wind chimes hanging from the trees clanged softly in the light breeze. Even the air here seemed to be alive, filled with humming and buzzing and chirping, like an invisible choir hidden among the leaves. Piled along the pathways were all sorts of things: bricks and wooden stakes, little sculptures and painted ceramic pots, buckets, children's toys, even an old toilet filled with purple flowers. A person could look around here forever, I thought, and still not see everything.

All the yards seemed to have one thing in common: rows of dirt sculpted into long hills and valleys, with plants the shape of fountains growing in the valleys. Whatever that was, it sure seemed popular.

I discovered one yard that was different from all the rest, surrounded by a high chain-link fence covered with flowers. There were bright pink and orange blooms, dark purple, golden yellow and pale blue, as though somebody had stirred up a rainbow and splattered it all around. Vines with deep red blossoms spilled over the fence, and giant tissue-papery petals towered on stalks overhead. I stood still for a while, peering through the fence as if through a kaleidoscope.

Finally, I continued down the path and discovered that it ended at an open area with a few picnic tables, a rusty metal shed, and one very large tree with branches reaching down to the ground. A striped brown cat with a missing ear appeared from nowhere and rubbed against my ankles, meowing.

"Hey," I whispered, bending down to stroke its back. "Do you live here?"

On one side of the big tree, the branches had been removed to create a doorway. Gasping in delight, I walked through the portal and found myself in a secret room with leafy walls so dense I could hardly see out. I turned in a slow circle, gazing at the canopy of leaves around me.

Suddenly there was a rustling from behind and I whirled around, startled to see someone entering the tree-room. In the opening stood a stout woman with a long denim skirt and faded T-shirt, partially gray hair tied in a bun and a large gold crucifix hanging around her neck.

"*Dios mío*, you scared me!" she laughed.

"Is—is it okay?" I stammered. "That I'm here?"

She nodded and laughed again, face melting into a warm smile. "*Claro*, yes yes yes, of course. You are new here, no?"

I nodded shyly. "Yeah. My name's Talia, but I don't really live here. My mom and I are just passing through."

She turned to peer through the opening in the leaves. "Ah, your mom is here too?"

"No, I'm just taking a walk."

Her brow furrowed. "By yourself, *mija*?"

I nodded. "We're staying in the motel down the street. It's okay, my mom said I could go."

She hesitated for a moment before breaking into another silver-toothed smile. "Well, you are welcome to look at the garden. My name is Ignacia, but everyone here calls me Nacha. Would you like to see my family's plot?"

I nodded again, excited, and followed her over to a yard with a fence made of sticks and string. Hanging above the gate was a frayed piece of yellow cloth painted with the words *Familia Jiménez*.

"This is where my husband and I have our garden," she told me. "We plant *maíz*, beans, *chiles*, watermelon, tomato, *hierbas*... *hierbas*, how do you say in English?"

She frowned a moment, then chuckled, shaking her head. "My English is not very good."

"Your garden's really pretty," I told her.

Nacha beamed. "*Que preciosa*! What a sweet girl you are."

She stooped to turn on a faucet beside the path, pulled a long hose through the gate, and placed her thumb in front of the water to make a gentle spray.

"What are you watering?" I asked, recognizing the rows of fountain-shaped plants.

She raised her eyebrows in surprise. "This? This is *elote*! El *maíz*! In English you call it, let me see... corn."

"Whoa, those are corn plants? It seems like everybody here planted some."

"*Claaaro*," she laughed. "This is our most important plant! In Mexico we use it to make everything. *Tortillas, tamales, pozole*... everything. Even in United States, we need to have our little field of *elote*, to help remember who we are!"

"So all those tiny plants are going to make corn?" I asked, trying to imagine. "Like corn on the cob?"

Nacha waved her hose over the small plants, causing them to sway and bend under the spray. "Yes, *mija*... but first, they will grow very strong and tall, higher than your head. And this is not corn for eating fresh. It is a special kind from México, for making tortillas."

"You make tortillas?" I tried to picture someone baking tortillas like giant cookies, instead of going to the grocery store.

"Yes… when I was a little girl, all the women in our town woke up early *early* in the morning to make tortillas for the families. I learned this from my mother, and she learned from her mother… back then, we did everything."

"Not anymore?"

"No. People buy from the store now, because it's easier." She looked at me and wrinkled her face. "But those are not the same. They have no flavor, like tortillas *hecho a mano*. You know, the ones made by our hands."

I bent down and touched one of the bright green leaves, now glistening with little droplets of water, trying to believe that someday this small plant would make entire corncobs. I guess I'd always known corn was something you could grow, but I never pictured tortillas coming from a garden too!

Nacha went to shut off the water and returned with a roll of string. "Now I'm going to tie up these tomatoes," she said, kneeling beside a row of bushy plants.

"Tie them up?" I repeated, puzzled.

She nodded and explained that some plants could support themselves, but others needed poles and string in order to stand up straight. *Support* themselves… the words reminded me of Mom and Uncle Jim's arguments, and I wondered if he thought Mom and I were like tomato plants growing on the walls of his apartment, needing support.

Nacha tied one end of the string to a metal stake in the ground, pulled it across the row of tomato plants, and held them upright while she tied the string at the opposite end.

"Do you want help?" I offered, noticing that it seemed difficult to hold everything in place at once.

She looked surprised and happily agreed, showing me where to hold the plants while she pulled and tied the string. I liked how the leaves smelled—sharp and fresh—and how they stained my hands bright yellowish-green as we worked.

Once we'd finished, Nacha stood and brushed her hands on her long skirt. "Now I'm going to pick some lettuce and *cilantro* for dinner and then go home to my husband. Don't stay too late here, *mija*, it's going to become dark soon. Would you like that I walk with you to the motel?"

I thought about Mom, lying in bed or sitting by the window, face pale and expressionless.

"That's okay," I told her. "I can go by myself. But thanks for showing me your garden."

She smiled and gave my head a little pat. "Thank *you* for helping me. Wait, take this to your mom." She pulled a folding knife from her pocket and cut a flower similar to the ones by the sidewalk but smaller. "Here is something to take when you leave, to remember El Chorro."

"Wow, thanks!" I reached out to take the hairy stem with its bright yellow bloom. "My mom will love this... I think it'll make her happy."

"God bless you, *mija*," Nacha called out as I walked back toward the main path.

I headed through the green maze of the garden, let myself out the gate, and for the second time that day, ran down the sidewalk back to our motel. The streetlights had turned on, the sky was fading to purple, and I hoped Mom wouldn't be worried that I'd been gone so long. I was excited to give her the flower and to tell about Nacha, the corn plants, and the huge tree with a secret room inside.

But when I opened the door and burst into our little room, I discovered that the drapes were closed, the food on the nightstand untouched, and Mom had already fallen asleep.

4

I RETURNED TO THE GARDEN the next day, once it became obvious that Mom wasn't getting up or calling for jobs. I'd already walked down the street to a gas station that morning to buy some muffins and orange juice, which, to my relief, Mom managed to eat. We sat together at the little table in our room, using the plastic wrappers from our muffins as plates.

On the center of the table was Nacha's flower, its stem cut short to fit inside a plastic cup from the bathroom. Mom kept her eyes on the bright circle of yellow petals as we ate, and I tried to cheer her up by talking about the garden. She listened patiently as I chatted about this and that, but her responses were still too quiet and her smile too sad. I knew there was nothing to do but wait.

I spent the rest of the morning watching cartoons on TV while Mom composed three more drafts of a letter to Hattie, all of which wound up crumpled in the bathroom trash basket. After the third failed attempt, she said "what's the point," sat with her face in her hands for a long time, then finally went back to bed.

When I got tired of watching TV, I ate a few stale pretzels left over from our bus ride, drank a glass of water from the bathroom faucet, stared out the window for a while, then took out my crayons and the brand-new red notebook Uncle Jim had given me. I opened it to the inside cover and drew a picture of a big white house with a chimney and light blue curtains, a grassy yard, and a dog chasing after a ball. Then I drew Mom and me standing together in front of the house beside some tall yellow flowers. As soon as we were settled, I decided, I wanted to plant our own garden.

I flipped through the Real Estate section of the newspaper, looking at houses for sale. Even the smallest ones cost a lot of money, but at least in Washington they would be cheaper. I could hardly wait.

But how would we ever go to Washington, if Mom didn't get out of bed? I tried again to persuade her, but she said she didn't feel good and please not to nag.

"Can I go back to the garden?" I finally asked, later that afternoon.

She was quiet for a long time.

"Mom?"

"I dunno, Tal... I mean, what if there are some not-very-nice people around there? I don't know if you should be walking around alone like this."

"Mom, the people I met there yesterday were super nice, I promise! It's not like L.A., remember?" Suddenly I had an idea. "Do you want to come with me and see the garden, and meet them?"

She sighed. "Tal, I don't want to talk to anyone right now. I don't feel well."

"Well, I'm bored," I complained. "We've just been hanging around here for two whole days."

"I know..." She pulled the blankets up to her neck and sighed again. "It isn't fair for you to be stuck here like this... none of this is fair to you..." Her voice broke and eyes filled up again with tears. "I'm so sorry, Tal."

"Don't worry," I said, putting one hand gently on her shoulder. "It's okay."

Mom managed a weak smile, telling me to go ahead but be careful. I nodded and bent down to give her a kiss.

"And don't stay too long, 'kay?"

"Okay."

Then finally I was out the door and free once again, running through the parking lot and down the sidewalk in the late afternoon sunshine, back to the garden.

∾

The old man was in the same place where I'd met him the day before, pouring water into the bowl-shapes of dirt around each plant. I stood quietly at the gate for a minute, watching. When the bucket was empty, he shook out the remaining few drops and turned around.

"Why hello! You are back." He smiled and made a little bow, heading over to the faucet by the gate. "Welcome again."

"Do you have to water those plants every day?" I asked.

He positioned his bucket beneath the faucet and shook his head. "Only when they are small and getting accustomed to their new home. We all need some extra care, when we are in a new place."

I pictured Mom in bed back at the motel and wondered if that's what was happening to her. Maybe she just needed some time and extra care too.

"Later," the old man continued, turning off the water, "their roots will grow down into the soil and make a home, where they can find their own water."

I peered over the gate as he watered each remaining plant.

"Would you like to come in and see the garden?" he asked once he'd finished.

I nodded eagerly, and he unlatched the gate and motioned for me to follow to where he'd been working. Beside the four *senburi* plants were more bowl-shapes of dirt with their own little plants in the middle. We squatted down to look closer, and the old man pointed with his finger to the places on each stem where curled-up baby leaves were just beginning to unfold.

"The longer you look," he said softly, "the more you will see."

It was true. Up close, I discovered that each plant had its own unique leaf shape and shade of green, and that some had tiny hairs while others were smooth and glistened with drops of water.

"This is *kuko*," he said, touching the leaves of one plant. "It helps those suffering from fatigue. And here is *shiso*, a tasty vegetable but also useful for inflammation. And this one is *oninyogara*, for curing headaches."

"Do you have a plant for curing sadness?" I asked, sort of kidding.

He looked up at me and raised his eyebrows. "Sadness? Hmm. Yes, over here." He motioned for me to follow down the gravel pathway, stopping to kneel beside a bush covered in delicate yellow flowers.

"Saint John's Wort," he said. "For easing depression."

I bent over and examined the small, oval-shaped leaves. "Does it work?"

The old man tilted his head from one side to the other, thinking. "Yes, I suppose. But it cannot do everything. We all have happiness inside us already, you see, and perhaps this plant can help us to find it." He stroked a leaf thoughtfully for a moment. "If we are looking."

He peered at me from under his wide-brimmed hat, squinting in the bright sunlight. "Are you feeling sad?"

I thought about it for a moment. *Was I?* There were plenty of things to feel sad about, after all. My friends were back in L.A., Hattie had turned out awful, and we had nowhere to go.

"Maybe a little bit," I said. "But it's mostly my mom."

"Then perhaps you can see if she likes this," he said, breaking off several twigs. "Just make a tea... boil water and put the leaves and flowers in for ten minutes, with the teacup covered, then take them out."

I reached out to take the leafy stems. "I'll try... I've never made tea like that before."

"Very easy," he said. "But hurry while they are fresh! If she likes it, I will give you more. A person must drink this tea for several weeks, before it can begin to help."

I nodded vigorously and thanked him, promising to do it right away. The old man smiled and bowed his head as I turned and ran down the main path toward the gate.

Back in our room, I stripped some flowers and leaves into a cup, then plugged in the electric coffee-maker to heat water. After covering the tea with a magazine for ten minutes as the old man had instructed, I removed the soggy leaves with a plastic fork and carried the cup over to Mom's bed.

"Here Mom, I made you some tea."

She opened her eyes, looking surprised.

"It's from a plant called Saint John-something. It's supposed to make you happier."

She looked up at me with a puzzled expression, but at least she took the cup.

"It's from that garden," I said. "Remember the man I met there? He knows how to use plants for curing all sorts of things, even sadness."

She looked down at the tiny remnants of leaves floating in the water and didn't answer.

"Like if you have a headache or need more energy, he knows which plant to use. I bet he has a cure for *everything*!"

"Well, remember not everything people say is true," she said, reaching out to pat my arm. "Thanks, though. You're sweet to make this for me."

"You should come see the garden," I told her. "It's so pretty. There are a zillion flowers, and all these food plants, and a tree that has a room inside! And the people there said I can come back anytime."

I kept talking about the garden as Mom slowly sipped her tea, and neither of us said a single word about Hattie or phone calls or where we were going next.

5

I DON'T KNOW IF it was the tea or not, but Mom seemed almost like a new person the next morning. I woke up to find her bed neatly made, the curtains open, and the sound of water running in the bathroom. *Maybe today we'll finally get out of here,* I hoped. *Maybe at least she'll start looking for jobs!*

And sure enough, when Mom emerged from the bathroom still wrapped in a towel, she blew me a kiss and began rummaging through her purse for the business card Hattie had given her.

"Wish me luck, Tal," she said, picking up the receiver.

I held my breath as she dialed.

"Hi, I got your number from my… um… friend, Hattie Johnson. She said you're looking for a cleaning lady?"

She paused, twisting the phone cord nervously around her index finger.

"Yes, I do… yes… mm-hmm… my own supplies? No, not right now, but— oh, yes, I see. Sure, that would be great! Let me just grab a pen. Is that near a bus line? My car's, um, in the shop right now… Sure, that's fine. At Fifth and Arlington? Okay, great."

I couldn't believe my ears. *Was she really getting some work?* Mom must have felt the same way, because she looked at me

and wiggled her eyebrows up and down. This was definitely
not the same Mom who'd been lying in bed listlessly the day
before!

"Oh, and do you mind if I bring my daughter along? She's
ten... yeah, very well behaved." She smiled at me and rolled
her eyes.

"Okay, great, we'll see you at two! Bye now."

She hung up the phone and let out a big breath. "Tal, she
wants to show me the house and have me clean *this afternoon,*
as a trial! Can you believe that?"

I jumped up from the bed and gave her a big hug. Mom
had spent week after week making phone calls back in L.A.,
without any luck. Could she really be getting a job so easily?
Maybe going to visit Hattie hadn't been entirely bad after all.

"Well, we'll see how it goes." she added hesitantly. "This
lady Denise sounds really picky."

"Do I have to go too?" I asked, lying back down and tracing
patterns on the bedspread with my index finger. "Couldn't I
just go back to that garden instead?"

She looked out the window and frowned. "Tal, that idea
worries me. I don't want you just hanging out in public places
alone... Come with me for today, okay?"

I sighed and rolled over to face the wall. It would be a
boring afternoon, but at least she might get a job.

We took one bus to the transit center downtown, then a
second bus to the neighborhood where Denise lived. It was
another hot day, and I lagged behind as Mom walked briskly
down the sidewalk, glancing every few minutes at her watch.
The houses here were fancy and farther apart, with big green
lawns and iron gates. Denise's gate was open, and we turned

and headed up the driveway. Pausing at the doorstep, Mom wiped her forehead with one wrist and smoothed down her hair. She was wearing her nicest blouse, hair tied up in an old-fashioned bun. A few dark strands had escaped and were plastered in sweat along her neck, and her face was flushed pink with the heat.

"You look really nice," I told her. "Don't worry."

She rang the bell, and a woman in bright blue jogging shorts and slippers opened the door, introducing herself as Denise and shaking both our hands firmly. She stepped back and invited us inside, where the air was cool and smelled like air freshener and laundry detergent. Standing in the entryway to a high-ceiling living room with a shiny piano and framed photographs above the fireplace, I thought everything looked spotless already. Did she even *need* a housekeeper?

I gazed around in curiosity as Denise explained to Mom about how their old "cleaning girl" had gone suddenly back to Mexico, so now a lot of people in this neighborhood were desperate to find someone new.

"The last girl we tried spilled a gallon of bleach all over the rug in the guest bedroom, can you believe that? And my friend Vicki had another girl steal some rings last week. It's just so hard to find someone you can trust anymore."

Denise motioned for us to follow her into the immaculate kitchen, where we drank with relief from tall glasses of ice water as she continued talking.

"This place is such a beast to keep up. It's older than it looks, and there are just so many nooks and crannies... I'll be glad if this works out, because I'm at the end of my rope!"

She gave Mom a bunch of instructions about all-purpose cleansers, vacuum bags, stain remover, furniture polish, and cat litter, and I hoped fervently that Mom would remember everything and do a good job.

"Well, I'll be in my office if you need anything," Denise finally said. "Talia, you can play in the living room or backyard while your Mom's working, okay Hon?"

So while Mom cleaned the already-clean house, I played outside, examined all the framed photographs on the living room walls, finished reading *Charlotte's Web* for the fifth time, and finally took out my red notebook from Uncle Jim and decided to make up a story of my own.

I wrote about a family who lived in a two-story, yellow house with a piano, a yard, and a dog named Waggles. One day, an old friend from long ago came to visit with her ten-year-old daughter. She couldn't find a job and needed help, and the family said, "Stay with of us, of course, there's plenty of space!" So for a while, they all lived together in the big yellow house, and the girl played with the family's kids and their dog Waggles every single day, until finally her mom saved up enough to buy their own house. They chose one in the same neighborhood, so they could still see their friends. Then they had a big moving-in party and got their own dog, named Waggles Jr., and lived happily ever after.

When Mom finished cleaning, I showed her my story. She smiled when I read the ending, but her smile still seemed a bit sad and tired. It had taken all afternoon to clean the house, and I hoped Denise wouldn't think she was too slow.

"There were a few little things," Denise commented, "but you'll get the routine. It's just great to have someone in here again. I'll have to tell my neighbors about you! Do you have any time next week? Thursdays are usually best for me, but I should get your number—" She pulled out her cell phone.

Mom took a quick breath and folded her hands together. "Oh, we just moved here a few days ago, so our phone line's not hooked up yet. Can I give you a call in a day or two, once we're more settled?"

"Oh, I see!" Denise pumped her head up and down. "Well I'm impressed that you could even *come* today, in the midst of moving and everything! Moving can be such a stressful time, I know."

Mom gave a small shrug. "It's nice to get work so soon. Thank you for—"

"Oh thank *you*. You have no idea what a big relief this is. Maybe things will finally get back to normal around here!"

She wrote a check, handed it to Mom, and walked us to the front door.

Heading back down the driveway, I held Mom's hand and swung it back and forth happily. "Isn't that good? You have a job!"

She nodded but still looked serious. "Cleaning just one person's house isn't enough, Tal. I need a real full-time job."

"But maybe you can work for her neighbors too!"

"Maybe."

I could tell she wasn't in the mood for talking, so when we reached the bus stop, I buried my head in my notebook and started another story. This one was about a magic plant that made people happy all day if they ate it for breakfast. I kept writing during the entire bus ride downtown and all the way back to the motel.

When we got to our room, I ran immediately to the desk to see what remained of the plant the old man had given me. It was like a fairytale, I thought. Like "Jack and the Beanstalk." *A stranger gives a girl a mysterious plant, and things start getting better for her and her mom.* I knew he'd said it wouldn't happen so fast, because a person needed to drink the tea for several weeks first… but still. I wanted to believe in magic.

"Would you like some more of that special tea from the garden?" I asked, starting to break off the remaining leaves and flowers. But Mom flopped onto the bed and shook her head, reaching for the TV remote and clicking absently through channels.

I looked down at the twigs in my hand, disappointed, and began to wonder if they were really anything special after all. The leaves had gone limp from sitting in the open air all day, and the little yellow petals had shriveled and fallen off. Feeling suddenly irritated, I scooped up the entire pile, walked to the bathroom, and dumped the remains of Saint-John-whatever-it-was into the wastebasket.

Then I curled up under the table and opened my notebook. My fourth grade teacher had said absolutely anything could happen in a story, so I wrote page after page about the magic plant that could cure sadness, make people kind to others, or help them find a job. Most important of all, it could magically lead people to the perfect home, just waiting for them. Then they could start a garden and put that plant in the ground to keep growing, and they could eat it for breakfast every single day and live happily ever after.

I breathed a sigh of satisfaction and closed my notebook. This time, I decided not to show my story to Mom.

6

AS IT TURNED OUT, three of Denise's friends wanted Mom to clean their houses too, and the next few days were nothing but a lot of waiting. Waiting for the bus, waiting while Mom scrubbed and vacuumed and mopped, waiting at the bank while someone told her about money loans and why we couldn't get one. ("Too complicated to explain," she told me again.) Waiting at the laundromat and Department of Social Services, waiting in line at the food bank to get cans of soup and boxes of graham crackers. Waiting to move to Washington. Waiting to have our own place. *How much longer*, I wanted to ask. *Will I spend the entire rest of my life waiting for things?*

Then, when it felt like I couldn't endure one more boring day, something lucky happened. Mom had finished cleaning in time to catch an earlier bus that afternoon, and we were sitting on the curb at the bus stop, eating tacos for dinner.

"Hey Mom…" I began hesitantly, "since you're done early, do you think maybe we could go over to the garden this evening? I really want to show you."

She looked tired and seemed about to say no, but then she reached over and ruffled my hair. "You've been an angel, Tal. I wish you didn't have to deal with all this. Alright, let's go see that garden you keep talking about."

The bus was crowded with other people going home from work, so I sat on Mom's lap until we reached the stop near the motel. The summer evening sun still hovered just above the tops of buildings, making us squint as we walked down the sidewalk toward the garden.

There were lots of people outdoors now in the neighborhood of colorful houses: some taking laundry off clotheslines or relaxing in lawn chairs, a few kids kicking a soccer ball in the street.

"Maybe we can live in a place like that someday," I said, pointing to one of my favorite houses.

Mom nodded wistfully, and I could tell she was dreaming about someday up in Washington too.

"Here we are!" I announced, when we finally arrived at the wall of sunflowers. I took Mom's hand and led her through the gate and down the main path. The old man with the medicine-plants was nowhere to be seen, but a few other people were around, kneeling on the ground or spraying water on their corn plants.

I explained to Mom that those fenced yards were called "plots," and that each plot belonged to someone who could grow whatever they wanted. Her eyes grew wide when we entered the leafy tree-room by the picnic tables, and she tilted her head back and turned in a slow circle, just like I had.

"Now let me show you the tomatoes I helped with!" I exclaimed, leading her back down the path.

To my delight, Nacha was there again, holding a rusty watering can above an assortment of plastic yogurt containers filled with soil. She looked up when she heard us coming, then broke into a big smile.

"*Bueno*, look who's here again! And I see that you brought your mom?"

I nodded happily. "Mom, this is Nacha."

"Hello, hello, it is a pleasure to meet you," Nacha said, coming over to the gate.

"This is a lovely garden you have," Mom told her.

Nacha beamed. "And this is a lovely *daughter* you have!" she replied. "Talia told me you here are in El Chorro only for a small time?"

"Yeah, we're on our way up to Washington," Mom said, sounding more confident than she had in a while. "But I have a few jobs here now, so we'll be around for a bit."

"Ah...it is just the two of you, no?"

Mom nodded. "Yep, just me and Tal."

"And you are going to work with your mom?" Nacha asked, turning toward me with raised eyebrows.

"Well, I've been taking her along for now. Tal's great about that," Mom said, giving my shoulder a squeeze.

"*Qué preciosa*," Nacha crooned. "You are a big help to your mama, I see."

Mom smiled at me and nodded.

"Well, you are always welcome here," Nacha went on. "I think Talia would enjoy to play with my *ahijados*—how do you say in English? Not nephews, but...hmm...godchildren, yes! They are here always on Saturdays. The little girl is almost the same age," she said, motioning toward me, "and she speaks very good English. And the boy too. Would you like to come tomorrow and meet them?"

I stood on my tip-toes and looked up at Mom. "Can I? *Please*?" Playing with other kids in the garden sounded way better than another day of housecleaning.

"And I will be here too," Nacha added, giving me a wink. "Don't worry, I will care for Talia like she is my own daughter."

"You'll be staying all day?" Mom asked hesitantly. "I'm working all the way across town, and I don't want to leave her alone..."

"No no no *claro*, don't worry. There is so much work to do, we always stay until night. Parents, *tíos*, the whole family, we all are watching the kids. I promise you her safety."

Mom smiled and seemed to relax a bit.

"The garden is good for the children," Nacha added. "It is good that they play under the sun and help their parents to grow some food, no? Saturday is a very good day here."

"Okay, I guess that sounds fine," Mom finally agreed. "Gosh, that's really nice of you. I'm sure she'll have a better time here than coming to work with me."

I jumped up and down, nodding my head. Tomorrow I could stay in the garden and play with other kids! I wouldn't think once all day long about jobs or saving money or getting settled. I wanted to run and throw my arms around Nacha.

"*Claro, claro*, no problem! Please do not worry at all," she repeated, picking up the watering can again.

The sun had already dipped below the trees, and Mom thanked Nacha again before we headed back down the path toward the entrance of the garden.

Isn't it nice there?" I asked her, as we walked down the sidewalk past the deserted truck yard.

Mom nodded. "I'm glad you'll be with some other kids tomorrow. Nacha seems like a sweet lady."

The evening air had finally cooled a bit, and mosquitoes buzzed around our ears as I held Mom's hand and skipped all the way back to the motel.

ॐ

"Vicki wants me to come every week," Mom said that evening, sitting on the bed while I rubbed her stiff neck and shoulders. "And Denise too. So maybe I can do that entire neighborhood for the summer."

"That's so lucky!" I exclaimed. "If you clean a house every day, can we still move to Washington and get our very own place before school starts?"

She reached back and gave my hand a squeeze. "I'll try my hardest."

Mom seemed tired and didn't say much else until we'd turned off the lights and were lying in bed.

"Tal, we can't keep staying here night after night," she sighed. "It's too expensive... almost everything I earned today went for food and another night in this place. I won't be able to save anything."

I stared up at the dim ceiling, my eyelids growing heavy. "Then where can we go?"

It was quiet for a long time, and I must have fallen asleep before she answered.

7

THE NEXT MORNING, Mom and I walked back to the garden, where we found Nacha kneeling beside her tomato plants. Mom thanked her several times, gave me a hug and kiss, and said she'd be back as early as she could.

I stood at the gate for a minute, feeling suddenly shy, until Nacha motioned to come inside. She introduced me to her husband, Victor, who didn't speak English but tipped his hat and smiled warmly.

They showed me how to pull out a plant called 'bindweed' from around the tomato plants, digging out the stringy white roots so any leftover pieces in the soil wouldn't sprout again.

"But do not take this one!" she said, pointing. "That is *verdolaga*, a weed that is good to eat. We like to cook it with onions and chiles all summer."

We had already finished pulling most of the bindweed when I heard kids' voices from somewhere in the garden.

"Ah, the family is here!" Nacha announced, brushing dirt off her hands. "Come, Talia, I will introduce you."

She led me to a large plot bordered by cactus plants as tall as trees, with pink oval fruits covered in spines. Inside the plot, two guys in baseball caps were pounding metal stakes noisily into the ground, while nearby, a woman with a long braid watered plants with a hose. On a small card table in the middle of the plot, a battery-powered radio blared static and bouncy Mexican music, and underneath the table, a girl with flip-flops and long dark pigtails crouched on the ground beside a pudgy, runny-nosed baby.

"*Buenos días!*" Nacha called out as we approached.

The woman turned in our direction and nodded with a smile, and the girl sprang instantly from under the table as the baby puckered his face and let out a wail. She turned around, hastily scooped him up, and ran to the front gate.

"Good morning, Lina!" Nacha greeted her. "Look, I have brought you a friend!"

The girl bounced the baby on her hip and stared at us with wide eyes. She was smaller than me, with skin the color of cinnamon, a missing front tooth, and gold stud earrings. The baby also had dark hair and eyes, and he seemed too heavy for the girl's thin arms.

"Is that your brother?" I asked.

"My cousin," she said in a soft, high voice, looking from me to Nacha and then back.

"Yes, this is Raulito our *bebecito!*" Nacha replied in singsong, reaching out to take the baby and gathering part of her skirt to wipe his nose.

Just then, a boy walked up from behind her, pushing a wheelbarrow full of dirt. He was a bit taller than Lina, with short hair sticking straight up, cut-off jeans, scabby knees, and untied sneakers without socks.

"*Hola* Pablo," Nacha greeted. "Look at you, working so hard today!"

He grinned proudly and came over to stand beside Lina.

"*This* is my brother," she said.

"Go ask your Mom if Talia can stay here and play with you for a while," Nacha said.

"Their mom does not speak good English," she explained to me as Lina ran back inside the plot. "And Spanish no, because they are *Mixtecos*. You know, Indians. They have their own language."

Lina came running back, flip-flops making little clouds of dust around her feet. "She said it's okay!"

Nacha smiled and waved to the woman with the long braid. "*Muchas gracias*, Dominga."

She handed the baby back to Lina and said to come find her if I needed anything. I nodded and watched as Nacha returned to her plot.

The baby had wriggled out of Lina's arms and was now sitting on the ground by her feet, putting little clods of dirt into his mouth.

"No, no, no," she said, squatting down to fish them out with her finger. I squatted down too.

"How old are you?" Lina asked, fixing her big eyes on me.

"Ten."

Her eyes widened. "That's old. I'm only eight, but when I have my birthday, I'll be old enough to get my very own bicycle." She paused to take another dirt clod from Raulito. "Do you like buttons?"

I shrugged. "I guess so."

Lina's mom came over to us with an even smaller baby, whom she handed to Lina, saying something in their language and smiling shyly at me before returning to her work.

"This is my little sister, María Rosa," Lina said, giving the baby a kiss on the cheek. She lifted Raulito in her other arm, and I followed them back to the shade of the card table in the middle of the plot. Lina spread a blanket and laid the baby girl beside her cousin.

I watched with curiosity as she pulled a plastic bag from her pocket and dumped the contents on the ground in front of us: all different shapes and colors of buttons, some chipped and scratched, others shiny and new looking.

"This is the best one," she said proudly, holding up a large blue button with a gold rim. "I traded it with Pablo for my four square reds. It's the best shooter."

She reached for a wooden board with faded marker lines across the surface and placed it on the ground between us. Setting down a small white button, she showed me how to push the blue "shooter" against its edge so the white button went sliding across the board.

"See? You have to get your guy to hit that orange one," she explained, "but if you hit any other guys off the board, I get to keep them. If I hit any, you get them."

She rattled off a million rules to the game, explaining what the different lines meant, how many points you got when your button crossed a line, and which "guys" were best to capture. After a while, Pablo came and crouched under the table with us, adding his own pocketful of buttons to the pile and helping catch Raulito whenever he started crawling away.

We played all morning, until I could shoot almost as well as Pablo. Nacha returned twice to check on us, peering over the fence and looking pleased when I waved happily from under the card table.

Later, an older woman with gray curly hair arrived at the gate, and Pablo and Lina immediately dropped their buttons and ran over to her, yelling "*Abuela! Abuela!*"

"Look at you angels, taking care of the babies," she said, taking their hands and entering the plot. Her face was almost as wrinkled as the old Japanese man's, and she wore a floppy hat with a ribbon around the rim, a pink blouse, and a pair of wire-rimmed glasses on a chain. Settling herself down at the little card table, she reached into her purse for a handful of hard candies, which she held out to Pablo and Lina.

"And who are you, Sweetie?" she asked, peering under the table and offering one to me as well.

"This is my new friend Talia!" Lina exclaimed. "It's okay, you can have one," she added, seeing my hesitation. "Abuela Jean always brings us candy."

Pablo's lips were already stained bright green from a jaw-breaker, and Lina crunched noisily on two peppermints.

"You kids are too adorable," the woman said, lifting María Rosa onto her lap. "I have a surprise for you today. See if it's okay with your mother to come visit me for a bit, okay?"

Pablo ran to where their mom was pulling weeds from the rows of corn plants, then returned to scoop up the babies and carry them over to her.

"Okay, we can go!" he said triumphantly, popping another candy into his mouth and bolting for the gate.

"*Abuela* means grandma," Lina explained as we ran down the path, "but we just say that 'cause our real grandma's in Mexico, and we can't see her. So we pretend."

"She says she'll be anybody's grandma who needs one!" Pablo added. "So lots of kids call her that."

Abuela Jean's plot looked like an old-fashioned painting: brick walkways lined with flowers and not a single weed in sight. Her tomatoes were neatly tied, her corn stood in three perfect rows along the fence, and a carefully trimmed hedge of purple flowers surrounded an iron bench in one corner. Along the paths were some fairy statues, two ceramic birdbaths, and signs saying *Welcome to my Garden* and *Gnome Crossing*.

Abuela picked up a plastic shopping bag beside the gate and suggested we go sit under the fig tree where it was cooler.

"And here is your surprise!" she announced, once we were settled on folding chairs in the giant tree-room. "This one is for Lina… this one for Pablo… and here's one to read to the babies. I think you kids will love these."

Lina and Pablo reached out to take their new books, flipping through all the pages and running their hands over the glossy covers.

"Thank you, Abuela!"

"Do you like to read too, Sweetie?" she asked, adjusting her glasses and looking at me.

I nodded vigorously.

"Excellent! Then this one is for you." She held out a small paperback with a picture of a tiger on the cover.

A few smaller kids appeared at the entrance of the tree-room, staring at us silently with wide, dark eyes. Abuela Jean smiled and invited them to come inside too, passing out candy and picture books to everyone.

"You, read?" one of the little kids asked quietly, in a way that sounded more like "wreathe" than "read."

She smiled again and opened another book to the first page, showing everyone the picture and beginning to read in a slow, clear voice as more kids gradually came inside and found seats around the tree trunk.

"Abuela used to be a teacher," Lina whispered in my ear, "so she likes reading to us. She even *taught* Pablo how to read last summer, 'cause he didn't know."

After three chapters, Abuela Jean cleared her throat and said she was feeling hoarse and that we would continue next Saturday. We emerged from the tree to find a bunch of people gathered around the picnic tables, talking in Spanish and that other language. The two guys in baseball caps, who turned out to be Lina's dad and older brother, sat at one table, drinking soda and heaping beans from a plastic container onto large tortillas balanced on their laps. Lina's mom came and set down a bowl of cilantro and lettuce in the center of the table, placed a gentle hand on my back, and motioned to the food. "Please, eat," she said softly. Mom had packed a peanut butter sandwich and graham crackers in a bag for me, but I left it untouched and eagerly helped myself to a tortilla with beans.

After lunch, Pablo and Lina showed me an empty field behind the garden, with nothing but weeds and old rusty cars and piles of rubble. In the middle of the field was a big cement slab, with broken boards and pieces of metal scattered around.

"This is where we play hopscotch," Lina said, pointing to faded chalk drawings on the cement.

At the back of the field was a barbed-wire fence covered in thorny plants, which Lina told me were blackberry vines. Next to the fence stood a low-branching tree that Pablo declared was good for climbing. He went first, then gave me and Lina a hand up. From our perch, we could see over the fence and past the railroad tracks, all the way to a construction site of bulldozers and brand-new houses down below. Beyond that, crop fields stretched into the distance, endless rows of brown and green, just like the ones Mom and I had seen from the bus.

"That's *las uvas*, the grapes, where our mom and dad work," Lina said. "And our brother Toño too."

"Next year when I'm twelve, I can work too," Pablo said proudly. "But sometimes when my dad's back is hurting, he can't go, so we tell the *contratista* that I'm twelve already.

"You only did that once," Lina said.

"So, it still counts!"

"You're just trying to sound grown up."

"Toño has been working for two years, and he's so fast," Pablo told me, ignoring his sister. "He can pick five boxes in an hour, almost as much as my dad. I can only pick three."

We sat perched in the tree together for a while, gazing at the fields and the grid of paved roads and half-finished houses.

"Hey, I have an idea," Pablo said. "Wanna build a fort? We could pretend we're builders, like *Tío*, and we're building our own house to live in."

Lina brightened, and we all jumped down from the tree and began searching for old boards, pieces of metal, and other building materials.

"It can be our own secret place," Pablo said. "And if we make it really strong, maybe it'll still be here when we come back next year."

"You're leaving?" I asked, surprised.

"In winter, we live in Coachella with our cousins," Lina said, "because the lettuce is ready to pick. And in summer we come here for the grapes."

"What are you talking about?" Pablo asked. "We're grown-up construction workers! We gotta build our house! C'mon!"

We took off running across the dry field to look for materials, the sun beating down on our backs and the afternoon stretching out wide and free all around us.

When we returned to the garden later, coated in a fine layer of dust and panting from our race across the field, the family's plot was mostly shaded by trees. Lina's dad sat at the card table with two people who she told me were her aunt and uncle, Raulito's parents. They were all talking rapidly in the language that wasn't Spanish, the aunt cradling Raulito underneath a blanket on her lap. As we approached, I noticed the old Japanese man standing just outside the gate of the family's plot, holding a basket filled with jars. His face lit up when he saw me.

"Hello again! I see you have found a friend."

I grinned and nodded.

"Good day, Li-chan," he said, turning to Lina with a small bow. "Will you please help me talk with your parents for a moment?"

Dominga came to the gate and motioned shyly for us to enter. The old man made a small bow to her as well, then lifted a jar of dry leaves from his basket and set it on the table.

"I brought more tea," he said. "How are the headaches? Do you think it is helping?"

Lina spoke rapidly to her parents in their language, and they smiled and nodded several times as they answered.

"Yeah," she finally told him. "They said it's good. They asked if they can pay you with something?"

The old man shook his head. "It is a pleasure to help you."

Dominga put her hand to her heart and murmured a quiet "Thank you."

"They sometimes get headaches after working in *las uvas*," Lina whispered to me, "so he gives a plant remedy to help."

The old man turned in my direction. "And you? Did your mother like the tea?"

I nodded eagerly, remembering that morning after Mom drank it and how everything started getting better.

"And *you* look happier too," he said, the smile-wrinkles deepening around his eyes. "Would you like some more?"

I nodded again and followed him to the herb garden near the front gate, where he cut more leaves and put them in a paper bag. Nacha came over to say that Mom would be returning soon, and seeing the old man, she waved and approached to talk with him.

Lina ran up and tugged at my sleeve. "C'mon! I want to show you something before you leave!"

Back at the family's plot, she led me to a large cactus-like plant in the far corner. It was more grayish-blue than green, with long spiny arms rising from the center above our heads and spilling down to the ground on all sides like a gigantic flower. Lina crawled into a narrow space between the fence and the massive plant, and I followed.

"This is my special spot," she said, eyes shining. "No matter what happens, ever, I'll always come back right here, because underneath this *agave* plant is my umbilical cord."

"You mean the thing that attached you to your mom's belly?" I asked, confused.

She nodded gravely. "When I was born, they buried it here, and that means it's my special place and I'll always come back, no matter what."

She pushed aside a broken chunk of concrete and began clawing in the moist soil until her fingernails scraped against something hard.

"What's that?"

"I'll show you," she said in a hushed voice. "But it's a secret." Bending so low that her pigtails brushed against the dirt, she unearthed a rusty metal lunchbox from a hole in the ground.

"These are my most specialest treasures," she whispered, wiping dirt off the lid and carefully opening the box. One by one, she showed me the rosary that was a gift from her real *abuela* in Mexico, a few baby teeth wrapped in a scrap of cloth, two shiny pink seashells, a wrinkled ribbon from a contest in second grade, and a photograph of herself in a lacy white dress on the steps of a big church.

"That was my First Holy Communion," she explained. "In Coachella. *Tía* gave me the picture."

"Why do you keep that stuff buried here?"

"'Cause," she said, placing the items back in the box. "It's safe. In Coachella, we sometimes live in a trailer, but sometimes we live with my cousins, and they'll take my stuff and mess it up. And in El Chorro we always stay in a different apartment, so I can't leave it there."

She carefully returned the box to its hole in the ground. "But no one comes over here except me. And besides, I have to come back to this spot my whole life, no matter what, 'cause that's how it works with umbilical cords."

"Wow...I never knew that."

"It's a secret," she reminded me. "But I wanted to show you, 'cause you're my friend. And you can make sure nobody touches it while we're gone."

"Oh, but I won't be here anymore," I told her reluctantly.

Lina's face fell. For a second, I thought she might even start to cry. "You won't? Are you coming back, ever?"

I started to shake my head. "Well, maybe to visit someday. But we're moving to Washington."

She sat there silently for a long time, slumped over and poking at the dirt with one finger.

"But don't worry, I won't tell anyone your secret," I promised.

I helped Lina scoop handfuls of soil over the little box and move the concrete chunk back into place, and then we returned to the card table to play buttons until Mom arrived to pick me up.

∽

Walking back to the motel that evening with my new book from Abuela Jean under one arm and a bag of tea leaves hanging from the other, I kept thinking about Lina's special place where she would always return. I wished I had a spot like that. In spite of our plans for a fresh start in Washington where everything was cheaper, I quietly, deep down, almost wished we could stay right here.

8

THE NEXT DAY, Mom and I headed out to look for a place she'd heard about that served free meals. Somebody at the downtown transit center pointed us to the correct bus stop, where a group of teenagers stood kicking a hacky-sack and hooting with laughter. In the shade of the bus shelter sat two men smoking cigarettes, an old guy in a wheelchair hunched over his newspaper, a couple leaning on each other's shoulders fast asleep, a young woman nursing her baby, and another woman with matted gray hair muttering to herself, arms wrapped around a huge plastic garbage bag. There was nowhere left to sit, so Mom and I stood on the sidewalk near the noisy teenagers and waited for the bus to come.

When it finally did, everyone tried to crowd in at once. It was another hot day, and a breeze from the open ceiling vents wasn't enough to remove the odor of cigarettes and sweaty bodies filling the bus.

Two little kids kept shouting and wrestling in the aisle, and the driver had to yell at them three times to shut up and stop pulling the yellow cord. The couple who had been sleeping on each other's shoulders began arguing at the back of the bus, and the little baby woke up and started crying, face cherry-red and hair plastered with sweat. Beside me, the old man in the wheelchair grumbled and swore under his breath about all the noise.

It was a relief when we finally arrived and everyone got off the bus. Mom took my hand, and we followed the others across a parking lot to a gray stucco building with a sign that read "J.R. Linden Day Center: Uvas County Social Services."

We joined the line outside the front entrance, standing behind the woman with the garbage bag, who seemed to be having a conversation with an invisible person beside her. The bulky plastic bag dragged along the ground in front of us as we inched forward.

"Your names, please?" asked a person at the front door.

"I'm Nora Trevino... and this is my daughter, Talia," Mom replied, a slight quaver in her voice. "We're just, um, here for some lunch."

"Have you been to the Day Center before?"

"No... we're not from around here."

"Okey-doke," the woman replied, writing something on her clipboard. "Are you planning to use any other services today? Laundry, shower, phone?"

"Um, I don't think so," Mom answered. "We just heard you serve lunch, so I was wondering if..."

"Yep, everyday at noon. Since you're a new client, you'll need to do an intake interview with our director, Francine. But she's gone on weekends, so don't worry about it for now. You can just line up over there by the kitchen."

Mom thanked her, and we headed over to the line at the opposite wall. The Day Center was mostly one big room filled with tables and chairs, like a school cafeteria. Some computer desks and bookshelves along one wall had been used to section off a little kids' play area in the corner.

It was loud inside, a hubbub of voices and clanging dishes, cell phones, the hum of laundry machines, and chairs scraping against the linoleum floor. Some people were sitting at tables playing chess or reading magazines, some napping on two chairs pushed together, others carrying laundry baskets or standing in line for the phone. The lady at the desk hollered twice for everyone to quiet down so others could hear their phone conversations. I stood quietly in the food line beside Mom, watching the commotion and imagining how it would feel to spend every day in a place like this.

A door beside us swung open and a tall woman with a magenta beach towel wrapped around her head strode into the room, followed by a toddler in swim trunks dripping water onto the floor. The woman scooped him up and patted him dry with her dress as they joined the line.

"Hold *still*, T.J.," she commanded. "Come on, we're gonna get lunch."

"Well, hey there, buddy!" a bald, cheerful man behind the food counter called out. "Givin' your mom a hard time?" He reached out and gave the toddler's cheek a poke. "Man, you got way too much energy there, little brother. Can I have some?"

"He took all mine," the woman chuckled in a deep, raspy voice. "How you doin,' Ted?"

"Oh, just trying to stay cool. Was it really this hot around here last year?"

She set down the fidgeting toddler and threw her head back with a roar of laughter. "Ha! You try livin' in Florida for a summer. This ain't nothin,' my friend."

"How about breaking up that party and serving some food?" someone yelled from the end of the line. "You got hungry people here!"

"Some folks got no patience," Ted whispered under his breath, winking at me and Mom as he slapped a big spoonful of spaghetti on each of our plates.

We got salad and bread and small Styrofoam cups of milk, then found a spot at one of the tables. Across from us sat the old man from the bus stop, hunched forward in his wheelchair, tracing the lines of a newspaper with one knobby hand. He looked up but didn't answer when we said hello.

"Archie don't talk," a man at the adjacent table informed us, leaning toward me with a grin. "He's a little. . . ya know. . . not all there."

The woman and toddler from the lunch line came to sit at our table too, followed by the mother and baby from the bus. "You stayin' at the church tonight, Lorna?" she asked, pulling up a chair.

"Yeah, looks like it."

"Me too, I guess. Dana says I can't stay at her place with the baby no more, now that she's crying so much at night."

Lorna pushed a forkful of spaghetti into T.J.'s mouth and gave a sympathetic nod. "Yeah, that teethin' phase, it's rough... hang in there, sister."

They started talking about bottles, teething, and diaper rashes, while Mom and I ate our spaghetti quietly and listened. Finally, the younger woman turned to us and said, "You're new here, huh?"

We nodded, and she reached a hand across the table and introduced herself as Christina. "And this is my baby girl, Skye," she added, moving the baby's hand in a waving motion.

I stroked Skye's pudgy arm with one finger as Mom shook hands with Christina and introduced us. The next thing I knew, Mom joined right in the conversation too, laughing at Lorna's jokes and adding her own embarrassing stories about when I was a baby.

I got up to throw away my plate and peek at the small backyard of the Day Center. It was just a square of grass with a few skinny trees and some picnic tables under the overhang of the roof, but it still felt nicer than being inside, so I slipped out and let the door swing shut behind me.

The sun was dizzyingly bright, and nobody was out there except a teenager sitting alone at one of the tables, chipping at something with a pocketknife.

"Hey," I said.

She glanced up and silently returned to her work.

"What're you making?"

"Nothing."

The girl dropped a small piece of wood into her pocket and wiped the knife clean on one leg. Her clothes were baggy, covered with patches and safety pins and little metal studs, with a chain dangling from one pocket. She had a freckled nose, silver lip-ring, and black hair with purple streaks that hung in front of her eyes.

"It sure is hot," I commented, sinking down onto a bench.

"Hot as hell," the girl muttered. "I hate El Chorro in the summer."

"Why don't you go inside?"

She shrugged again. "My mom's in there. I hate her too."

"Oh." I swung my legs back and forth, not knowing what else to say.

The girl shook the hair off her face and squinted at me. "Where'd *you* come from?"

"My mom and I just came here for some lunch."

"You stayin' at the church?"

"No, we have a mo—" I stopped short, remembering what Mom said about the motel being too expensive. Now that she had a job here in El Chorro, we had to stay somewhere... but where? I began to feel all panicky inside. "What church?"

"You dunno anything, do you. There's no real shelter in this stupid town, so people stay at a church."

"Do you?"

She kicked at the bench with one foot. "Yeah, for now, since my mom's boyfriend threw us out."

"How come?"

"You ask a lotta questions. Jeez. They broke up, okay?"

I looked down at my lap, feeling bad for having asked. "My mom and I used to live at my uncle's apartment," I offered hesitantly. "But I guess we all broke up, too."

"Oh yeah?" One corner of the girl's mouth twisted upward, as if she thought this were funny. I watched as she pulled a cigarette and lighter from her pocket and flicked the metal wheel to make a flame.

"How old are you?" I asked, surprised, because she seemed too young for cigarettes.

"Fifteen, why do *you* care? God I can't wait 'til I'm eighteen and get outta this dump."

"Do you really smoke those?"

She sighed and let the flame go out, slowly rolling the cigarette between two fingers, and frowned at me. "Wanna know a secret? I hate them. Don't ever do this, okay? It'll kill you."

"Then why are you doing it?"

She snorted and put the lighter back in her pocket. "You wouldn't understand."

Why did older people always say that? I slid off the bench without another word and started for the door.

"Hey, I'm Blade."

I stopped and turned back to face her. "That's a cool name. Is it because of your pocketknife?"

She nodded, flipping the knife out again in one swift motion. "I can do *anything* with this sick blade. But you better not tell anyone here, they'll take it away from me."

I nodded. "Promise."

She made the same crooked half-smile again. "Who are you, anyway?"

"My name's Talia," I said, feeling suddenly plain and un-interesting. "I don't have a cool nickname, or anything like that."

Blade shook her hair to one side, pulled the baggy T-shirt down, then rose from the table and headed toward me.

"Wait up, T-cat," she said, dropping the cigarette in her pocket and following me to the door.

∾

Mom saw us come inside and ran over to me. "Sweetheart, are you okay?"

I nodded. "Yeah, I was just looking around."

She smiled and ruffled my hair, then knelt down for a face-to-face talk. "Tal, listen... I'm thinking maybe we could go back to the motel this afternoon and get our clothes, so we can do laundry here?"

"Sure," I agreed with a shrug. *Why was she asking me?*

"And..." Mom hesitated and lowered her voice a notch. "Well, Lorna was also talking about this church where she's staying... maybe we could go tonight too, just to see how it is?"

She bit her lip and looked into my eyes with a hopeful expression. "It's just a free place to sleep, so I can save money faster and pay uncle Jim back what I owe him, you know? Does that sound okay, Sweetheart?"

I thought about it for a moment and nodded slowly. If we stayed at the church for a night, did that mean we were officially homeless? Like those people sitting on the curb with cardboard signs? I repeated the word a few times in my head, but it sounded strange, like a description of somebody else.

"That's really fine," I said, trying to smile a bit so she wouldn't worry.

We rode the bus back to the motel, packed our stuff, and checked out at the front desk. Our little room had almost started to feel like home, I realized, but now we really had nowhere to be. *Homeless,* the voice inside my head kept repeating, but I tried to ignore it. This would just be for tonight, or maybe a few nights. Just until Mom could save enough to get back on our feet. And the church would be sort of like a motel too, right?

When we returned, the Day Center was less crowded than before, and the lady at the desk just smiled and gave a little wave to come in. I followed Mom to the laundry room and helped her load our clothes into a washing machine, then crawled under a computer desk and opened my red notebook, considering ideas for a new story.

By the time our laundry was finished and we'd repacked everything into bags, it was almost five o'clock. "Closing in ten minutes sharp!" the woman at the desk announced. "Shuttles to the church will be here soon. Please remember to take all your personal belongings!"

We carried our stuff out to the parking lot and stood on the curb with everyone else. Soon the shuttles arrived—three big vans that everyone crammed into, pulling bags and suitcases onto our laps. Mom and I squeezed into the back row and shared a seatbelt, sandwiched between T.J.'s child-seat and an older woman who coughed through the entire ride.

The church was one of those big, old-fashioned kinds with a bell tower and stained glass windows, and in the parking lot was a more ordinary, square building with lots of people gathered around the door.

"Welcome to home-sweet-home!" Lorna laughed as we climbed from the van, throwing a backpack over her shoulder and taking T.J. by the hand. We grabbed our stuff and followed them up the ramp to the building.

"Have you two been here before?" asked a man behind a table at the front door.

Mom shook her head.

"Alright, the rules are all posted up there, but let me explain a couple of things," he said. "Absolutely no alcohol, drugs, smoking, or violence of any kind will be tolerated in this building, please limit your showers to five minutes each, we have lights out at ten o'clock and quiet hours until six in the morning... um... dinner from six to seven, *no* saver plates. If you want food, you have to be here. Shelter doors close at nine p.m., no clients go in or out after that, *no* exceptions. There's a chore list on the kitchen door, we'll get you signed up... and please remember we expect everyone to clean up after themselves here. Fresh towels and sheets are available, just have someone unlock the closet for you. Our volunteer chaperone Lisa will be on duty all night, so go to her if you have any questions. Remember, doors close at nine p.m., so if you leave after that, you won't be allowed back in. Got it?"

Mom nodded, and we carried our bags through the door.

"He makes it sound like *kindergarten*," I whispered. "Or maybe jail."

The room we entered was like another big cafeteria with white plastic tables and chairs, three refrigerators, and tall metal cabinets lining the walls. A woman in a denim dress with a sticker reading HI MY NAME IS LISA half-walked and half-skipped over to us, smiling brightly.

"Hey guys, welcome! Wanna see where you can set down your stuff?"

She put away her clipboard and helped carry our bags down a narrow flight of stairs to the basement, which was mostly one big carpeted room filled with folding cots. Many of the cots already had sleeping bags, suitcases, stuffed animals, purses, and backpacks strewn across them.

"Let's see..." Lisa said, glancing around the room. "Let's find a good spot for you guys."

She walked over to the far corner, where two empty cots stood side by side. "How about here?"

Mom dropped our heaviest bag onto the thick canvas with a thud and said that was fine.

"We do have storage lockers for clients," Lisa offered, "if you're interested in leaving stuff here during the day?"

Mom hesitated. "Oh, I don't know…I mean, um, we're just trying this out for tonight. I think we'll keep everything with us."

Lisa waved her hand in the air to brush it off. "No problem. Just let me know if you change your mind."

She led us to the linen closet to pick out clean sheets and towels, then pointed out a small room with couches and a television set. "You can hang out and watch TV or play games or whatever…we turn out the lights around ten o'clock, but until then it's all yours."

"There's also a playroom," she added, turning to me. "But I bet you're too old for that stuff, right?"

I nodded, remembering the Day Center playroom filled with shrieking toddlers. I was grateful that Lisa could see I wasn't a baby.

"Well, they're serving dinner upstairs right now, if you feel like heading up. It's gonna be good tonight, curry or something. We always have awesome food when those folks from the Islamic Center do dinner. Just let me know if you need anything else, alright?"

Mom and I thanked her and headed back upstairs, where the dining room was now a bustle of activity. I noticed Blade and her mom sitting at a table in the corner, heads bent over their plates, not talking.

We got food and sat at another table, across from a man and woman with two little boys who kept bickering and touching the food on each other's plates.

"Sibling rivalry," the woman said to Mom, rolling her eyes with a sigh. "Gotta love it, huh?"

While we ate, she told a story about how her family lost their house, the previous year. "After Brad's back injury, he couldn't work for six months, and there went all our savings," she said, shaking her head. "I still have my job at the supermarket, but you can't support a family on that, you know? ← Not with medical bills... but we're praying those disability payments will kick in soon, and things'll start looking up."

I chewed my food and listened quietly, wondering if one job would be enough for *us* to afford a place of our own.

After dinner, we got towels and stood in line for a shower, then returned to the basement. A few people were already lying down, reading magazines or trying to sleep. I spotted Christina sitting on the edge of her cot, holding a bottle of milk to the baby's mouth and rocking gently back and forth. The sounds of television and muffled voices filtered in from the lounge, and preschoolers in pajamas ran squealing in and out of the playroom, where another television played cartoons with the volume turned up high.

"Alyssa, get back over here *now*," someone demanded. "You heard what I said."

A little girl with tangled hair shot past us in her underwear, followed by a scowling woman in a bathrobe. "*Alyssa*, you're gonna get it."

"Can somebody tell that woman to shut up?" muttered a voice from beneath a sleeping bag.

Mom and I peeked briefly into the lounge, but neither of us wanted to sit with a bunch of strangers watching a scary TV show, so even with the basement still brightly lit and full of activity, we decided to go to bed early.

"Thanks for being willing to try this, Sweetheart," Mom whispered, kissing my forehead and tucking a perfume-scented blanket around my neck. "I promise it won't be long... we'll have our own place, with our own beds to sleep in. 'Kay?"

I nodded, hoping she was right, and watched as Mom returned to her cot and climbed under the blanket with a long sigh. She seemed to fall asleep right away, but I lay awake, staring at the fluorescent lights and thinking of ideas for a new story. It would be about a roaming band of superheroes who built free houses for anyone who needed somewhere to live. Every house would have a yard for gardening, so people could grow lots of food for themselves and the builders, and nobody would have to worry about getting money for meals. Everyone would have plenty to eat, and eventually, everyone in the whole world would have a home too.

The sounds of voices and television faded into the background as I lost myself in this new idea. First thing the next morning, I told myself, I would write it down.

But when morning came, there was no time for stories. Someone turned on the lights at six o'clock, a few alarm clocks started beeping, Skye began to wail, and soon the whole room became one giant bustle of movement and voices, unzipping bags, folding blankets, and the clanging of cots stacking up against the walls.

"You can keep the same bedding if you're coming back again tonight," Lisa told us, walking around with her clipboard to sign people up for morning chores.

Mom hesitated and glanced at me with questioning eyes, then replied that we'd like to leave our stuff on the cots for another night.

We signed up to sweep and vacuum the basement, and after finishing our chores, went upstairs for a breakfast of cold cereal and milk. Lisa showed us a locker where we could store our stuff for the day, and by 7:15 we were out on the curb with everyone else, waiting for the shuttle to take us back to the Day Center.

It wasn't until later that morning, while Mom was having her "intake meeting" with the center director, Francine, that I finally had a chance to think about my new story again. Crouched under the picnic tables outside, I opened my red notebook and gradually let myself disappear from the J.R. Linden Day Center in El Chorro and into my own imaginary world, where anything was possible.

9

THE NEXT WEEK was boring, boring, boring. I went along for two more housecleaning jobs, read the book from Abuela Jean three times, wrote more stories in my red notebook, and waited in what seemed like a million lines. There were lines to check in at the shelter and get lunch, lines to do laundry and take showers, lines to get on the bus. I knew that Mom was trying her best, so I bit my tongue and didn't complain, even when the sticky heat and constant waiting were almost more than I could bear.

Every day, after Mom finished her work or errands, we returned to the Day Center so she could use a computer and make phone calls before riding to the church. The routine became familiar: sign in at the door, eat dinner with Lorna and Christina, stand in line to shower and use the bathroom, then fall asleep to the sounds of creaking metal cots, snoring, fussing babies, and hushed, irritated voices.

But at least Mom seemed in a better mood. Ever since she got more cleaning jobs and began to save money, she had returned to her old talkative and hardworking self, full of ideas for the future. Even after a long day of work, she would volunteer to help wash dishes in the church kitchen, and later she and Lorna would sit on a couch in the lounge and joke around, Lorna's raspy bellow resonating throughout the basement and Mom's light, high giggles rippling like a fountain above it. I was glad she'd found a new friend and felt happier again, even if the days were long and boring.

When Friday finally arrived and Mom had no cleaning jobs or errands, we went to the park and had our own special day off. Mom sat under the slide with me and helped build a sand house, complete with twig fence and acorn chimney. We even used tree moss to make little curtains on the windows.

"Maybe this is what our own house will be like, in Washington," I said hopefully. "Can we plant a garden in the yard?"

Mom said that would be lovely, and I ran to gather bits of grass to make a garden at the sand house.

When it got too hot to be outside, we headed across the street to the public library. I wanted to get my own card and check out books, but the librarian said we needed proof of a permanent address in El Chorro. Mom tried to explain that we were just passing through for a short time, but the librarian shrugged apologetically and said library cards were for local residents only. So we went and sat in big chairs by the window and just enjoyed the air conditioning, while Mom flipped through magazines and I skimmed over a pile of kids' books, wishing I could read them all.

"Do you think we could go to the garden again?" I asked later, as we were leaving the library. "Maybe I can find that lady with all the books and trade with her for a new one."

I knew Abuela Jean probably wouldn't be there, and I wasn't sure what we'd do at the garden all by ourselves on such a hot day, but that didn't matter. It just felt nice being in that bright green maze of plants and flowers, where everything seemed perfect in the world.

Mom must have felt the same way, because she thought about it for a moment and then agreed. We took a bus and walked through the neighborhood of colorful houses, past the noisy truck yard and weedy field to the garden.

At first, it seemed like nobody was around, but as we neared the giant fig tree, I spotted the same old man with the straw hat. I tugged Mom's arm in excitement.

"That's the guy who gave you the tea!"

He stood bent over a row of small logs by the rusty metal shed, but looked up and smiled as we approached.

"Why, hello again. Is this your mother?"

I nodded happily, pulling Mom's hand.

"Thanks for the tea," she told him. "That was really nice of you."

"It is my pleasure to give it," he replied in the calm, steady voice I remembered from before. He bowed his head slightly and reached out a hand to Mom. "My name is Masahiro—I am glad to meet you."

Mom shook his hand, and I suddenly realized that until that moment, I hadn't even known the old man's name. *Ma-sa-hiro.* I liked the sound of it.

"What are all those for?" I asked, pointing to the rows of neatly cut logs leaning against the shed.

"These are for growing *shiitake*," he replied. "Do you know *shiitake* mushroom? It does not grow in soil, but on wood."

He pushed a small peg into one log and hammered it gently. "This is like planting seeds," he told us. "You see, these pegs are covered in fine invisible roots. They will grow inside the wood and produce mushrooms on the surface, like flowers."

"Wow, that's cool," I said, stepping a bit closer to look.

"In a few months, when it rains, they will produce," Masahiro added. "You are welcome to come again and try home-grown *shiitake*."

We both thanked him politely, not mentioning that we wouldn't be here anymore by that time.

Masahiro smiled and returned to his work, and Mom and I set off through the garden, winding our way down the bright green paths in the late afternoon sunlight. I showed her Abuela Jean's tidy plot with its brick walkways and little statues, then Lina's family's giant cactus with spiny pink fruits. When we came to the plot with the chain-link fence and hundreds of flowers, Mom stopped and stared, just as I'd done the first time.

"Isn't that *amazing*," she breathed. We both stood still, peering through the vine-covered fence. There were even more kinds of flowers than I remembered—red and yellow bowl-shaped flowers with petals like wrinkled tissue paper, upside-down hanging trumpets, bushes of fuzzy orange blooms like fireworks, and a sea of fluttering light blue petals so thin the sunlight came right through. There were clusters of purple blossoms hanging like grapes, bright pink pom-poms, red and yellow pinwheels, and fountain-like flowers of velvety purple with yellow antennae rising up from the center. It seemed like every possible color and shape of flower in the whole world must have been growing right there.

"You lost or somethin'?" A low, scratchy voice came from somewhere behind the fence.

Startled, I peered harder through the vines and noticed what I had missed before. In the middle of the plot was a lopsided wooden desk with stacks of buckets and vases piled all around. Seated at the desk, practically hidden by jars and containers, was the person who had spoken.

"Oh, we're just looking around!" Mom called back. "Your flowers are beautiful."

"Well, so long's you don't pick none," she grumbled.

"Don't worry!" I replied, even though I had secretly been thinking about making a bouquet for Mom.

It was quiet for a moment, and then a deep, rumbling laugh bubbled up from inside the plot. "Is that a *child* I hear?

Well, Lord have mercy, you can come right in if you want to. You don't sound like no thief to me."

We looked at each other in surprise.

The next thing we knew, a padlock clicked and the gate beside us swung open. Standing on the other side, hands on her hips, stood a huge woman in overalls and rubber boots, with a round, stern face the color of chocolate, bright red lipstick, and dangly gold earrings.

"Well?" she asked, staring down at us. "You wanna look or don't you?"

We stepped tentatively through the gate, into the garden filled with flowers.

"Whoa…" I gasped, looking around in awe.

"Six months now somebody's stealin' my flowers," she muttered, shuffling along a footpath back to the cluttered desk. "Just when my dahlias started bloomin'—*gone*. Those scoundrels. Can't trust nobody these days."

She settled back into her chair with a groan. "But I can see plain it ain't you two. Where you come from anyway?"

"Oh, we're just here briefly, on our way up north," Mom explained. "We were staying at a motel down the street, and my daughter fell in love with this garden. "

The woman chuckled. "Ain't that somethin!' *Tourists*."

She pulled a stem from the bucket beside her and stripped off its leaves in one swift motion, leaving a bare stalk with a bright orange bloom on top. She placed this in a vase on the desk, chose another flower stem, and repeated the process.

"Why are you doing that?" I asked.

"You never seen someone make a bouquet, child?"

I shook my head.

"Well, rule number one is you gotta strip 'em, see? Can't have all that green in the way of your color. Keeps 'em fresh longer too."

She slid two large sturdy fingers down another stem.

"Gosh, you must be making a lot of bouquets," Mom said, surveying the array of bins, buckets, jars, and vases.

"Yep. Big weddin' tomorrow. Those folks call me up and say 'Mrs. Murphey, can you make us twenty-five bouquets and corsages for next Saturday?' and I says to them, 'Well of course I can, if my flowers ain't all stole and gone by then!'"

She shook her head and let out a chortle that rocked her entire body. "You seen them padlocks on my gate? Ever heard of somebody lockin' up *flowers*? Yep, that's what the world's come to. And those thieves still find some way in. That's why I'm sayin,' you can't trust nobody these days. 'Specially not that good-for-nothin' Bill Mitchell, always loitering here with his mangy cats for no good reason. He don't even give a lick about gardening... never grew nothin' in his life. Can't trust the scoundrel."

For all her talk about scoundrels and not trusting people, Mrs. Murphey seemed to be enjoying our company. We stood quietly beside the desk and watched as she stripped one flower stem after another, arranging them in jars according to color.

"Do you just grow flowers here?" I asked after a while. "Not food?"

Mrs. Murphey chuckled and shook her head. "Believe you me, this here's just as important as food. This here feeds the *soul*."

"You mean by looking at them?"

She reached for another stem and shrugged. "Dunno how, but it works. You start makin' all these flowers bloom around you, and things start changin' in *here*." She patted one big leaf-stained hand against her chest. "Least, for me it did."

"It made you feel happier?" I thought about what the old man had said about having happiness inside us already, but needing something to help find it.

"Yeah... after losin' my boy, I never thought I'd see no part of happiness again."

"Your son?" Mom's face creased with concern.

Mrs. Murphey nodded, fingers moving slower. "Yeah, my boy Lester... he died in Iraq." Her voice dropped, becoming even more gruff and scratchy than before. "Couldn't see no reason to keep goin' in the world after that, for a long time. Just went down to the cemetery and sat by him, every day."

Mom stared at the flowers in Mrs. Murphey's hand, looking like she might start to cry herself.

"And then you started a garden?" I asked.

"Yep." Mrs. Murphey kept her eyes glued to the flowers. "I'm tellin' you, the Lord does business in mighty strange ways... but I got that message, loud and clear. 'Don't you worry 'bout how to go on livin',' ma'am,' he said. Those pretty flowers never worry about nothin', and the Lord makes every one of them perfect, don't he? If he got enough attention for them, you better believe he's gonna take care of things for you too!'"

She chuckled. "Oh yes, I got that memo straight outta heaven. First it was just a few plants on the windowsill, for Les' grave, but then I just kept plantin' more and more, 'til I finally got this plot here. And then the life started comin' back into me, just a little. Can't explain it."

She shook her head, continuing to strip leaves swiftly off one stem after another, the buckets and vases around her filling with an array of red and orange, dark purple, magenta and more shades of yellow than I knew existed. She was right, I thought—just looking at all those colors was like the biggest, tastiest feast in the world.

∾

Later, as we headed back down the main path to the gate, I heard someone calling out from behind. It was Nacha! She came hurrying after us with a bulging plastic shopping bag swinging on one arm.

"Nora, Talia, hello! I have a gift for you!"

She reached into the plastic bag and pulled out a handful of yellow-orange balls. "The first tomatoes of the summer."

"Those are *tomatoes*?" I asked in surprise.

Nacha nodded, smiling. "Yes *mija*. Cherry tomatoes, sweet like candy. Here, try."

I took one of the tiny yellow fruits and cautiously nibbled at it, juice squirting down my chin. To my amazement, Nacha was right! It didn't taste like an ordinary tomato at all, but more like a piece of tangy fruit candy.

"Whoa," I laughed, popping the rest into my mouth and licking the juice off my face. "You should try one, Mom."

Nacha beamed at us. "Here, this bag is for you."

"Are you sure?" Mom asked hesitantly, but Nacha laughed and held out the bag, insisting that soon there would be too many tomatoes for anyone to eat.

"Tomorrow is Saturday," she said, giving me a wink. "Are you coming back again, to play with the children? We will be here all day."

I looked up at Mom, who, to my surprise, agreed right away. Maybe it was just my imagination or the rich light of the garden at sunset, but at that moment, standing on the path eating cherry tomatoes and grinning at Nacha, Mom looked happier than I'd seen her in ages. It was as if the brightness of Mrs. Murphey's flower garden had somehow gotten inside of her.

10

MOM AND I RETURNED to the garden the next morning, catching a bus from the church and walking through the quiet neighborhood in the still-cool morning air. We found Mrs. Murphey in the same spot as the day before, sitting at her desk, muttering and stripping stems off more flowers. Mom didn't have any cleaning jobs that morning, so she stayed at the garden for a while. At Mrs. Murphey's insistence, she pulled up a stool and began helping with the flower corsages. Mrs. Murphey demonstrated how to cut the stems at an angle so the flowers would last longer, and how to choose buds that were barely beginning to open, so they'd be fresh for the wedding that afternoon.

"See?" she said, pointing to a Mexican Hat with its petals still half-folded around the center. "That one's in her prime right now, but tomorrow she'll be a saggy old thing like me." She chuckled. "So pick 'em young, it don't last."

I watched them work for a while, trying to memorize the names of all the different flowers, then went off to look for Nacha or Lina. Their plots were still empty, so I decided to go exploring by myself.

Just past Masahiro's medicine garden was a dense grove of plants with rustling leaves, like a forest of giant grass. I'd seen the striped cat disappear into that forest before, and I was curious to see where he had gone. Moving slowly like an explorer in an unknown land, I headed down the footpath and suddenly found myself in another world, separate from the rest of the garden. The path through this grass jungle curved around several times, then opened into a small clearing. To my surprise, there in the clearing was Masahiro! He sat cross-legged on a flat rock, beside a small oval-shaped pond with floating lily pads. It took me a second to realize that the pond was actually an old bathtub buried in the ground, and that the smooth rocks were slabs of broken concrete.

Masahiro sat on a mat made of woven straw, hands resting in his lap, eyes closed. He must have sensed me standing there, because after a moment he opened his eyes and turned in my direction.

"S-sorry," I stammered. "I didn't mean to disturb you."

He smiled gently and shook his head. "That is not any problem. Welcome."

"It's... really beautiful here," I said, looking around the little clearing. Morning sunlight filtered through the leaves, making quivering flecks of light on the water's surface. Bright orange and white fish came up to the surface occasionally, mouths open and fins swaying gracefully in the water.

"Yes," Masahiro agreed. "One might say this is my church, here by this little pond in the bamboo grove."

"Were you praying?" I asked, remembering how he'd been sitting with closed eyes.

Masahiro thought for a moment. "Perhaps that is one way to say it."

Slowly, he uncrossed his legs and refolded them the other way. "This little pond is where I come to be still, to be with life as it is. We call it meditation. But I believe it is similar to praying... another path up the same mountain."

He motioned for me to sit on another slab of concrete be-side the bathtub. Closing his eyes again, Masahiro took a long breath, held it for a moment, then exhaled even more slowly.

"No matter what else is happening," he said, "our breath is always here. Being still and paying attention to that is one way to find peace."

"This is a peaceful place," I said, gazing at the dense foliage surrounding the bathtub-pond.

Masahiro opened his eyes and looked at me with a soft smile. "Yes," he agreed. "But the most peace is *here*." He held a wrinkled hand to his chest. "When I come to sit beside this little pond, it is my own peace inside that I seek."

He was quiet for a long time. "Perhaps that is difficult for you to understand, right now," he said at last, "but it is okay. Just as the koi fish take many years to develop their bright colors, there are things we learn with time."

He took another deep breath and closed his eyes again. "I simply meant to tell you this place is for stillness. If you are quiet and still, you are welcome to sit here anytime."

I nodded, and Masahiro swayed back and forth for a mo-ment before becoming still again. We sat in silence for a long time, no sound but the slight rippling of water when larger fish came to the surface. Finally, feeling a bit restless but not wanting to break the hypnotic spell, I rose to my feet and walked quietly back down the path without a word.

On my way to the fig tree, I passed the same striped brown cat with the missing ear. "Is this your home?" I asked, bending down to stroke its soft fur. "Do you live here at the garden?" *Cats are lucky,* I thought to myself. *They don't need money, or houses.*

Two more cats suddenly appeared and began rubbing against my legs, purring, and a smaller one circled cautiously at a distance, eyeing me with round green eyes.

"Looks like you've got some friends," came a deep voice from behind. I turned and saw a tall man in army camouflage clothes and duct-taped boots, with a ponytail and thick grey beard, walking toward me. Trailing behind him came a parade of even more cats.

"Are they yours?" I asked.

He grinned, revealing a row of yellowed and partially missing teeth. "Nah. Other way around."

"Why do you bring them all with you to the garden?"

He threw his head back and laughed. "They just follow me. From the trailer park over that-a-way."

So this must be the guy Mrs. Murphey was talking about, I realized. I wondered quietly whether he actually liked to steal flowers.

"Do you have a plot in the garden?" I asked him.

The man shook his head. "Nah, I ain't no gardener. Just like to come sit under that tree. That tree is heaven on earth, ya know?"

I nodded.

"Some folks here, they don't want me around," he said, dropping his voice to a hoarse whisper. "They think this place is just for growin' vegetables, and nothin' else. Well, you know what? I don't even *like* vegetables! I'm a meat-and-potatotes kinda guy, alright? But I sure do like that tree. That's where I get my peace."

He bent down and picked up one of the cats that was clawing against his pants, a small orange and white spotted kitten with no tail, and cradled it against his chest. "I seen some crazy things in this world," he went on, "things you don't wanna know about, but I tell ya, this place is where I get me some peace."

"It's fine with *me* if you come here and don't have a plot," I said. "That's what I do, too!"

He cocked his head for a minute and then grinned. "Well, ain't that somethin'."

Then he headed off toward the fig tree with a slight limp, still grinning, the line of cats following behind.

I spent the rest of the morning playing buttons with Pablo and Lina, and later—once the babies were asleep—working on our fort. "This is gonna be a good strong house," Pablo said, wiping the dust off his hands as we lay down chunks of broken concrete for the foundation. "I think it'll last all winter."

The whole family went home early that day to prepare for María Rosa's baptism the following morning, so I wandered back toward the bamboo forest and found Masahiro in his herb garden, trimming leaves into a basket with a pair of scissors.

He looked up from beneath the wide-brimmed hat and smiled. "Why, hello again."

"Would you like any help?" I asked.

Masahiro seemed pleased by this idea and handed me another basket and pair of scissors, demonstrating how to snip the small fuzzy leaves from the top of each stem.

"This is for making tea," he explained. "Also, to keep the plants smaller. *Gennoshouko* will crawl over the whole garden, if we let it!"

"*What's* it called?"

"*Gen-no-shouko*," he repeated slowly. In English this is... geranium, I think. But a different, Japanese kind. The name means 'help immediately,' because if you have a stomachache and drink this tea, you will feel better very quickly."

When our baskets were full, Masahiro showed me how to tie the trimmings into bunches and hang them from tree branches to dry. Then we returned to the herb garden and began cutting leaves from a tall, thorny plant along the fence.

"This is *ukogi*," he told me. "I do not know the name in English."

"Is it for making tea too?"

Masahiro nodded as his scissors went snip, snip, snip and the leaves dropped into his basket. "Yes, *ukogi* tea is good for people with weakness or infection. It gives the body more energy to heal itself."

"You get more energy? Like coffee?"

"Even better," he said, laughing, "because it lasts a longer time. But you already have the energy and quickness of three children, Tali-chan! I do not think we will need *ukogi* tea for you today!"

I laughed too, and we continued snipping our way along the fence. When our baskets were full, we went over to the shed and poured the leaves into shallow boxes made from old window screens, and put these in the shade to dry as well.

Then Masahiro led the way back through the rustling bamboo forest to the meditation pond, where we knelt beside a plant with splotched yellow and green heart-shaped leaves. Masahiro demonstrated how to cut the stems back almost to the ground, assuring me they would regrow in the blink of an eye. As we snipped, the air filled with a strong, sharp smell, and I put one leaf up to my nose and made a face.

"Ah yes," Masahiro said. "Some people call this herb 'fish-mint,' because of the smell."

"Yuck!" I made another face. "Who would drink fish-mint tea?"

Masahiro chuckled. "It is not bad. When the leaves dry, there is no more smell of fish. In Japan, this plant is also called *juuyaku*, 'ten medicines in one,' because it will help with so many problems. Cough, fever, snake bite, swelling, pneumonia, to stop bleeding... even for a tumor."

"Whoa! One plant can do all that?"

"This is because *juuyaku* helps to clean out the body," he explained, "so it can heal itself."

We continued working silently while I thought about this. Mom had said not to believe everything I heard, but Masahiro sounded so sure about these things.

"How do you know what all the plants do?" I finally asked. He stopped snipping for a moment and gazed into the dark water in the little pond. When he spoke again, his voice was even more slow and quiet than usual.

"I learned this from my grandmother—my *obaachan*, as we say in Japan. She was a very wise person... it is because of her that I am alive."

"Were you sick?"

Masahiro nodded and resumed cutting the purple stems. "Yes, very sick, and my family was too poor to pay for a doctor. My parents had arrived here in America only a few years before, you see. They worked hard in the fields and did not have a lot of money."

He paused and looked over at me. "Did you know that in the past, most of the farmworkers here were Japanese?"

I shook my head, surprised.

"Yes," he went on, "many people came from Japan to work in the fields. We all lived in this part of town, so it is called the *Nihonmachi* District. This means Japan-town."

"Like the name of the garden!" I said, remembering the painted sign by the gate.

"Indeed." Masahiro smiled. "To me, this will always be the *Nihonmachi*, even though most people here now are from elsewhere."

"Did your grandma live here too?"

"No," he replied, "she stayed in the village of Takamura, in Japan, in the home of my father's brother. But I was a very sick child, with tuberculosis and fevers, and a doctor said I might not survive another year if this continued. So I was sent to Japan, for *Obaachan* to take care of me."

"You went all by yourself?"

He shook his head. "I accompanied a rich man who was returning to seek a wife. You see, in El Chorro my parents belonged to a *kenjin-kai*, a club of people from the same part of Japan, and they all helped to buy a ticket for me."

I stared at him. "So your family just sent you away?!"

"Yes... we were very poor, Tali-chan. I was the youngest of three brothers, and my parents could not pay for more doctors and medications which had not helped. But my father had seen *Obaachan* cure people of terrible illnesses, so this was our final hope."

He rose to his feet and moved to another sprawling patch of *juuyaku* across the pond, knelt down again, and continued snipping leaves methodically into his basket. I had stopped working and was staring wide-eyed at Masahiro.

"So you went all the way to Japan without them?"

"Yes." He leaned back for a moment, a far-away look in his eyes. "I remember that day, leaving with the rich man Okuda-san, on a big ship. It was summertime, and I thought I might faint with so much heat and sadness. My life energy—in Japanese we call this *qi*—was very stagnant until I went to live with *Obaachan*."

"Did she make you better?"

Masahiro smiled and patted his chest. "As you see, here I am. She treated me with plant-medicines and healing foods, and slowly I became stronger. We would go together into the hills to gather wild plants."

He gestured toward the *juuyaku* and herb garden. "In Japan, all of these plants grow by themselves, like weeds. *Obaachan* taught me how to find and use them. I learned many things from her."

"Wow," I said. "That's really cool."

"Indeed. Soon, I grew just as strong and healthy as my cousins. After school, we would help to collect firewood for cooking, harvest rice and spread it on mats to dry, weave *tatami* mats from rice straw... all these things I learned to do. When I first arrived in Takamura, I was just a pale, sickly boy who knew nothing. But in a few years, I became like all the other boys in our village."

"In a few *years*?" I repeated, surprised. "You stayed there that long?"

He nodded. "My parents feared that I might become sick again, in America. *Obaachan* kept my *qi* flowing with many herbs and special practices. But also..." He lowered his voice a notch, as if to share a secret. "I believe she requested that I stay, in letters to my parents. You see, *Obaachan* wanted to give her knowledge to someone, but my cousins had no patience to learn such things. 'The young people have changed,' she often said. 'They want to grow up and live in the city, and they do not care about the old ways. But you are different, Ma-chan.'"

"Why were you different?" I asked.

Masahiro shrugged. "Perhaps because I was ill for so long, I learned to be patient. *Obaachan* would take me into the fields to gather plants, and because they had healed me, I wanted to learn."

"But didn't you miss your family?"

He sat back on his heels, closed his eyes for a moment, and nodded. A hot breeze rustled through the forest of bamboo around us.

"Yes," he said at last. "I missed them very much, at first. I would lie on my *tatami* mat every night and dream about my parents and my brothers. But in time, my uncle's family became a home to me, while the others in America became a smaller and smaller memory."

He leaned forward again to cut the last remaining stems into his basket. "Also, I had much respect for *Obaachan*, who cured me. It would have been ungrateful, asking to leave."

He rose and motioned for me to follow back to the fig tree, where we tied more bunches of *juuyaku* with string.

"When did you come back to America?" I asked, curious to know the rest of the story.

"Well," Masahiro answered quietly, hanging a newly tied bunch of *juuyaku* on a tree branch, "I stayed in Takamura long enough to care for *Obaachan* until she died."

"You took care of *her*?"

"Yes. She had been correct—most of my cousins left for the city, and I was the only one who learned how to use plants for medicine. So finally, I took care of *Obaachan*, just as she had cared for me."

"Wow, that's perfect," I said.

He nodded. "Just as you must take a step with your left foot and then with your right, when one thing happens in life, something else happens to balance it. Not always a thing we prefer, of course, but something to make balance."

"But that's not balanced, because when she took care of you, *you* got better!" I pointed out.

"Yes, that is true." Masahiro sighed. "But I was young, and she was old. *Obaachan* had already passed her wisdom onward. It was her time."

I looked down at the ground, sad to imagine Masahiro saying goodbye to his beloved grandma.

"It's okay, Tali-chan!" he said, noticing my expression. "You see, it was my time to move on, too. I was no longer a child. I wanted to see more of the world than our little village...so I traveled to America to reunite with my parents and brothers."

He shook out the remaining leaves from his basket and reached for mine with a smile. "And here I am. And here are the grandchildren of plants in Takamura village, from seeds I carried in my clothes all the way across the Pacific Ocean."

I tried to picture Masahiro as a young man, traveling alone on a ship all the way across the ocean with seeds tucked inside his clothes, returning to a country and family he could hardly remember. It was like something from a movie.

"So there is a long answer to your question!" he concluded with a laugh.

"Wow," I exclaimed. "That's one of the best stories I've ever heard."

Masahiro looked at me with a thoughtful expression, tipping his head slighty to one side and then the other. "Sometimes the best stories are your own life," he eventually replied.

∾

Later that afternoon, on my way back to find Nacha, I stopped to gaze at an especially large plot I'd noticed a few times before. It was covered in rows of plants like a striped blanket, each row a different shade of green. Two women in cut-off jeans, faded T-shirts, and sunhats knelt beside one row, pulling leaves and tossing them into plastic bins at their sides.

I stood at the fence, watching curiously as they carried the bins to a metal sink, dumped out the contents, then returned to pick more leaves, chatting and sometimes laughing as they moved gradually down the row.

As they came closer, one of the women noticed me and waved, and the other came over with a handful of greens.

"You like spinach?" she asked, popping a leaf into her mouth and chewing.

Before I could answer, the other woman laughed aloud. "Grace, did you ever see a kid who liked to eat plain spinach?" She picked up her bin and joined us at the fence. "It's okay girl, you don't have to take it," she said, dropping her voice to a pretend whisper. "Just ignore my sister, she's such a weirdo."

"Hey!" said Grace. "What do *you* know? The kid's been standing there watching us harvest spinach for the past five minutes—maybe she'd like to try some, okay?"

She held out a handful of leaves over the fence. "Me and Rowena grow the best spinach in this town."

I reached out tentatively and took a leaf, turning it over to examine the bumpy, plastic-looking surface. Both women watched intently as I nibbled at its edge.

I never liked when Uncle Jim forced me to eat vegetables, but to my surprise, the spinach tasted good! It was crunchier and sweeter than I expected, and sort of earthy, like eating a piece of springtime.

"Wow," I said, taking another bite.

"See?" Grace declared triumphantly. "What did I tell you? I'm not a weirdo."

"Well, you've apparently got a special case here," the other woman said with a shrug. "What's your name, girl?"

"Talia."

"Hmm... Talia... any relation to Popeye the Sailor?"

This time they both burst out laughing, which made me smile too.

"What are you doing with all those?" I asked, pointing to the tubs of spinach leaves.

"That's for farmers' market," Grace explained. "We harvest on Saturday so we can set up early next morning."

"Ever been to the market?" asked the other woman, who I guessed must be Rowena.

I shook my head.

"Really! Well that's the perfect place for a spinach-loving kid like you. It's where the farmers set up tables downtown to sell produce. Ask your folks, they probably know about it."

"Are you guys farmers?" I asked, impressed.

They both laughed again. "Not really," Grace said. "We just grow too much to eat, so we started selling at market."

"But you can call us farmers if you want," said Rowena. "I like the sound of that."

"Yeah, would you like to come see our *farm*?" Grace asked, grinning.

She unlatched the gate to let me inside, and I followed the two women over to the big metal sink, where they dumped their spinach into a bath of water. Rowena began washing the leaves and packing them in waxed cardboard boxes, and Grace picked up two more empty bins from beside the sink.

"I'll start on carrots," she announced. "Wanna help?"

I nodded enthusiastically.

"Oh, I see, putting her to *work* now, hey?" Rowena said.

"You just wish you'd thought of it first!" Grace joked back, giving me a wink. She led the way to a row of lacy, fern-like leaves and jabbed a pitchfork into the ground next to them, making the soil loosen and the plants lift up. To my amazement, buried in the dirt at the end of all those delicate stems were tons of carrots! Not just the typical orange ones, but all colors: purple, yellow, white, and deep red-orange. I never knew so many kinds of carrots existed!

Grace pulled out a handful and showed me how to tie the bunch together tightly with a piece of string. Crouching on either side of the row, we made bunch after bunch of multicolored carrots and stacked them in the plastic tubs. A few were funny shapes, twisted around each other like they were hugging, or split into two halves like little dancing legs. Grace held these up to show me, and we laughed some more.

When both bins were full, we dragged them back to the sink and sprayed off the carrots with a hose. With all the dirt removed and the fresh roots glistening with water, the carrots looked even more colorful than before, like bunches of oddly shaped party balloons.

Next, the three of us walked over to a row of yellowish-green vines sprawled across the ground. Hidden underneath the prickly leaves were green fruits with wrinkled skin, the way my fingers looked after staying in the bath too long.

"What are those?" I asked, as they began picking the fruits and tossing them into bins.

"People call these 'bitter melons,'" Rowena said, "but in the Philippines, where our family's from, they're called *ampalaya*."

"Are they actually bitter?" I wanted to know.

Rowena nodded. "Yep. But we grew up eating 'em, so we like it."

"Ha!" Grace hooted. "You like it? You used to complain every single time Mom made *ampalaya*! Remember the time Joel caught you feeding all your *ampalaya con carne* to the chickens?"

"I don't know what you're talking about." Rowena turned to me, shaking her head in mock dismay. "See how she picks on me?"

"If you do it right, they're not so bitter," Grace explained, tossing another melon into the bin. "You gotta harvest them young, like this one here, and soak them in salt water to get out the bitterness, and then use the right spices for cooking them. All the old Filipina ladies in town love our *ampalaya*."

I helped to rustle through the dense vines, looking for camouflaged fruits like in an Easter egg hunt. Soon our bins filled up with *ampalayas*. By the time we finished, the late-afternoon sun had already dipped below the trees and dragonflies swooped through the air above our heads.

I was helping carry boxes of vegetables out to Rowena's truck when Mom arrived to pick me up. The sisters both shook her hand enthusiastically, said it was great to meet us and what a hard-working helper I was, and asked if we'd like some vegetables to take home.

Mom thanked them and said maybe sometime, not mentioning that we didn't have anywhere to cook our own food. Grace shrugged and said that was fine, and if we ever wanted anything—especially some spinach for "Talia the Sailor Girl"— we should just ask.

I was bursting with excitement to tell Mom about my day, about the bathtub-pond and the man with all the cats, Masahiro's story, and the vegetables for farmers' market, but she looked so tired that I decided to wait. All the way back to the church, my head kept swimming with images of rainbow carrots and camouflaged *ampalayas*, hanging bundles of herbs, and the hidden pond of lily pads and koi fish in Masahiro's forest of rustling bamboo. It was like walking straight into the best story ever.

11

BACK AT THE DAY CENTER Monday morning, we had a meeting with a caseworker named Alicia, whose job was to help people get back on their feet. She was a short, perfume-smelling woman with curly black hair and fake eyelashes, who spoke fast and seemed to be in a hurry. After shaking both of our hands firmly, she led the way to a small office at the back of the room and invited us to sit down.

"Alrighty, so hopefully we can work together to get you guys housed as soon as possible. That's the goal, right?"

Mom looked unsure but nodded anyway.

"And I see you've only been here since June?"

Mom sat up straighter in her chair. "Yeah, um, we're actually planning to head up to Washington, where it's cheaper."

Alicia nodded. "Yeah, affordable housing is pretty limited in this town… There's that new subdivision going in, across the railroad tracks, but they won't be on the rental market for a while. So, do you guys have connections up there in Washington? Friends, family, any kind of support system?"

Mom shook her head.

Alicia frowned slightly and leafed through papers on her desk. "I see you were down in L.A. before this… and you had employment down there?"

Mom nodded.

I gazed out the office window, not wanting to think about L.A. and our last few months at Uncle Jim's. I knew he was having a hard time too, worried about losing his job, but did he really have to make us leave? Mom's and Alicia's voices faded into the background as I stared at the skinny trees outside the window and tried not to think about it. I let my mind wander back to the garden, remembering Masahiro's story about being sent away from his home as a kid too.

Suddenly I felt Mom nudging my shoulder. "Tal? Did you hear what Alicia asked you?"

I shook my head, embarrassed.

"She'd like to talk with us separately for a few minutes. Is that okay with you, Sweetheart?"

I nodded hesitantly, and Mom got up to leave, the office door clicking shut behind her. Alicia glanced at her watch and then looked at me.

"So, Talia, I thought we could just talk a little about how all this has been for you," she began, "and it might help me understand how I can better help you and your mom. How does that sound?"

I shrugged.

"Well, let's just give it a try," she prompted. "Remember, this is so we can figure out the best way to help you guys get a place to live, okay?"

I shrugged again.

"So, I'm wondering, how was it at your uncle's place in L.A.? Did you like living there?"

"Yeah."

"And living with your uncle? Did you like that too? How did he treat you and your mom?"

"He's nice," I said, not wanting her to get the wrong idea about Uncle Jim. *Why did she need to know that, anyway?*

"He just didn't have space for us anymore," I said, "'cause his girlfriend was moving in."

I felt a bit guilty lying, but that was the story Mom said to tell anyone who asked.

"And do you remember the last job your mom had, down there?" Alicia continued.

I stiffened. What should I say? I didn't want her to know how many times Mom had been fired, or how long she'd tried unsuccessfully to get a job.

"Yeah, at the YMCA," I said.

"Can you remember what happened, when she stopped working there?" Alicia probed. "Or why she stopped?"

I stared down at my lap. What would happen if she found out? If she knew how sad Mom sometimes got? Too sad to get out of bed and go to work, or eat food, or do much of anything at all... What if Alicia decided to take me away to live with someone else, like Uncle Jim warned could happen?

I picked at a scab on my knee, trying to think of something to say. "She got sick."

Alicia nodded, earrings dangling back and forth. "And she was sick for a pretty long time."

"Yeah."

"Do you remember if she went to the doctor?"

I shrugged again, feeling trapped.

"Do you remember anything she did, during that time?"

"Stayed in bed," I replied nervously. *Wasn't that what everyone did when they were sick?*

Alicia glanced at her watch again. "Talia, it sounds like your mom has had some challenges keeping a job because of her health. And I'm wondering how it is for *you* when she's not feeling well... do you often help out with extra stuff?"

I nodded.

"Like preparing food, cleaning, going to the store... ?"

I nodded again.

"And are there ways you try to help Mom feel better?"

"Well..." I looked up to the ceiling, deciding what to say. "Sometimes I make tea. But mostly she just needs time."

Alicia shuffled through her papers. "So, Talia, I understand that when you were younger, you once stayed with another family for a few weeks when your mom wasn't well. Do you remember anything about that time?"

I shook my head firmly. "No, I was too little. That was a really long time ago." I did actually have a few dim memories of living in a house with other people when I was four, but I didn't want Alicia getting any ideas about that.

She kept asking more questions, and I tried to respond with normal-sounding answers, until finally she thanked me and said it was Mom's turn. I sank with relief onto a chair outside the office and waited while they had their private meeting, which dragged on and on forever.

The morning rush of people leaving for work had passed, and the regular lunch crowd hadn't arrived yet, so the Day Center seemed a bit quieter than usual. A woman with long grey braids was singing along to the radio and frying hash browns on a plug-in skillet by the microwave, and a small group gathered around her as the room filled with the aromas of coffee and frying grease.

"Hey, what's a five-letter word for *flexible*?" someone doing a crossword puzzle at one of the tables called out, but nobody seemed to hear.

Archie sat across the room in his usual spot, slouching over a magazine and tracing lines of print with one knobby hand. The garbage-bag woman was digging through a crate of donated clothes in the corner and muttering to herself, and a man with a silver cross around his neck was arguing loudly in Spanish on a cell phone.

Through the window, I could see a skinny guy with dreadlocks and feathers sticking out of his hat perched on one of the picnic tables, playing a wooden flute. He was wearing a Hawaiian shirt and leopard-print leggings, sunglasses, and a leather jacket with fringe swaying back and forth. The door of the center opened as someone walked in, and for a moment I could hear the flute player's music—fast, light, skipping notes like a flock of birds—before the door swung shut again.

At a table nearby, Christina sat feeding baby Skye from a bottle and talking with a new couple who had just arrived the day before: a tall, redheaded man and a small woman with a pale face and dark circles under her eyes. She sat quietly, stroking the bulge in her tank top, and I realized she must be pregnant.

"We been staying in a tent down by the railroad tracks," the man was saying, "you know, so we can be together. Those idiots at the church don't care if a couple's married, it's men upstairs and women downstairs, no exceptions."

Christina shook her head with a sympathetic sigh. "That's messed up."

The man nodded. "Yeah, tell me about it. But Kimmy's four months along already, so she needs something better, so we thought we'd try for a night or two." He reached out and gave the woman's shoulder a light squeeze.

"Don't call me Kimmy," she retorted, pushing his hand away. The man shrugged, scooted his chair back, and got up to join the group around the skillet, leaving Christina and the new woman talking quietly together.

Another man with matted hair emerged from the bathroom and hobbled toward me with a lopsided smile. One of his eyes was squinted almost shut, oozing a thick yellow liquid, the other eye open extra wide as if surprised. As he approached, I suddenly realized that he had only one real leg, the other a complicated apparatus of metal and plastic with a worn sneaker at the end. I smiled at him and tried not to stare.

"Hey," the man said, coming so close I could smell his warm, cheesy breath in my face. "Lookey."

He held up a plastic mosquito-eye kaleidoscope like those prizes at the fair, lifted it to his good eye and looked at me through the hole, turning it slowly in circles. Then he held the toy out to me with one leathery hand. I took it tentatively and peered through the hole, seeing hundreds of tiny one-legged men looking back at me with their one good eye.

"Cool," I said, handing it back to him.

The man nodded and grinned even wider. "Cool," he repeated. "Lookey."

Francine, the director of the center, hurried past with a walkie-talkie in one hand but turned back when she saw me and the man with the mosquito eye. "Peco, go sit down and leave that girl alone," she said. "Talia, where's your mom?"

I pointed to the meeting room.

Francine frowned. "Alright... why don't you go into the playroom for now, Hon. You're not allowed to hang around unsupervised."

I sighed and slid off my chair, heading reluctantly toward the playroom with the annoying, screaming toddlers. It seemed like forever until Mom finished her meeting and appeared in the doorway looking for me, face tense and drawn.

"C'mon Tal," she said in a low, quiet voice. "Let's go somewhere."

I could see she was upset, so I followed without asking questions. We crossed the Day Center parking lot and didn't bother waiting for a bus, just headed down the shoulder of the busy street toward town. I watched as Mom's sneakers crunched little twigs in the dry dirt, her head and shoulders slumping lower with each step.

"What happened?" I finally asked.

She heaved a long sigh and began walking even slower. When she eventually spoke, her voice was low and flat, barely audible.

"Apparently Alicia thinks I'm crazy."

"What? What do you mean?"

Mom sighed again. "She wants me to go and get tested by a psychiatrist... because if I have some mental problem, we might get on a list for cheaper housing."

I frowned. Getting a cheap house sounded great, but not if someone was calling Mom crazy!

"Why does she think that?" I asked. "Just because you sometimes get sad and don't feel well?"

Mom shrugged, head hanging toward the ground. "I don't know, Tal... I just don't know what to do..." Her voice broke, and tears slid silently down her cheeks.

We walked down the roadside for a long time without saying anything, no sound except Mom's ragged breathing, the crunching gravel beneath our feet, and the constant whirring of traffic. It was already midday and my neck and forehead were dripping with sweat, but Mom still wore her sweater and didn't even seem to notice. We trudged onward through the heat in silence.

I wanted to shout that *Alicia* was the crazy one, and that we shouldn't have anything more to do with her. But on the other hand, what if she actually could help us get money for a house? Wouldn't that be worth it?

We finally reached downtown El Chorro and walked all the way to the public library, where we drank from a water fountain and sank onto chairs in the air-conditioned coolness. Mom had stopped crying by now, and her face looked blank and tired. I wanted to say something to cheer her up, but I couldn't think of anything.

After a while she went to use a computer, and I folded my legs beneath me in the big chair and took out my notebook to begin a new story.

This one took place in a magical kingdom far away, where the king and queen had a special group of people called the Happy-Sad Council, who helped them to know how things were going in the kingdom. The council members got happy and sad very easily, so whenever something was wrong or out of balance in the kingdom, they always felt it. Even when the common people were going about business as usual, a council member might suddenly get filled with sadness. Then the king and queen would know something wasn't right, and they could fix it before things got worse and *everyone* started to notice. When the entire Happy-Sad Council was laughing joyfully again, everyone in the kingdom would celebrate with them. The council was highly respected, because they had such an important job.

I was starting to write a new part about the Happy-Sad Council's children, when Mom returned and said it was time to go. I reluctantly put away my notebook and followed her out the double doors of the library, into the still-hot late afternoon. We walked in silence to the transit center and caught route six to the church, where Mom went straight downstairs to prepare for bed, skipped dinner, and didn't say another word for the rest of the evening.

12

MOM CALLED DENISE the next morning, to say she was feeling sick and wouldn't be able to work. She didn't go the following day either, or the next. We hung around the Day Center while she flipped absently through magazines and took naps at the picnic tables outside.

"Are you going back to work soon?" I asked a few times, worried that she might lose her new jobs.

But Mom just sighed, telling me that she didn't feel well and please not to nag.

So I spent the days wandering around, re-reading my new book, playing checkers with anyone who would play, and doing extra chores out of sheer boredom. I wrote a long story about some kids who traveled around the world to all sorts of exciting places, having adventures everywhere they went, and another story about a family that broke up but changed their minds and got back together again. I wrote page after page in my red notebook, not showing these stories to anyone.

On the third day of hanging around with nothing to do, thinking I might collapse with boredom, I suddenly had an idea. I walked right up to the director's office, knocked on the door, and asked Francine if I could make a garden out in the yard.

"A garden?" Francine repeated, squinting down at me. "What exactly do you mean?"

"A vegetable garden," I replied, suddenly feeling embarrassed. "Where I could plant a few things, like carrots and tomatoes... maybe flowers. I would just need a little spot."

She frowned and thought about it.

"Other people might like it too," I added hopefully. "It could give them something to do."

"Hmmm," she finally said. "Well, I guess you could dig around by the utility shed, where there's no lawn. But keep it clean, okay? No mud puddles, please."

I pumped my head up and down excitedly and bolted outside to look at the location of my new garden. It was no bigger than a picnic table, strewn with pebbles and cigarette butts and tiny pieces of broken glass, but it was *mine* to use.

This was different from having a plot at the community garden, I told myself. A tiny patch of dirt at the Day Center wasn't like a real plot in a real true garden... so it would be easy to leave behind when we moved away to Washington.

I cleared away the trash, then used a stick to break up the ground as best I could. It was already moist from the sprinklers that watered the lawn, but more gravelly than the soil at the garden. I was still picking out small rocks when I heard someone come up behind me.

"'Wassup, T-cat."

It was Blade, hands shoved in pockets, staring down at me from behind the curtain of purple-streaked hair. "Diggin' up the yard or what?"

"To plant things," I replied.

She made that face halfway between a smile and a frown and didn't say anything.

"I'm going to plant sunflowers, and little tomatoes that taste like candy!" I continued, eager to tell someone my plans.

Blade just stared like I was the weirdest kid she ever met.

"Do you want to help?" I offered, but she shook her head and turned to go back inside.

As I removed more rocks and pieces of broken glass from the dirt, someone else came over and quietly crouched beside me. To my surprise, it was Kim, who had hardly spoken a word since the day she and her boyfriend Jared arrived at the Linden Day Center.

"Hey," she whispered, resting one hand on her pregnant belly while reaching out with the other to pick up a clump of soil, crumbling it slowly between her thumb and fingers. "My mama always used to have a garden," she said quietly. "I used to help her sometimes, weeding and stuff."

"How come you stopped?"

Kim let the last crumbs fall to the ground. "She died when I was fourteen."

I looked up, startled, not knowing what to say.

"I ran away the year after that," Kim went on, "hopping cargo trains, hitchhiking… Got here somehow."

"Whoa."

She returned the other hand to her belly and stroked it silently for a moment. "I just wish she could meet the baby."

We both stared at the bare patch of gravel for a while without speaking.

"I always wanted to go back and plant some hollyhocks around her grave," Kim said at last. "That was her favorite flower. But we don't have the money to get back there now."

"Where?"

"Boone County, Kentucky. That's where I grew up, where my Mama's buried."

"Do you want to plant some hollyhock flowers *here*?" I asked, brightening at the idea. "I know it's not the real place… but you could pretend."

Kim fixed her big green eyes on me and didn't speak for a while. "Really?" she said at last. "You think I could do that?"

"Sure, I'm allowed to use this spot to grow anything. And I even know someone who might have hollyhock seeds!"

"Well..." she said slowly, reaching for another clump of soil. "I don't know how long we'll even stay here. But if you really think it'd be okay... yeah. I'd like that."

I nodded vigorously. "I'm sure! And then when the baby's born, you can show it the hollyhock flowers, and that'll be sort of like introducing the baby to your mom."

Kim ran her fingers through the dirt, the corners of her lips twitching a little. "Alright." she agreed. "That'd be fine."

With the patch of soil all ready, now I just needed some seeds. I looked hopefully over at Mom, who was sitting at a picnic table fast asleep, an untouched plate of food beside her on the bench. There was nothing to do but wait.

When she finally awoke later that afternoon, I got a nice surprise. "Sure, let's get out of here for a while," she said in the same flat, quiet voice she always used when she wasn't feeling well. I was so excited to finally be going somewhere that I almost forgot to grab my red notebook and a plastic grocery bag for seeds. We took the bus downtown, then waited and took another bus to the *Nihonmachi* neighborhood.

As we walked past the old white building near the motel, I was surprised to hear someone call out to us from beneath a pine tree in the yard. It was Masahiro! He was sitting at a picnic table with three other men, sipping iced tea and playing a board game.

"Hello, my friends," he said in his usual soft voice, when we reached the tree. "Are you walking to the garden?"

"Yes!" I burst out, eager to tell him. "Today, I started making my own little garden at the Day Cen— at the place where we're staying. So now I just need seeds to plant!"

He looked puzzled for a split second, then smiled. "Why of course, Tali-chan. I will be going to the garden soon myself, and would be happy to help you."

"What's that?" I asked, pointing to the board and pieces spread out on the picnic table.

"Ah, this...It is a very old game from Japan, somewhat like chess. We call it *Goh*."

The others around the table gave small nods and smiled. They all had wrinkly faces, narrow eyes, and white hair like Masahiro's, and I realized they probably all grew up together here in the Japan-town neighborhood of El Chorro.

"You folks working over at the garden?" one of the men asked us.

"Yep," I said cheerfully, deciding not to explain that we didn't really live here or have our own garden plot.

Mom stood silently and let me do all the talking, as she usually did when she wasn't feeling well. "Do you?" I asked the man who had spoken.

He chuckled and shook his head. "Nope. Ever heard of a green thumb? Well, I got a *black* thumb. But our friend here Tanaka-san, man oh man, he just looks at a plant and it grows!"

Masahiro smiled and shook his head. "It is a partnership between myself and the plants, Ikeda-san. Everything wants to live." He turned to me and Mom. "I would like to introduce you to my friends: Mr. Ikeda, Mr. Goto, Mr. Furukawa."

Each of the men gave a polite nod toward us, and I tried to keep smiling and talking cheerfully so they wouldn't notice Mom's quietness. *Could other people tell something was wrong? Or were her moods invisible to everyone except me?*

☙

When Masahiro arrived at the garden later that afternoon, he took us to the shed and pulled out a cardboard box of neatly labeled envelopes, filled with seeds collected from plants he'd grown. It was still too hot for planting carrots, he explained, but I could try out some sunflowers and basil, and perhaps Mrs. Murphey would have hollyhock seeds.

"You need compost, too," he said. "Come, this way."

He led us behind the shed, to a row of wooden bins made from shipping pallets. Most of the bins held piles of dry leaves and grass, but one was filled with moist, dark soil.

"If you want to grow plants," Masahiro said, picking up a handful and holding it out to me, "this is the secret."

I looked up at him, puzzled. "Dirt?"

Masahiro smiled. "This is only one part of the soil, the part made from plants." He pointed to a pile of dry leaves.

"You mean all *that* turns into *this*?"

He nodded. "Worms and other small creatures eat the old plants, turning them into soil again. We call this compost."

"That's like magic!" I exclaimed.

Masahiro smiled again. "Yes. All of life is magic, if you look closely."

He poured the dark, crumbly compost into my hands. "You see, soil is mostly made of tiny rocks. But this is the *living* part of the soil. In your hands are billions of creatures, too small to see, which help the plants to grow. We must always be careful, after taking some life away from the soil, to give some back."

"Taking some life?" I repeated, confused.

Masahiro picked up a bucket and began filling it with compost. "Yes. When a plant grows, it takes some life energy, *qi*, from the soil, turning it into leaves and fruits. And when we harvest those things, we are taking the life for ourselves."

"Oh!" I jumped in. "So if you harvest something that's alive, you have to put something alive back to replace it!"

"Exactly," he said with a broad smile. "That is why we

make compost. It is like a big meal for the garden, to give it new energy."

He held out the bucket to me. "And here is some compost for your own little garden!"

Masahiro brushed off his hands and pulled a tarp over the bins, then disappeared into the shed for a moment and emerged with three wooden-handled knives. "Would you like to help me harvest a few things? I have too many vegetables for one person to eat. I would be honored to give you some, or perhaps you would join me for supper this evening."

I turned questioningly toward Mom. Her eyes still looked tired, but a bit of color seemed to be returning to her cheeks. She stared back at me with something that wasn't quite a smile but still made my heart surge with hope.

"Are you sure?" she asked hesitantly. "That's really kind of you..."

But Masahiro was already nodding and handing us each a knife. "It is a true pleasure. Come, my vegetable garden is this way."

We followed him down the path to another plot, where he patiently taught us how to harvest each plant: delicate fan-shaped leaves of *mitsuba*, Japanese spinach, lacy *shungiku* or chrysanthemum leaves, and dark reddish-purple *shiso*. He demonstrated how to pull up green onions, pushing the tips of our knives into the soil to loosen them and then pulling gently from the base of each stem. We watched as he bent down and pulled an entire large plant out of the ground, shaking the soil off a huge white root almost as big as my arm.

"Wow, what's that?" I asked in amazement.

"This is daikon," he replied. "It is a radish, very common in Japanese cooking."

Even Mom looked impressed. We put all the vegetables in Masahiro's basket, then headed back out to the sidewalk.

It was early evening, and a light breeze stirred the air as we walked past the abandoned buildings and quiet truck yard.

But instead of turning into the neighborhood of colorful houses where Mom and I usually walked, Masahiro continued farther down Ito Street, where the road became wider and lined with old-looking buildings. We turned the corner by a large, boarded-up building with the words PALACE HOTEL in faded paint along one side, then headed down a street of mostly empty storefronts with graffiti and plywood covering the windows, separated by an occasional lit-up gas station or corner market. Almost all the signs had Spanish names: *González* Auto Repair, *Panadería Oaxaqueña, Guadalajara* Super Discount, and *La Hacienda* Ag Labor Services. When we passed a tall church with stained-glass windows and the words *Nuestra Señora de Guadalupe* in gold cursive lettering over the doors, I couldn't help picturing everyone in line for food at the church shelter across town. This was the first time since we began staying there, I realized, that Mom and I had eaten dinner anywhere else.

Just down the street from the church was a small brick storefront with colorful posters in the windows and a sign reading *Las Lupitas* TIENDA MEXICANA. Masahiro stopped in front of the store, looked up, and gave a small nod.

"Here." He led us behind the narrow brick building and up a rickety wooden staircase. When we reached the landing, he carefully removed his shoes and stepped into a pair of house slippers, then pulled a key from his pocket and unlocked the iron screen door. Mom and I followed his lead, untying our shoes and stepping inside.

It took a moment for my eyes to adjust to the dim light. The apartment smelled of old books, incense, and something familiar that I couldn't name. It had a high ceiling and tall narrow windows looking out onto the street below, with long beams of late-afternoon light filtering in. Below the windows were two rocking chairs with flowery cushions that matched the pale yellow and green wallpaper, and along another wall, a worn brown sofa sat beside a bookshelf filled with both English and Japanese titles.

Beside the door where we'd entered was a cabinet of ornately carved wood, decorated with a whole assortment of things: candles, sticks of incense in tiny metal bowls, framed photographs, a basket of fruit, a little bronze sculpture of a laughing man, and two glass bowls of water. I stood there for a moment gazing at this peculiar display, then followed Masahiro and Mom across the room to set down our baskets.

"Please feel at home here," he told us, the word *home* echoing in my ears as we followed him into the small adjoining kitchen.

There was barely room for the three of us to squeeze in, but Mom and I wanted to help, so Masahiro smiled and agreed that we would cook the meal together. Mom washed vegetables at the sink while Masahiro showed me how to chop them finely on a cutting board, holding the knife loosely in one hand while lifting and lowering the handle in a rocking motion.

Crunch, crunch, crunch went the cabbage and daikon and *mitsuba*, filling the kitchen with such a fresh, delicious scent that it seemed like you could eat a meal just by breathing. I helped cut spinach and *shiso* into little pieces and added them to the pot, which Masahiro filled with water from the kitchen sink and put on the stove.

"That's it?" I asked, surprised that making a whole dinner could be so easy.

"Yes," he replied with a small shrug. "*Miso-shiru* is simple. Just vegetables, water and miso. In Japan, people eat this way almost every day."

Mom and I watched as he moved gracefully around the small kitchen, washing cutting boards, taking dishes from a cupboard, and checking a pot of rice on the stove. It had been so long since we'd prepared a meal ourselves in a real kitchen that the whole thing seemed like a special occasion.

"In Japan, we usually made this soup with sea vegetable, mushroom, and tofu," Masahiro explained, "but I prefer to make *miso-shiru* with everything in the garden. Whatever I have today, it goes in the pot!"

He opened the lid to peak inside, letting out a plume of steam and rich aromas. "My mother used to say, 'This is not *miso-shiru*! What has America done to you, Ma-chan?'" He chuckled and carefully turned down the flame under the pot. "But she always ate it with a smile on her face."

A few minutes later, he turned off the stove and let me peek into the soup pot, where the water had turned clear green and simmered in tiny bubbles around the brigh-colored vegetables.

"It is important to stop cooking as soon as they are soft," he explained. "If you cook too long, they will become dull and loose their *qi*. Their flavor, their life."

He went to the fridge, took out a tub of light brown paste that looked like peanut butter, and scooped a teaspoon into each of our bowls. "This is *miso*," he explained. "A fermented paste of soybean, for the broth."

Mom and I watched as he spooned hot vegetable water over the miso, stirring until it dissolved into a cloudy broth, then added a ladle of vegetables to each bowl. He looked over at us and smiled. "There! Fifteen minutes ago you had a basket of vegetables— now you have soup."

"It's like fast food from the garden!" I exclaimed, and we all laughed.

Masahiro scooped rice into three ceramic bowls, which he placed on the table beside the soup bowls, along with small platters of sliced cucumber and ginger. Then he switched on a dim yellow lamp hanging above the table and motioned for us to sit down. "*Gohan desu yo!*" he said with a smile. "This is what we say in Japan, to begin a meal. It means 'rice is ready,' because for us, every meal is eaten with rice."

"Gosh, thanks so much for having us over," Mom said, looking at the steaming bowls of food spread out before us. For a moment, I thought she might start to cry. But instead, she giggled as she clumsily tried to lift a piece of cucumber into her mouth with a pair of chopsticks.

"Like this," Masahiro said patiently, giving a lesson in how to hold the wooden sticks between our fingers. I wasn't much better at it than Mom, and I had to keep picking up fallen rice and vegetables from my lap as we ate.

"Whoa, that's delicious!" I said, after following Masahiro's example and lifting my bowl to sip the broth.

He smiled. "I am glad you like it, Tali-chan. This is something you can always make, when you grow a garden. Very easy and nourishing."

Mom nodded in agreement. "I've never had Japanese food before, but it's really good." I suddenly realized it was the first time in three days that she'd shown interest in food, and it was a relief to see her eating a full meal again.

I was also hungry and began slurping the soup eagerly, taking large mouthfuls of rice and sliced cucumber. But then I noticed how calmly Masahiro ate, just as he seemed to do everything in life, carefully selecting each bite and chewing for a long time before taking another. Feeling a bit embarrassed, I slowed down and tried to do the same.

"Have you lived here a long time?" Mom asked Masahiro.

He finished chewing a mouthful of rice and nodded. "Yes. This has been my home since I came to America, a very long time ago."

"You mean when *Obaachan* died and you left Japan?" I asked, remembering the story.

"You have a good memory!" he said, brightening. "Yes, when I came to El Chorro to reunite with my parents and brothers, they lived here in this apartment. The store beneath us was my father's grocery."

"But didn't your parents work in the fields?"

"Yes. They worked very, very hard in the fields for many years, and like other Japanese laborers, they also rented a small plot and grew their own crops for market. They saved money until finally my father could start his own business."

His eyes got a far-away look. "The *Nihonmachi* was very different in those days. All the businesses on this street were owned by Japanese people... we had a fish market, two grocery stores, a barbershop, the *kabuki* theater, the Buddhist Church, even our own school. It is just a few blocks, but everything you needed was right here. The *Nihonmachi* was like a small town back in Japan, where the streets were always full and everybody knew everybody."

He paused to take a sip of broth. "But this all changed, after the war."

"Why?" I asked.

Masahiro's face grew serious. "Those were the years when we were forced to leave, when all of the Japanese people were sent away."

"Sent *away*?" I repeated, astonished by his words. "How come?"

Masahiro remained quiet for so long I thought he might not have heard, but at last he answered, speaking even more carefully than usual.

"People in America were scared, at that time, Tali-chan. The Japanese army had attacked this country, and people feared that another attack might happen, that we might be spies for

Japan. They had gone blind from their fear... they could not see that we were loyal Americans too."

"So you had to go away?" I couldn't imagine this. How could people like Masahiro be punished, if they hadn't done anything wrong?

He nodded, lips pulled tightly together and eyes intent on a spot on the table. "Yes. Soldiers came to the *Nihonmachi* and forced us to get on buses... everyone. Parents, children, babies, grandparents. We had to leave everything behind: our homes, schools, businesses, our pets, everything that would not fit in a single suitcase. Ah, yes... I will never forget the confusion and crying on that day."

He looked out the window at the darkening sky outside, as though still seeing crowds of anxious people with suitcases in hand, boarding buses in the street below. "We did not know where they were taking us, or if we would ever return."

"That's horrible!" I blurted. I looked worriedly over at Mom, whose face was etched with sadness.

"You have not learned this in school, Tali-chan?" Masahiro asked. I shook my head.

He sighed. "That is too bad... Many people do not like to talk about that time, because it is so painful. But I believe we must tell our stories."

"Where did everyone go, on the buses?" I asked.

Masahiro took another bite of rice, chewed for a long time, and washed it down with a sip of broth before answering. "The soldiers took us on a train with the curtains pulled down, so we could not see out. Finally we arrived in Arizona, at a place called Gila River Relocation Camp. This was like a town in the middle of the desert, made of simple buildings and surrounded by barbed wire and guard towers, like a prison. That is where we stayed for the next three years."

"*Three years?*" I could hardly believe it.

Masahiro nodded gravely. "Yes, until the war ended. I lived with my parents and elder brother Kazuo in one small room in Block Twenty-four, Building Two. My eldest brother, Haruki, lived with his wife and baby in the same building, separated from us by a thin wall. We had cots to sleep on, a small woodstove, and whatever we had carried in our suitcases… nothing more."

"What about a kitchen? How did you eat?"

Masahiro finished the last bite of grated ginger and laid his chopsticks down across the small platter. "We could not prepare food at Gila River. This was one of the hardest things, waiting in long lines every day, to eat in the mess hall. How I missed quiet suppers at home with my parents and brothers, eating *miso-shiru* as we were accustomed! But now everyone sat crowded together for meals, eating unfamiliar foods with a fork and spoon."

A slight smile crept across his face, the wrinkles around his eyes deepening. "But we did have daikon radish. It can grow a root more than one foot long, in just forty-five days. So we planted many acres of daikon at the camp and ate it with every single meal, even breakfast. When the war ended and we finally left Gila River, I thought I would never wish to eat daikon again in my life!"

He chuckled lightly. "But then, I had a surprise. When we came home, everything looked and smelled and tasted different. At the camp, daikon tasted like prison. But back home, daikon tasted like *freedom*. Then I finally understood what the old women in our village meant, when they used to say 'better than a feast elsewhere is a meal at home of rice and tea.'"

He was quiet for a moment, seeming to gaze at something far away, then cleared his throat and pushed back his chair from the table. "Speaking of tea, would you like some? Then we will have enjoyed a truly Japanese meal."

Masahiro gathered our dishes and carried them back to the small kitchen, motioning for us to relax. A few minutes later, he returned to the table with a teapot and three small cups without handles. Holding the pot carefully, he poured us each a tiny amount of steaming lime-green liquid, then returned to each cup and poured a little more. This way, he explained, everybody's tea would have equal flavor.

He raised a cup to his lips with both hands and took a sip, then sat back in his chair with a long, satisfied exhale.

"But why did everything change after the war?" I asked. "Didn't everyone just come back home?"

Masahiro took another sip of tea. "Well... the government allowed people to leave the camps early, if they promised to move far away. My eldest brother Haruki was very eager to leave, so he and his wife and their child moved to New York. Many others did this too. And for those of us who returned, we found things very different here. Our businesses had been sold... large companies had taken over our farms... and many houses were destroyed by fire, or the possessions stolen. There were new people living in the *Nihonmachi* now, and they ignored us in the street, refused to serve us in their shops, even threw bricks at our windows. This is why many people decided to leave El Chorro for the big city, to start over."

"How come you stayed?" I wanted to know.

"We were very lucky," he replied. "My parents had some good friends who protected our building, while we were gone. These people, the Quakers, helped us during that time, guarding our homes and even bringing us supplies in the camp. When we returned, many who lost their homes stayed in the Quaker meeting hall, or in my family's empty grocery store, until they could find someplace to go."

"And then you started the store again?"

He shook his head. "No, my parents were quite old, by

this time. And unlike my brothers, I am not a businessman. So we rented it to someone else. Life went on, but much had changed... the *Nihonmachi* felt like a foreign land. And we had changed, too. We were not the same people who'd left three years before." He sipped his tea and let out another long sigh. "I suppose, in some ways, we never came back."

We sat together around the small wooden table in silence for a few minutes, drinking our tea and listening to the soft tick-tick of a clock in the living room. Outside the window, the sky had deepened to a dark, velvety blue and the street-lights came on.

"Did you feel homesick there?" I asked.

"Yes," he replied slowly. "But the *Nihonmachi* in El Chorro was not truly my home, either. I missed Takamura village in Japan. I knew my place was now here in America... but still, it did not feel like home."

Mom cleared her throat and spoke for the first time in a while. "Did it ever get easier?"

He nodded. "Yes, when I began to grow plants. I still had those seeds I carried in my clothes from Japan, you remember? So I decided to put them in the ground and tend a small garden, as *Obaachan* had taught me when I was a boy."

"You got a plot at the community garden?" I asked.

Masahiro smiled and shook his head. "No, Tali-chan, the garden did not exist then. But do you remember that tiny patch of ground behind this building, near the stairway? That is where I started."

He leaned in toward us, eyes growing wider, as if to tell a secret. "Then something remarkable happened. As the plants grew, putting their roots down into the soil, I too began to feel more rooted and at ease in this place. I discovered that a true home cannot always be found, but is something you can *grow* yourself, like a garden, right where you are."

Mom stared into her teacup without saying anything, and I wondered what she was thinking.

Masahiro tilted his head back to sip the last drops of tea. "Are you sure you would not like a small plot of your own, to garden while you are here?"

Mom raised her eyebrows toward me questioningly, but I shook my head. A little square of dirt by the shed at the Day Center was one thing, but a real garden plot would be too hard to leave behind when we moved to Washington.

"Maybe I could just take some seeds, like you did from Japan," I suggested. "Then, when we move, I can use them to start a garden at our new house!"

He smiled. "Okay, Tali-chan, if you prefer. And of course you are welcome to come to the garden anytime, to learn and gather seeds." He turned to Mom. "I go there every day, quite early. There is a bus stop one block from this apartment, and Talia is welcome to come anytime. I will meet her there, and we can walk to the garden together."

I turned to Mom with excitement. Maybe I could finally stop tagging along to cleaning jobs, and could go to the garden during the long weekdays instead!

"Gosh, that's awfully nice of you," Mom said. "Maybe sometimes, if you're sure it's okay…"

"I promise you, I would enjoy it very much. It is a gift to have such an eager student."

After finishing our tea, Masahiro walked me and Mom to the door, saying it was a pleasure to have our company and that we were welcome to come again. Walking through the living room, my eyes were pulled again to the shiny, intricately carved wooden cabinet with its strange assortment of objects.

"Have you ever seen a *butsudan*?" Masahiro asked, noticing my curiosity. "It is a Buddhist altar, to honor those whom we love."

In the center of the altar was a gold-framed photograph of a woman with dark hair in a bun, a fancy dress with a high lace collar, and a wistful gaze. Just beside this was a smaller black-and-white photograph of several people lined up in a row, wearing formal clothes and staring into the camera with serious faces.

"That is my family," Masahiro said, pointing. "When I was a small boy, before leaving for Japan. You see? There I am, and there are my parents and elder brothers Haruki and Kazuo."

"Who's that?" I asked, pointing to the other photograph.

"That is my wife, Kiyo," Masahiro said quietly. "It has been a number of years now since she died."

He gently touched another photograph in a small oval frame. "This is our wedding photograph. We met at Gila River Relocation Camp, and were married in the church barracks there."

I stared at the little photo of Masahiro standing arm in arm with a young woman in a white bridal dress, on the steps of a long wooden building. I thought it would be sad to get married in a prison town, with no honeymoon or idea when they'd be free again, but when I looked up at Masahiro, he was smiling at the photo with a twinkle in his dark eyes.

"Kiyo," he whispered. "Wasn't she beautiful?"

∽

That night, lying on my cot in the church basement, listening to an old woman's snoring and Skye's occasional cries, I thought about Masahiro as a young man at Gila River Relocation Camp. I tried to imagine him standing in line for showers and meals, or sleeping in the crowded barracks with all the noise of other people's arguments and crying babies coming through the thin walls. I pictured him lying on his own cot and wondering if he would ever have a place that truly felt like home. *Just like us.* I also remembered what he said about "growing a home" anywhere you happened to be, just by planting seeds there. I wished we could plant a house from a seed.

13

THE NEXT DAY WAS SATURDAY, and Mom woke up like her old self again. We rode the bus to the garden, where she dropped me off with Nacha before leaving to clean houses for the day.

I went immediately to the herb garden and meditation pond to look for Masahiro, but he was nowhere to be seen. Lina and Pablo hadn't arrived yet either, and on my way back to Nacha's plot I spotted a heavy-set man with a long black ponytail and a bandana wrapped around his head, standing by the shed talking with two teenagers.

"Hey kid!" he called out as I approached. "You lookin' for Masahiro? He said to tell you he's at a meeting, he'll be back later. Wanna help us instead?"

I hesitated. I'd seen this man in the garden before, usually hanging out with a bunch of high school kids, and I'd always felt a bit scared by their tattoos and metal chains. But his voice sounded friendly, and I was glad he'd offered me something to do until Pablo and Lina arrived.

"C'mon," he said, "grab one of these trowels. We're gonna head over and sow some beans." He gave me a hand-sized shovel and led the way to a corner of the garden, where he opened a small metal gate. Like the other plots, his was covered mostly with rows of corn plants as tall as my knees. On a table by the gate were three plastic cups of beans soaking in water.

"Seen you around here lately," he said, handing me one of the cups. "What's your name?"

For a second I considered introducing myself as T-cat, but nothing came out except my own plain name.

"Talia, awesome. Glad to meet ya." He put up a fist and bumped his knuckles lightly against mine. "I'm Bill Tava. And these are my buddies—Manny, Díaz."

The two high school guys gave small nods but didn't say anything. They looked like younger versions of Bill: dark, muscular shoulders, loose tank tops, chains around their necks, and sharp squinting eyes. The one named Manny had a shaved head with a cloth wrapped over it, and Díaz wore a baseball cap turned backwards. They both kept their eyes to the ground, shoulders slumped.

"Alright, guys," Bill said, handing us each a cup. "So you got some tepary beans there, and we're gonna sow 'em right next to this corn. Watch." He knelt beside a corn plant at the end of one row, pushed his trowel firmly into the soil, dropped in a bean, then patted down the dirt on top. "That's it," he told us. "In a few days those beans will sprout and start climbin' right up the corn."

"That's how Nacha's doing it too!" I exclaimed.

"You bet," Bill replied. "That's what people here on this continent have been doin' for thousands of years. 'The Three Sisters,' they call 'em— corn, beans, and squash."

He turned to look at the boys. "You two guys probably wouldn't be standin' here today, if it weren't for those three plants, ya know that?"

Manny shrugged, and Díaz remained silent. I wondered why they came to the garden, if they seemed so bored with everything.

"Alright, so pick a row," Bill commanded, "and pop 'em in. One for each corn plant."

We squatted between the rows and started burying our beans in the ground. Underneath the dry, crusty surface, the soil was soft and moist, and it was easy to push my trowel down and drop a bean into each hole. I scooted along on my hands and knees, planting one bean next to each cornstalk and imagining tall vines climbing into the air. It was hard to believe, as Nacha had promised, that soon these stalks would be taller than any of us!

The sun was getting hot, and halfway through the first row Manny stripped off his tank top and used it to wipe his forehead. Díaz stood and took off his shirt too, tossing it by the fence and heaving a great sigh as he knelt back down between the rows of corn. They both worked without saying a word, but I had lots of questions.

"Is this the type of corn for making tortillas?" I asked Bill.

"Pretty much," he said. "But this is a kind the Yaquí—that's my people—grow out in Arizona. We make these corn-cakes called *taskari*, sorta like tortillas… and boiled corn with beans, called *posorimme*… all kindsa stuff. Corn's like the main food out there."

"Is that where you used to live?"

"Yep, I grew up in the city, but spent a lotta time at my grandparents' place on the rez. Ya know, the Yaquí Reservation." He turned to look at Manny and Díaz. "You think this is hot? Try *that* for a summer."

The boys kept their heads bent low, dropping one bean after another into the soil.

When we finished planting, Bill gave us all high fives and said thanks for our help. Manny and Díaz pulled wrinkled papers from their pockets and handed them over, and Bill scribbled something before handing the papers back.

"Service hours," he explained to me, after they'd gone. "You know, 'cause they got in trouble."

"That's why they were here?" I asked, the boys' sullen expressions suddenly making sense. "Because they had to?"

He nodded. "Well, they gotta do somethin', right? And this is better than scrubbing toilets in the park, that's for sure."

At that moment, we heard an uproar of voices from the picnic table area, and I followed Bill down the path to see what was happening. It wasn't lunchtime yet, but people had already gathered around. Abuela Jean sat in a folding chair near the fig tree, reading a picture book to a little boy with scabbed knees and a runny nose. I spotted Grace and Rowena with an elderly woman in a wheelchair, and they noticed me and waved.

"What's happening?" I asked, running over to them.

"We're having a meeting with some people from the city," Rowena said. "You know, because they're deciding whether to sell this land."

"You mean the *garden*?"

She rubbed some dry, caked dirt off her fingernails and nodded. "Yeah, nobody told you?"

I shook my head.

"A man wants to buy this land, to build apartments or something. He offered to pay the city a lot of money."

"Right here?" I asked in disbelief. "On top of the garden?"

"*If* the city sells it to him," Grace jumped in. "Nobody's made any decisions yet. We're seeing if we can get them to change their minds."

Just then, someone let out a high whistle and we all grew quiet. Nacha and Masahiro stood at the head of the picnic tables beside two women in business suits.

"Hello everyone," Masahiro said in his usual calm voice. "I would like to introduce Ms. Anne Patterson and Ms. Andrea

Dominguez, from the City Planning Commission. Thank you both for coming today."

The two women smiled and nodded as Nacha, looking a bit nervous, translated Masahiro's words into Spanish. Then one of the women stepped forward to speak.

"Thank you, Mr. Tanaka. And thank you all for inviting us today to see your garden. We know this space is very important to you, and we are committed to hearing the positions of all stakeholders in any land-use decision. We acknowledge your efforts over the years to transform a run-down, abandoned lot into a productive and thriving garden." She paused for Nacha to translate. A ripple of murmurs and whispers spread throughout the group as Ms. Patterson cleared her throat and went on.

"However, we are now investigating ways this historic district may present significant growth opportunities for the city of El Chorro. Redevelopment of the *Nihonmachi* could potentially bring new jobs, homes, and revenues for our city's growing population."

Nacha translated again, and Ms. Patterson continued. "As you know, every opportunity comes with both benefits and costs. Our responsibility as city planning commissioners is to make recommendations to the city council that would maximize the benefits and mitigate the costs. We assure you that in the possibility of this lot being rezoned, we will make every effort to compensate you and provide a new site for your program to continue. We invite you to attend a public hearing on September fourteenth at seven o'clock p.m. in the city administration building, and we thank you again for the opportunity to visit today."

Nacha translated, and another wave of hushed comments swept through the group. Masahiro stood up to shake hands with the two women and thanked them politely for coming.

"Would anybody like to ask a question of Ms. Patterson and Ms. Dominguez?" he asked, turning to all of us.

"Who is this developer that wants to take our land?" Bill Tava shouted out. "Can't we talk with him ourselves?"

"I can provide you with contact information for his staff," Ms. Patterson replied. "I can't guarantee they will speak with you, but you are welcome to try making contact."

"Where would you relocate the garden?" Nacha translated for one of the gardeners who didn't speak English.

"No decision has yet been made," Ms. Patterson answered, "but a potential site near the freeway on-ramp at East Clifford Street has been suggested for evaluation. We would invite you to partner with us in the site-selection process."

After a few more questions, Masahiro thanked the commissioners again and said he would like to present them with a gift from the garden. Grace rose to her feet and slipped under the fig tree for a moment, emerging with a large basket of beautifully arranged vegetables, which she held out to the two commissioners. Rowena stood on a bench and snapped a photo as Ms. Dominguez reached out to take the basket.

As soon as the two women left, everyone began talking at once, raising their hands and asking questions in rapid, high-pitched Spanish. Masahiro waited at the end of the table until people quieted down and turned their eyes toward him.

"I realize you are confused right now," he said, "and possibly afraid, not knowing what will happen. But there is hope. There are many things we can do."

Nacha translated and the gardeners remained silent, eyes intent on Masahiro. "In six weeks," he continued, "the planning commission will have a meeting where we may all stand up to speak. Then they will vote about the 'zoning' of this land, which means the way it can be used. If the zoning is changed, then the developer, Mr. Richards, may build his shopping mall and condominiums here. But if the zoning remains as it is, he cannot do so, and the garden will still be ours."

Masahiro waited again for Nacha's translation, then explained that we still had time to make signs, start a petition, write to the newspaper, and maybe even get on TV, so other people in El Chorro would know what was happening and would come to the city meeting to help us.

Someone suggested gathering again the following week, and everyone agreed to meet at the picnic tables and discuss their next steps.

"*Viva la huerta!*" one person called out. "Long live the garden!"

"We're gonna save this sacred ground!" Bill bellowed, lifting both fists into the air.

❧

I spent the rest of that afternoon with Pablo and Lina, putting the final touches on our fort and then later playing a game of buttons while watching the babies. When *Tía* Yolanda had to run an errand to get new diapers for Raulito, she poked her head under the card table and asked if we'd like to go along. Pablo jumped up, grinning. "Yeah, we get *paletas!*"

"Popsicles," Lina explained to me. "The special kind from Mexico. *Tía* always gets us one."

We set off down Ito Street, Yolanda pushing Raul in a stroller as Pablo and Lina and I raced ahead. We turned by the boarded-up Palace Hotel on Masahiro's street, and to my surprise, stopped right in front of his apartment building. Then I remembered the grocery store. Las Lupitas TIENDA MEXICANA, read the neon green sign on the awning. Above it, almost too faded to decipher, was the outline of old painted letters on the brick: *Tanaka & Sons Grocery*.

It was unlike any store I'd ever been in, a long narrow room with every single inch of space filled with *something*. Around the shelves of typical grocery store items were colorful displays of Mexican candies, tall white candles with paintings of Jesus and the Virgin Mary, sacks of cornmeal piled as high as my head, shelves of sugar-sprinkled rolls, beer advertisements with flashing neon lights, and colorful piñatas hanging from the ceiling. Along one wall stood a display case filled with sausages, fish with their heads still on, something that looked like cow hooves, and enormous discs of white cheese. Lively accordion music came over the speakers, and a group of men in cowboy hats stood around one of the cash registers laughing and talking in rapid Spanish. I could hardly believe that on the other side of the ceiling, above all this color and noise, was Masahiro's quiet, orderly apartment.

Tía Yolanda let us each choose a popsicle from the freezer case by the cash register. There were all sorts of flavors I'd never heard of: *Dulce de leche*, watermelon, coconut milk, *tamarindo*, and Lina's favorite, guava.

Skipping back through the *Nihonmachi* streets with my two friends, licking our popsicles and leaping over cracks in the sidewalk, I almost forgot about the meeting earlier that afternoon. It felt as if summer would go on exactly the same forever, with bean planting and games of buttons, *paletas* and new books under the fig tree, me and Pablo and Lina building our fort and playing amidst the growing jungles of corn.

It wasn't until we arrived back at the garden and found Rowena photographing everybody's plots that I suddenly remembered what was happening, and how the perfect little world we'd created might suddenly be pulled right out from beneath our feet.

14

THAT WEEKEND was a big celebration called *Obon* at the El Chorro Buddhist Church, and Masahiro had invited me and Mom to go. The yard of the old building was decorated with streamers and handmade paper lanterns strung between trees, a stage, and long tables covered with plates of food. We spotted Masahiro standing under a pine tree talking with Mr. Goto and Mr. Furukawa, the same two friends he'd introduced to us before.

"Welcome to *Obon*!" he called out as we approached, reaching to take the bowl of chips and dip we'd brought.

"Our dish isn't really Japanese..." Mom apologized.

Masahiro smiled again and shook his head. "*You* are not Japanese either, but we still wanted you to come!"

Mr. Goto, Mr. Furukawa, and Mom all laughed.

"Did I tell you why we celebrate *Obon*?" Masahiro asked us, and Mom and I shook our heads.

"Ah, that is important to know. This is when we remember our family members who have died. In Japan, it is believed that the spirits of the dead return on this day, so we welcome them home with lanterns and delicious food."

"All the dead people come back to life?" I asked, wrinkling my nose.

Masahiro shrugged slightly. "When we invite them, even in our memories, perhaps they are here with us. That is for you to decide."

Just then, we heard a loud bang and turned to see a group of costumed people beginning to dance on the stage, holding sticks and beating huge wooden drums so hard it shook the ground beneath our feet. People gathered around to watch the performance, and everyone cheered when the first piece was over. One of the drummers came up to the microphone and introduced the group as the El Chorro Taiko Drumming Ensemble, explaining that taiko was a very old tradition for protecting the crops and giving thanks for a plentiful harvest.

"By teaching the art of *taiko* drumming to our youth," he said proudly, "we're keeping our Japanese heritage alive here in El Chorro."

Several kids in costumes came on stage for the next piece and started drumming alongside the adults. I was surprised that some of them didn't even look Japanese, but Masahiro explained that some just had one parent or grandparent from Japan, while the rest of their family was from somewhere else.

"Many people come back to El Chorro for this special day," he told me after the performance was over, "just like in Japan, where everyone returns to their villages in the countryside for Obon. In America, many families come back to the *Nihonmachi* to remember relatives who lived here long ago."

It seemed like everybody at the festival knew Masahiro. People kept coming over to us, giving him long handshakes and calling him *Tanaka-san*, which he explained was a way of showing respect. A few people even called him *Ojiisan*, grandfather, even though he wasn't their real grandpa.

Mom and I hung around for a while as he greeted old friends, held their grandbabies and great-grandbabies, told stories, and laughed at jokes we couldn't understand. When what seemed like the fiftieth old lady came shuffling over with a long bow and the usual "*Saaaa*, Tanaka-san, so good to see you," Mom headed for the food tables and I went to look inside the building.

The church was mostly a big empty room with a wood floor, tall windows, and a polished, ornately carved *butsudan* against the far wall, like the one in Masahiro's apartment. Lining the walls were framed black-and-white photographs and faded newspaper clippings. I stood on my tiptoes to examine a picture of the building when it was new, with a group of men in suits on the front porch.

"Aha! I remember that!"

I turned to see Mr. Furukawa standing behind me, pointing his cane toward the photo. "You see that man right there? That's my father. He helped build this place, back in 1914."

"Whoa, almost a hundred years ago!"

"Yes," Mr. Furukawa agreed with a chuckle. "Has your friend Mr. Tanaka told you the story of our church?"

I shook my head.

"Well now," he began, closing his eyes for a moment and rocking back and forth on his cane. "My father and those other men built this place. Tanaka-san's father too. Back in those days, we used it for everything. This was the center of our world when I was growing up. Weddings, funerals, important meetings... Japanese lessons after school... *shibai* recitals, when we performed old songs and dances for our parents." He smiled wistfully and gazed around the room, as though watching a scene from his childhood.

"Yep, the center of our whole world alright. Sometimes for holidays there were big potlucks, a few hundred people all crowded in here. The men would sit over there, and the women on that side, with us kids running between the tables, causing mischief. We were a big community in those days."

"Until the war?" I asked, remembering Masahiro's story.

Mr. Furukawa shrugged. "I guess so...and times just changed. The older people died, the kids moved away for school...or they married non-Japanese and live across town, and don't come here anymore. Except today, of course! *Obon* is very important, because it helps us remember our history."

He paused and closed his eyes for another moment, then finally said, more quietly, "Yeah, that's true, it was never the same after the war."

"Did you go to Gila River too?" I asked timidly.

Mr. Furukawa nodded. "Yep. I am sorry to say."

He beckoned me to follow him to the opposite wall and pointed to a photograph of several men and women posing in front of a plain building with a sign reading *Furukawa Bros. Produce Company.*

"See? That was my family's company," he said proudly, tapping the tip of his cane lightly on the wooden floor. "We were among the lucky few, like the Tanakas, whose businesses were protected by friends while we were gone."

He gazed at the photo quietly for a moment. "But everything changed. See, before the war, we got vegetables from lots of Japanese farmers in El Chorro. We washed and packed everything for shipping it away by train. That building in the picture was our packing shed. Many vegetables eaten all over the United States, in those days, came from Japanese farmers and packers in El Chorro!"

"Why did that change?" I asked.

"Well..." Mr. Furukawa replied slowly, "A big company, U.S. Produce, took over the small Japanese farms while we were gone, to grow food during the war. And the land was never given back."

He moved farther along down the wall and pointed to a photograph of a family with three children, posing stiffly in front of a small house beside an old-fashioned tractor. "Many friends who used to sell vegetables to us—like the Hiramatsu family right there, you see?—went to *work* for U.S. Produce after the war. Skilled growers, who once operated their own successful farms, just working as laborers in the fields!"

He squeezed his eyes shut and shook his head several times. "It was a rough time for us."

I stared at the photo of the family in front of their home. "So those people never got their farms back?"

"Nope. Most folks moved away, looking for better jobs."

"But you decided to stay here?"

Mr. Furukawa nodded, running his gaze slowly along the row of photographs. "Yep... we stayed. My brother and I took over the family business for a while. But then those big growers started using their own refrigerated trucks, instead of shipping by train. U.S. Produce got its own big packing shed, with vacuum coolers the size of the moon... and they'd just send the vegetables straight there from the fields, thousands of boxes per day. So what could we do?"

"What *did* you do?" I wanted to know.

"Well," he sighed, "in '73, my brother and I shut the place down. All the other packing sheds too, just abandoned... I got an office job, and my brother started driving trucks for U.S. Produce."

He stopped in front of a black-and-white aerial photo of some long buildings along the railroad tracks. "See right there? That was our company. And right there was Pacific Selected Vegetables, our friends the Ikeda family. But it's all gone now, those places that used to be our whole life. And that's where your friend Tanaka-san made his garden."

"Oh!" I exclaimed, everything suddenly making sense. *The big field of rubble behind the garden... the cement platform where Lina and Pablo played hopscotch... all those rotting boards we used for building our fort.* "So the garden is right where your packing buildings used to be!"

Mr. Furukawa nodded. We had now reached the altar at the far end of the room, and he extended two fingers to stroke the little bronze statues surrounded by incense and candles.

"So you see, nothing in this world stays the same. In our religion, we try to remember that."

"Who is that person?" I asked, following his gaze to a little statue on the altar.

Mr. Furukawa looked surprised. "Right there? That is the Buddha!" he replied. "He is our greatest teacher. A man who saw things as they are, and was at peace with the world."

Kind of like Masahiro, I thought to myself.

Just then, Mom came through the doorway of the church and rushed over with a worried expression.

"Did you see this, Tal?" she asked, holding out a photocopied sheet of paper.

SAVE THE NIHONMACHI COMMUNITY GARDEN!

Please help preserve our vegetable gardens in historic El Chorro. Every signature counts!

I looked at the long list of names on the page, then up at Mom, wondering if she'd be upset that I hadn't told her yet.

"I know—" I began.

"Would someone actually tear down that beautiful place?" she asked incredulously.

I glanced at Mr. Furukawa, remembering what he'd just said about nothing staying the same. "Masahiro says there are lots of things we can do," I told her hopefully.

Mom was already signing her name furiously on one of the lines. "Well there's one more for the list!"

A scratchy warble of music came through the speakers outside, and Mr. Furukawa's face lit up. "Aha!" he exclaimed. "Time for the *Bon Odori,* our ceremonial dance!"

We followed as he made his way slowly to the door and hobbled carefully down the front steps of the church. It was hard to imagine that Mr. Furukawa had once been a little boy here in this building, running around and making mischief with other kids.

Out on the lawn, a group of dancers in colorful robes and sashes moved slowly together in a circle, waving their arms in synchronized patterns while everybody else watched and clapped to the strange-sounding music. After the first two dances, someone went to the microphone and invited those who wanted to join in.

"Don't worry!" he said. "Anyone can learn the *Bon Odori!* Just watch the dancers in the middle and follow along!"

On a raised platform in the center of the lawn stood a single taiko drummer, along with four older women poised to lead the dance. Others from the crowd began forming a big circle around them.

I looked up at Mr. Furukawa, who smiled and shook his head. "Nope, my dancing days are done," he said, tapping his cane against the dry grass. "But you go ahead and try!"

I tugged at Mom's hand with a grin, pulling her toward the circle of dancers. She tried to protest, but Mr. Furukawa gave her a playful prod with his cane and said, "Hey it's *Obon,* it only happens once a year." Finally she gave a resigned laugh and joined the circle.

The music started again and we followed along, lifting our arms to one side and then the other, giving a gentle clap and repeating the pattern as the circle slowly started to move. Onlookers swayed and clapped their hands, a hundred paper lanterns swung from the trees above our heads, and for a moment, it was easy to pretend we were all Japanese and living back in the days Mr. Furukawa had described, when the El Chorro Buddhist Church was the center of the world.

15

AS MASAHIRO HAD OFFERED, I began going to the garden on weekdays while Mom did her cleaning jobs. In the morning, she would ride with me to the bus stop near Masahiro's apartment, where he always stood with a thermos of tea in hand, waiting to walk to the garden together. When we arrived, he usually headed straight to the bamboo forest to meditate, while I wandered off looking for somebody to help.

Grace and Rowena both had office jobs and only came to the garden on evenings and weekends, but sometimes I went to their plot anyway and pulled weeds to surprise them. Next to it was a smaller plot with raised wooden boxes filled with soil and plants. This belonged to Grace and Rowena's mother, Mrs. Matapang, who was very old and pulled herself along in her wheelchair between the planter boxes, picking weeds and talking to herself in a language called Tagalog, from the Philippine Islands where she was born.

We soon became friends, and whenever she saw me nearby, Mrs. Matapang would call out in a sharp voice and ask for help with something, like carrying over a pail of compost or filling up a watering can. Then she would start telling stories about "the island," the vegetable garden she tended as a girl, recipes she learned from her mother for strange foods with names like *kangkong* and *upo*, and tricks for making a small amount of food into a big meal that could feed six hungry kids. I would stand quietly beside the wheelchair listening as Mrs. Matapang warbled on, her voice rising and falling like a songbird. Sometimes she even seemed to forget I was there, and would look up suddenly and scold herself for being such a chatterbox.

"Maria Matapang, you talk too much! You're going to talk this little girl's ear off!" she would laugh, shaking her head. But then she always flew straight back into her stories. One of her favorites to tell me was the story of coming to America.

"I was only eighteen years old when the war ended," she began, eyes glazing over with memory. "Only eighteen, can you believe such a thing? A baby! And already married and saying goodbye to my husband, so he could go to America and save money to bring me... He fought in the war, you see, so they let him come. And did I complain, those two years waiting all alone? No, I did not! Not a single word!"

At this point, Rowena and Grace would usually roll their eyes and go back to work as I stood transfixed by their mother's side, her stories rolling on and gathering momentum like a runaway train.

"And do you know how that is, to leave your home and everything in your whole life behind, like I did? No! People do not understand this! But I said to myself, 'Maria, you are a strong woman. If someone else can do it, then you can do it. You can learn to be an American too.' And I worked very, very hard in the packing sheds, sometimes even in the field beside my husband. I was a very, very good wife to him, yes I was. We make our mistakes, María Matapang is no exception, but I can say that I was a very good wife."

She would nod her head emphatically, picking with agile fingers at the weeds in a planter box.

"And he was a good husband too," she always added next. "He joined the strike when the grape pickers said 'Enough! We will not pick another grape until you treat us better!' And I said to myself, 'Okay Maria, this is your time to stand up tall. This is not a time for fear.' So I stayed alone with the kids, while those workers marched all the way to the state capitol... and we marched in the streets and fought very hard, and did we ever give up? No! We fought until we won! Some people say I am an old woman who is crazy in the head, but they do not know what I have seen in my life." She clicked her tongue and said something in Tagalog, then laughed shrilly. "They do not know María Matapang!"

Another favorite story was about the garden's beginning, when Masahiro got permission from the city to start growing vegetables in an empty field near the closed-down packing sheds. Mrs. Matapang was the first person to join him, and they used to carry buckets of water all the way from their apartments each day to the rocky little plots with poor soil at the edge of town. But eventually other people started asking for a space too, and over the years, the soil improved and the garden expanded. Mrs. Matapang used to bring her kids to the plot every weekend to help tend vegetables, insisting that they learn how to prepare Filipino foods and be proud of where they came from, no matter what anybody else said.

"Aren't my girls wonderful?" she asked one day, watching Grace and Rowena at work in the neighboring plot. "And oh, how they used to complain! 'We don't live on the island, Mom,' they would say. But see them now? Growing the best *ampalaya* and *talong* in this town, and making good money too! Ha! So who was right?"

∽

One morning when nobody else seemed to be around, I ran over to Bill Tava's plot to see if our beans had sprouted. *There they were!* Beside each corn stalk was a small green shoot with two open leaves and a third beginning to unfold in the middle.

I knelt to look closer, marveling at how an entire plant could magically start existing from a tiny seed, when I heard the gate opening behind me.

"'Sup kid," Bill called, striding into the plot with a group of bored-looking teenagers trailing behind.

"Look!" I pointed with excitement.

"You bet." He knelt beside me and pointed to the spot where the original bean was still attached, split in half to let the stem emerge from its center. "Crazy, huh? Look at this, guys!"

I noticed that Díaz was in the group, his eyes widening slightly when he saw the bean sprouts. The other kids stood around with shoulders hunched and hands shoved in pockets, making quiet jokes to each other and snickering softly. Díaz bent over for a second to touch one of the tiny plants, then straightened up and shoved his hands into his pockets too, looking embarrassed.

"Alright guys, circle up," Bill commanded, and the high school students gathered in a small group around him.

"You guys know what it's like in the Sonora Desert, in Arizona?" he began.

Nobody answered.

"Dry as dust," Bill told them. "Nothin' but rocks and dirt and sun. But my people have been growing corn and beans in that desert for thousands of years, right outta the sand. You bet those plants don't have it easy. It's a bad deal for a corn plant. But they grow up anyway, and most years they thrive."

The teenagers were silent, staring down at the ground or blankly into space, but Bill didn't seem to mind.

"I didn't care about that stuff, either, when I was a kid," he continued. "Who cared about the ancestors? I didn't wanna be like them, coaxin' scrawny plants outta the desert my whole life. So when I turned eighteen, I stopped going to the rez, and got in a whole lotta trouble... in and outta prison three times. I thought, 'Hey, I'm just a poor Indian kid from a poor family, with parents who drank too much, and no skills but playin' some basketball—I got no future, man. You can't do nothin' with a background like that.'"

A few of the kids looked up at Bill, squinting and frowning into the sunlight. He stared back at them for a moment before going on.

"And it took me a long time to realize *we're* like that corn in the desert. We're just born somewhere, right? And some folks are born in the tropics with lots of water, and some of us come up in the desert, in a year without rain. We gotta struggle. Things that are easy for someone else, we don't have. You know what I'm sayin'?"

A couple of the high schoolers nodded slightly.

"So we gotta put our roots way, way, way down," he continued, "to get any water. We gotta suck out every drop we can. We depend on ceremonies and prayers for rain. We take our chances. People look at us and say, 'Yeah right, you can't grow nothin' in that place. You got no future, man.'"

He reached into his backpack and pulled out two ears of corn, one with dark purple-blue kernels and the other creamy white. "But look at this! You guys see these? They came off my grandma's garden at the rez, in one of the driest years they ever had. Those plants had a tough life. They had all the cards in the deck stacked against them, right? But they grew up and produced a crop anyway."

We all looked at the two large corncobs in Bill's hand, outlined against the bright sky.

"And here's what I want you to think about, guys. Is this corn weaker, comin' from poor soil without enough rain? Or is it maybe *stronger*, 'cause it came from there and survived anyway?"

He pressed his thumb against the ear of white corn and popped off several kernels into his other hand. "Now I'm gonna pass this around, and everybody take a few. You can plant 'em, or just keep 'em as a reminder, whatever you want."

He passed the cob to the kid nearest him, who turned it over a couple times, popped off a few kernels, and put them in his pocket.

Bill Tava bowed his head silently and turned in a slow circle, pausing in each of the four directions for a moment, as the ear of corn moved around the circle.

"You know how long it took me to even think about that stuff?" he asked me and Díaz and a kid named Jordan later that afternoon, as we hoed weeds from around the chile peppers. "I had to sit in prison, bored outta my skull for two whole years before I even started thinkin' about it. There was a Native American garden in the prison yard, and we Indians were the only people who could go in there. Real peaceful spot, corn and cleome flowers and squash climbin' up the fence, and benches where you could sit… it reminded me of my grandma's garden back on the rez. And ya know, that's the first time I felt glad to be who I was. Proud to be *Yoeme*, a Yaquí man."

Díaz and Jordan kept working in silence, scraping the metal blades of their hoes through the soil and leaving clumps of severed weeds to wither in the hot sun.

"So then I found out they had this program for inmates, in that garden, so I started helpin' out. And instead of some good-for-nothing criminal with no future, I started to see myself a bit different, like a person who could actually do somethin.' You know what I mean? I could take care of a plant and make it live. And those plants needed me. They didn't know about my past, and they didn't care."

Díaz paused and looked up from his hoeing.

"Yep," Bill said. "Instead of being so angry at the world for what it didn't give me, I started gettin' excited about what *I* could give! I thought, 'Hell, maybe I actually could have some kinda purpose in life.'"

Now even Jordan had stopped working and looked over at Bill, who wiped the sweat off his forehead and leaned against his hoe handle.

"I thought I could never be nothin' but a failure, a prisoner, a total loser, ya know? But now I was somethin' else. A *gardener*. When I got out two years later, I started workin' for this place up in San Francisco, growin' nursery plants and vegetables. You know what it's like, to get outta prison? Let me tell you guys, it's hell. Nobody wants to hire a dude with a criminal record. Your opportunities look like *zilch*, got that?"

The boys stared at him silently.

"But that's why this place I went is so awesome," Bill went on. "It's for ex-cons, people like me gettin' outta jail. We got to grow a bunch of plants, learn about workin' a steady job, takin' care of money, some volunteer stuff for the city... we worked real hard out there. Some folks didn't make it, and they're back in prison now. But some of us, like me, we got free."

"Why did you stop working there?" I wanted to know.

"Well, I finally got a job in landscape maintenance for El Chorro City College, so I moved on down. But that took twenty years outta my life just gettin' here, ya know? You guys don't wanna learn how I did."

Bill wiped his forehead again and returned to hoeing, and the boys followed his lead. When all the rows were finished and nothing remained but neat lines of pepper plants and limp weeds strewn in the paths between them, he signed everyone's papers, gave a few high fives and fancy knuckle-handshakes, and thanked the high schoolers for an awesome day.

As everyone was leaving, Díaz hung back, looking shyly down at his loose, untied sneakers.

"Hey man," Bill said casually, picking up the hoes and shovels to put away.

"Hey," Díaz echoed. He cleared his throat a couple times. "Hey... uh... all my hours are done."

"Way to go," Bill said. "Been great havin' ya."

"Well, um... I was just wondering..." Díaz shifted from one foot to the other, looking a bit embarrassed. "I was wondering if you could use any help, I mean, with anything, any other time."

Bill broke into a wide smile and gave Díaz a hard slap on the back. "Hey, you mean you *like* it here?" He threw back his head to laugh, and Díaz smiled shyly and gave a small shrug.

Bill took a scrap of paper from his pocket, scribbled on the back, and handed it to him. "There's my digits, call me up anytime, alright? Or just show up on Saturday, you know where I'm at."

Díaz took the paper and nodded. "Cool... thanks."

At the end of those long days in the garden, Mom came to pick me up and go back to the church for dinner, or if it was early enough, to the Day Center to do laundry and use the computer. The routine became familiar, and eventually we got to know most of the other "clients" at the shelter.

There was Lance, the crossword puzzle genius who knew every single word in the dictionary but never talked; Sergio, who made jewelry out of thin copper wire and seashells; and Jocelyn, who was hitchhiking across the country on her way to meet up with friends in Phoenix. Jocelyn seemed to be in love with Sun Dragon, the guy I'd seen playing flute out at the picnic tables a few weeks before. I often saw them sitting together on a worn blanket downtown by the bus stop, with a can of dollar bills and a tattered cardboard sign promising good karma in exchange for random acts of kindness. Sun Dragon would blow his flute, beginning with slow notes that grew until he was playing with his entire body, rocking back and forth, the muscles in his arms flexing and a whole chorus of trills filling the air.

And best of all, there was Cathy, the older, gray-haired woman who liked taking care of T.J. and Skye and the other little kids, and who was always offering bits of mothering advice to Lorna, Christina, and Mom. She would help fold people's laundry and iron their work shirts, put bandages on scraped knees, wipe runny noses, read bedtime stories, and turn on the coffee pot in the kitchen every morning. "Where would we all be, without Cathy our den mama?" Lorna often said with a chuckle.

One afternoon, Mom and I arrived at the Day Center to find two police cars pulled up outside the entrance. There on the sidewalk in front of the officers, head hanging low, was Blade! She shot me an angry look as we passed by, and I lowered my eyes, wondering what had happened.

"Mind your own business," she muttered later, when we were sitting out at the picnic tables.

"I was just worried if you're okay…"

Blade dug the tip of her pocketknife into a piece of bark and scowled. "Well, quit worrying."

I shrugged and slid off the bench, wondering why people had to act so mean, when suddenly I noticed Blade's shoulders were trembling. Tears fell from beneath her shaggy curtain of hair, and she flicked the pocketknife open and closed, open and closed, without saying anything.

I stood awkwardly beside the table, not knowing what to do. I never realized that tough big kids like Blade *could* cry.

Her breath came out in short, ragged heaves, and she coughed several times. "I never even wanted to do it," she sobbed. "Those stupid jerks talked me into it..."

"Into what?" I asked hesitantly.

She closed the knife and buried her face in her hands, shoulders shaking even harder. "God, my life *sucks*. Nobody understands. I owe Sting-Ray for cigarettes, and... and other stuff...and now the cops are on my back, so I'll never be able to pay up. It's totally my fault we got caught, too. They're gonna hate me."

She kicked the picnic bench with one boot, then kicked it again harder. "Why am I even telling *you*. You're just a little kid, you wouldn't get it."

I put my hands on my hips indignantly. "How do you know? Maybe I would." I stared at her and thought for a moment. "I do know what it's like when everything you care about just starts disappearing, and you wonder if things are ever gonna be okay again."

Blade lifted her head a bit and peered at me from behind her hair, with dark smudges of eyeliner and tears staining her cheeks. "Yeah," she said in a small voice.

We were both quiet for a moment. "Are you scared you won't have friends anymore?" I asked cautiously.

She nodded and buried her face in her hands again. "I already don't. Everybody hates me." She choked on a sob but kept going. "And it doesn't even matter, 'cause I'm grounded. How can you be grounded when you don't even have a house, huh? And I also have to do these stupid community service hours, so I'll never be able to hang out anyway…and those jerks that got me into this in the first place, they don't even give a—"

"You have to do community service?" I asked, suddenly getting an idea.

Blade heaved a long, shaky sigh and nodded. "Yeah. My life sucks."

"Wait, I know somewhere really cool where you can do it!" I blurted out. "Growing stuff in a garden!"

I started telling her about Bill Tava, and how Díaz and Jordan and the others got to work and hang out and listen to Bill's stories for their service hours.

"And I don't hate you," I added, hoping she'd believe me. "I bet he wouldn't either."

Blade slowly raised her head again and wiped her face with the back of one sleeve, smearing the eyeliner even more. "Really? You think maybe I could do that?"

I nodded. "I'll ask him."

"Jeez. Thanks, T-cat."

She rose and followed me over to the patch of ground beside the shed, where tiny hollyhock plants were now surrounded by a dense carpet of newly sprouted basil. I knelt and ran my hand across the top of the seedlings, then began "thinning" as Grace and Rowena had taught me, pulling out some plants so others had enough room to grow.

Blade watched silently for a moment. "How do you know which ones to pull or leave alone?"

I shrugged. "I just guess."

Then, to my surprise, she bent down and plucked one of the little plants herself, grinning in that lopsided, almost-frowning way.

"Smell it," I told her, crushing one seedling between my thumb and forefinger.

Blade copied me, and the air filled with the sharp, pungent, sort of minty aroma of fresh basil.

"Dude," she said, holding it up to her nose.

I took a long whiff and grinned. "Cool, huh? Every single plant at the garden has a different smell, but I think basil's my favorite."

Blade stayed and helped me thin the rest of the plants, saying nothing more about her troubles with the police. After a while, Kim joined us too, settling down beside the young hollyhock plants as she did every day, just to look at them.

Sun Dragon sat on a nearby picnic table watching us and playing his flute. "Did you know plants grow more if they hear music?" he called out. "No joke, they've done studies. Some folks think I'm just bummin' around, but they don't see I'm liftin' the whole vibration of this place. So are you, kid! Just keep on manifesting, alright? That's all you gotta do."

Blade rolled her eyes, and Kim kept staring at the plants as though in her own private world. The door of the Day Center slammed shut and Peco came wandering across the yard, stopping to stare at our plants through his plastic mosquito eye. "Lookey," he laughed.

Even Francine came over after a while to see what we were all doing, but instead of scolding about being unsupervised by adults, as I'd expected, she just smiled and said the little plants were "darling."

Later, Cathy took a photo of us with her cell phone, and Sergio picked out a few pieces of broken glass from the soil for making his jewelry. When Blade and I finished thinning the basil, I brushed off my hands with a sigh of satisfaction. Everybody at the Day Center seemed to be enjoying this tiny garden in some way or another.

16

ONE MORNING WHILE I was harvesting *edamame* soybeans with Masahiro, Nacha came and beckoned him over to the fence, where they spoke together in low voices.

"We are praying that he will be alright," I overheard her say before leaving. "May *la Virgen* send angels to be with him."

Masahiro returned with a serious expression and asked if I would like to accompany him to the Rivas home to visit Pablo, who was sick. He'd gone to work again in the vineyards the day before, and fell ill shortly after arriving home.

"Will he be okay?" I asked, watching as Masahiro used his knife to cut big leaves off a loquat tree.

"I suspect he is suffering from too much heat," Masahiro replied. "Or perhaps exposure to chemicals. So we will take *juuyaku*, for detoxifying the body, and *hatogumi*, for energy to heal… and these *biwa* leaves, for cooling."

I followed him around the herb garden as he harvested from one plant after another, explaining the purpose of each. Then we set off across the back field, through a rusty wire gate, and down the embankment to a dirt path along the railroad tracks. I gazed out at the fields of grape vines, where groups of workers in hats and long sleeves were gathered around stacks of boxes.

"It is very hard work, in the fields," Masahiro said, watching them too. "I remember."

This surprised me. "*You* used to work out there?"

"Yes... after the war, this was the only work many Japanese people could find."

I remembered what Mr. Furukawa had said about people becoming farmworkers after the war. But it never occurred to me that Masahiro could have been one too!

"Did you do it for a long time?" I asked, trying to imagine him out in the sun-scorched fields, filling boxes with grapes.

"It seemed long... almost two years. Very difficult work, repeating the same motion all day long. Not like gardening." He paused for a moment and gazed out at the endless rows of vines. "So I know how hard it is for our friends."

"How come you got to stop, after two years?" I wanted to know.

"Well... something happened." He shook his head, lips pursed. "After the war, farmers began using many chemicals in the fields. They told us it was safe. But we saw what happened to workers who were exposed to those chemicals."

"Did they get sick?"

Masahiro nodded. "One day, there was an accident on our crew. The plane spraying insecticide came too close, and the chemicals fell down on us like rain. Many people became ill that day—fever, skin rashes, vomiting—and those who tried to wash themselves in the irrigation ditch only became worse."

"That's terrible!" I exclaimed. "What did you do?"

"Well," he continued softly, "nobody came to help us. Then I remembered a remedy that *Obaachan* taught me, for poisoning. I hurried back to my tiny plot behind the grocery store and cut leaves and roots to prepare this remedy. In time, we all recovered... but I decided I would not work in the fields anymore."

"And your wife too?"

Masahiro nodded. "At first, nobody would hire Japanese teachers, but finally she got a job. And for myself, like other men in the *Nihonmachi*, I found work tending people's yards. Soon there were no more Japanese people in the crop fields, only Mexican and Filipino. But the same problems continued for those new workers... and we continued trying to help."

"How?" I thought back to Mrs. Matapang's stories about her husband and the other grape pickers walking all the way to Sacramento.

"We organized big marches," Masahiro said, "and told people not to buy from companies that treated farmworkers poorly. We arranged meetings, published articles, sometimes picketed in front of stores."

"Did it help?"

He thought for a moment. "Yes. But there are still many struggles. Even for those who have stopped working in the fields, it still affects us..." A look of sadness came across his face. "I always wondered if perhaps that is why my wife and I could not have children."

The path along the railroad tracks ended at a neighborhood of bumpy gravel roads lined with trailers and mobile homes. At the end of the road stood a group of buildings similar to the motel where Mom and I had stayed, which Masahiro said were apartments for the migrant fieldworkers and their families. The long narrw buildings were surrounded by dusty cars and pick-up trucks, and along the rows of identical doors were an assortment of lawn chairs, barbecues, and piles of mud-caked sneakers and boots. Many of the windows were open, with the sounds of clanging pots and Spanish TV commercials drifting into the hot afternoon.

Masahiro led the way to one door and knocked lightly. After a moment, Lina appeared, balancing María Rosa on one hip and holding a bottle of milk in the other hand. Her face lit up with surprise when she saw us, then grew serious.

"Pablo's really sick!"

"Yes, Li-chan." Masahiro gave her shoulder a gentle pat as we stepped inside. "I brought something that may help."

The air in the apartment was even hotter than outside, smelling of maple syrup and diapers. Raulito sat in a highchair by the window, smearing something all over his face with a slobbery grin. As my eyes adjusted to the dim light, I was surprised to see how tiny the apartment was. It really *was* like the motel room where Mom and I had stayed, but with two double beds and a small kitchenette with a sink full of dishes. Taped to the walls were a bunch of school assignments and crayon drawings, curled gluey ribbons of flypaper, and a small faded painting of the *Virgen de Guadalupe*. It was hard to believe the entire family lived in such a small space! Toys, clothes, backpacks, and books were scattered around the floor, and we stepped carefully over to the bed where Pablo lay, eyes half open. Masahiro bent down to touch his forehead and hands.

"Pa-chan? Can you hear me?"

Pablo made a small moaning sound, and Masahiro spoke again in a voice so soft I could barely hear.

Suddenly Raulito let out a wail, and Lina unlatched his high chair and lifted him down to the ground with her one free arm. He immediately set off crawling toward the front door, which she ran to shut before he could escape. "No, no, Raulito, stay in!"

"Do you take care of both babies every day?" I asked.

"It's easy when Pablo and I do it together," she said. "But now he's sick."

"Did he get poisoned?"

Lina made a worried frown. "Poison? I don't think so..."

He got too hot, that's what *Tío* said. My dad's back was hurt, so Pablo went to work, and he's not used to the sun yet."

Masahiro asked if he could boil a pot of water, to make the remedies. Lina nodded eagerly and handed María Rosa to me. The baby's face puckered for a moment, but when I bounced gently as I'd seen Lina do many times, she poked her tiny fingers into her mouth and settled down. Lina washed a cooking pot, and we both watched with curiosity as Masahiro brewed some tea, strained out the leaves, and set this on a nightstand beside the bed.

"It must cool first," he said. "Then he must sip it slowly throughout the day. *Biwa* leaves can help to cool the body. With rest, he will be able to heal by himself."

To my relief, Pablo did get better, and Masahiro and I began going to the farmworker apartments more often. He took lots of tea and dried herbs to people there, and I would spend the afternoon playing with Lina and Pablo, helping them care for the babies while their parents and Toño were at work.

One afternoon, Antonio and Dominga came home looking very upset. I continued playing with Raulito on the floor while everyone else sat on the beds talking in Mixteco for a long time in hushed, serious voices.

"*Tía* and *Tío* got deported," Lina told me afterward, her face drawn and eyes wider than ever. "They had to go back to Mexico, 'cause they don't have papers."

"Papers?" I was confused.

Pablo jumped in. "She means they're illegal. Like they don't have permission to be here, and they got caught."

I stared at my friends' frightened faces, taking in the news. Raulito squirmed in Pablo's arms, and he set his little cousin down on the floor.

"But are they coming back?" I asked. "What about Raulito?"

"We don't know," Lina said in a small voice. "They're gonna try as soon as they get enough money."

"But it's really hard to get back here," Pablo said, "'cause you have to walk in the desert for a long, long time, and it's dangerous."

Dominga came and put an arm around Lina's shoulders, patted Pablo on the head, and whispered something in Mixteco. Even though I couldn't understand the words, I knew she was saying that everything would be okay.

That night, I wrote three new stories in my red notebook, all about farmworker families who got their very own land to farm. They didn't have to work in vineyards anymore, and could rest during the hottest part of the day, and could live in one place all year long. They were excellent gardeners and knew how to grow all sorts of food, and they produced such delicious corn and beans and squash and chile peppers that the government gave them papers to stay in America forever.

17

THE REST OF THAT SUMMER, I spent almost every day in the garden. I harvested vegetables for farmer's market with Grace and Rowena, stripped flower stems for Mrs. Murphey's bouquets, helped barbecue young cactus pads called *nopales* from the Rivas family's plot, and learned most of Masahiro's healing plants and their uses. When the other kids and I got scratches from thorns or splintery boards in the field, I rubbed the yellow sap of *ashitaba* plants on our skin to help it heal faster, and when the days were hottest I prepared *biwa* tea to cool us down after long mornings playing in the sun.

I got to know each of Bill Mitchell's cats by name, and I sat under the fig tree on hot afternoons listening to Abuela Jean read books and teach kids how to read. Some of the farm-worker children moved around too often to stay in one school all year, she explained to me. Besides, it was harder learning to read in English, which they barely even spoke yet. So Abuela would sit under the fig tree every Saturday with stacks of colorful picture books and a crowd of children around her, making sure everyone took a turn to read aloud.

"It never occurred to me," she once told Mom with a laugh, "when I retired from the classroom, that my favorite teaching position was actually about to begin!"

As the weeks went on, I got to know the other gardeners too. There was Felipe Sánchez, Pablo and Lina's great-great-uncle or something like that, who always sat in the shade of his plot strumming a small guitar and singing to his corn plants. Sometimes he sang so loudly that other people working in their plots would smile and hum along, joining in for a few lines of a familiar song.

I became friends with Masahiro's old friend Mrs. Ikeda, who was nearly blind but still tended her plot almost every day, sometimes bringing homemade Japanese pastries called *manju*—little buns with sweet red bean paste in the middle— for us as a treat. We would sit in the shade of the fig tree and sip cold barley tea, with a snack of salted soybeans and *manju*, as Mrs. Ikeda and Masahiro discussed the progress of their gardens.

And of course there were the many farmworker families, who picked grapes during the week but still came on evenings and Saturdays to care for their plots of towering corn. Even on scorching days that could turn a person's arms and legs to lead weights, the kind of heat that hammers you down like a nail until it's almost too hot to breathe, the farmworkers still came to work in their plots. They wore wet towels draped over their necks and large bandanas hanging down from their hats, to soak up sweat and protect their skin from the sun. Sometimes they would take long breaks in the shade, but they still came to the garden, no matter how hot it was.

One day we all had a party for Lina's birthday, with her mom's homemade *tamales* and a *piñata* hanging from the fig tree. Pablo taught me "Happy Birthday" in Spanish, and Felipe strummed his guitar as Lina blew out all nine candles at once.

Just as Nacha promised, the corn had finally grown high over our heads, the ground beneath it a thick mass of sprawling squash plants with giant platter-sized leaves. Bean vines spiraled up the cornstalks, their curly tendrils rising into the air above the pollen-coated tassels. It was like every plot had its own miniature jungle, buzzing with insects and glowing almost neon green in the sunlight. Corncobs gradually fattened along the thick stalks, with pale tender silks poking out the top like uncombed hair. Large patterned spiders hung upside down from webs between the plants, white cabbage moths fluttered in and out among the squash vines, and orange and black ladybug larvae crawled slowly along the leaves, devouring aphids. All those once-bare patches of dirt with their tiny seedlings had somehow transformed into bustling cities of life!

One week in the middle of summer, everyone's tomatoes suddenly ripened as well. Some were ordinary red tomatoes like at the grocery store, but there were also stripey Green Zebras, big yellow Hawaiian Pineapple tomatoes, Cherokee Purples, skinny San Marzanos and monstrous Brandywines, Rainbow Beefsteaks with ribs and folds of multicolored flesh, spotted Tigerellas and Zapotec Pinks, heart-shaped Orange Russians, and little Sungold Cherry Tomatoes as sweet as candy. In almost every plot, unruly tomato plants sagged from the weight of hundreds of fruits, with even more falling and rotting on the ground beneath. I learned how to eat fresh tomatoes just like apples, biting into the sweet, soft flesh with juice dripping down my chin.

One of Masahiro's tomato plants was growing in a large plastic bucket, instead of in the ground. He told me it was an experiment to see if he could create a tomato plant that was *perennial*, staying alive year after year like a tree.

"Tomatoes die in winter because of frost," he explained to me. "But in warmer, tropical places, like the island where Mrs. Matapang is from, tomato plants can live for many years. They become like bushes, with woody trunks."

"Whoa, a tomato *bush*?"

Masahiro smiled with a twinkle in his eye. "Yes. So I am doing an experiment, to see if I can create an Everlasting Tomato in our part of the world. For two years, I have brought this plant inside my apartment for the winter, to keep it alive. You see? It is beginning to form a tough stem."

I looked where he pointed, noticing how the main stem of the plant had become brown and hard, twisting around like the bark of a gnarled tree.

"Someday soon," Masahiro went on, "I will transplant it, to see if this plant can survive winter in El Chorro. Imagine, a perennial tomato! Everything *wants* to live, you see. And we can find ways to help. If this tomato is placed near sheltering plants, with good sunlight from the south and a thick blanket of straw on the ground, it just may thrive."

"Whoa," I said again, reaching out to stroke the leaves of the two-year-old tomato plant.

Masahiro laughed lightly. "It is just an experiment."

One day, Abuela Jean invited some of the gardeners to her house for a "canning party." We stood around the kitchen table, slicing tomatoes and tossing them into large pots, as Abuela told stories about long days canning over a hot stove as a child on her family's dairy farm in Illinois.

"If you wanted food to eat in winter," she explained, "then you had to can it, in summer. No supermarkets!"

When the tomatoes had boiled down into a thick, reddish-orange pulp, we carefully ladled it all into clean glass jars, screwed on the lids, and boiled the jars to sterilize them for storage. By the end of that afternoon, the kitchen counter was lined with shiny jars of tomato sauce, which could sit in a

cupboard for years without spoiling. Abuela Jean sent everyone home with several jars and said she'd be happy to host
another party anytime.

"Apples will be ripe in a month or two," she said, winking
at me. "I can always use help canning applesauce."

ॐ

Masahiro had his own ways of preserving the surplus
vegetables and fruits in the garden. One day in early summer,
I helped him fill buckets with unripe yellow-green fruits and
carry them back to the apartment for making a special kind of
pickle called *umeboshi*. First we cut out the pits from each fruit,
then packed the pieces tightly into clay pots with bunches of
red shiso leaves and salt water.

"These are not real *ume* plums," he told me, "like in Japan.
They are close, but not the same. Here in America, I have never
seen a real *ume* tree." He pulled another clay pot from the
cupboard and took out a wrinkled red *umeboshi* for me to try.
I nibbled it and scrunched my face as the tangy, super salty
flavor spread over my tongue.

"Yuck!"

Masahiro laughed. "It is an acquired taste, I suppose. In
Japan, we used to eat *umeboshi* with breakfast every morning,
for cleansing. It is very good for digestion."

He showed me his large cupboard filled with clay pots
of pickles, not just from *ume* plums but all sorts of things. On
afternoons when it was too hot to work in the garden, we
sometimes carried baskets full of vegetables back to the cool,
dim apartment to make *tsukemono*, pickled vegetables. The
kitchen table would become a rainbow of color as we chopped
up daikon radishes and turnip leaves, carrots and Chinese
cabbage and small *kyuri* cucumbers, sprinkling them all with
salt and packing the mixture tightly into clay pots.

"This is how we kept food from spoiling," he explained, "before the refrigerator. Even here in America, my mother always had a crock of *tsukemono* in the pantry."

∿

After many weeks of meetings in the little office at the Day Center, Alicia finally convinced Mom to meet with the psychiatrist who offered free testing at the church. Later, Mom went to see him for a second appointment and got a prescription for some sort of medicine to help her not get sad anymore.

"Is there really something wrong in your brain?" I asked cautiously one morning, as she unwrapped a little white pill to swallow with her oatmeal.

Mom was quiet for a moment and then shrugged. "I don't know, Tal... I just don't know anymore."

She chewed a spoonful of cereal, placed the pill in her mouth, and washed it down with a gulp of orange juice. "But Alicia says we might qualify for a special program to get a place to live, if I take these... so it can't hurt to try, right?"

I nodded hesitantly. A house sounded great, but I didn't want anyone thinking Mom was crazy. Didn't some people just get sad more easily than others?

Mom *had* seemed happier in the last few weeks, but I couldn't tell if it was because of the pills or because we'd been spending so much time at the garden, relaxing under the fig tree and harvesting vegetables with Grace and Rowena and making flower bouquets with Mrs. Murphey. Mom had turned out to be an expert flower arranger, combining the different shapes and colors into elaborate masterpieces that even impressed Mrs. Murphey herself.

"Your mama's got a gift from God," she told me one day. "That woman's an honest-to-goodness artist."

By the middle of August, I realized all Mom's promises about being settled by the time school started were not going to work out. Even though I loved everybody at the garden, it wasn't the same as being somewhere we could stay forever. I wanted to plant our very *own* garden, at our own home that we'd never have to leave behind. So I was still praying for some sort of miracle, for a whirlwind to lift us into the sky and drop us down at the perfect house of our very own in Washington, like Dorothy landing in Oz. My heart sank with disappointment when Mom broke the news that it was time to enroll me in school for sixth grade.

"In El Chorro?" I asked innocently, even though I knew she meant in El Chorro.

At that moment, I made a decision. The next day in the garden, I told Masahiro that I'd changed my mind and would like to have a plot for myself and Mom after all. He smiled with a touch of sadness in his eyes, as if he understood exactly what that meant.

"I believe this is a perfect place for you," he said, leading the way to an empty plot overgrown with weeds and partially shaded by the low-arching umbrella of a mimosa tree. "It has good partial shade in the summertime, and good winter sun when the mimosa loses its leaves. It has not been tended in many years, so the soil is well rested and has much life to give."

He spoke and moved a bit more quickly than usual, so I could tell he was getting excited. "I have many seeds to share with you and your mother. And please ask if there is any help you need."

I thanked him, beginning to feel excited too. I had been determined not to start a garden until we settled down for good, so we'd never have to leave it behind... but kneeling to run my hands through the matted weeds and crusty soil of our very own plot, I couldn't help a rising thrill in my chest. This was *our* little piece of earth, for now. Our square of soil, with its billions of tiny living creatures to take care of. We could grow anything we wanted!

When Masahiro returned to his work and nobody was watching, I flopped down on my back in the tall grass, looked up at the lacy green leaves of the mimosa tree fluttering in the afternoon breeze, and laughed aloud. Who cared if it wasn't forever, if we had to leave our first garden behind and start a new one? This was ours for now, a place of our very own, and that was all that mattered. I lay in Mom's and my new garden, looking up at the sky through the branches of the mimosa tree, and laughed and laughed and laughed.

18

A FEW WEEKS LATER, I began sixth grade in Mr. Parker's class at Chorro Elementary. I hated being the new kid, not knowing anyone, and trying to make sure nobody figured out we were homeless. I buried my nose in my notebook on the school bus, stuck to myself at recess, and was always the first one out the door when the bell rang at the end of the day.

When Mom didn't have cleaning jobs, she would meet me at the downtown bus stop after school and we'd head to the garden together to work in our new plot. First, we cleared out the weeds and hauled wheelbarrows full of dry grass to the compost piles behind the shed. Then we watered the hard, dry soil to soften it.

Masahiro explained that good soil has both sand and clay, with clay holding water like a sponge, and sand letting water pass through. "Just like a happy life," he said, "there must be a balance between holding onto things and letting them go."

He showed us how to tell when the ground was ready to dig, pressing together a handful of soil and bouncing it gently in his palm, causing it to crumble and spill through his fingers.

"See?" he explained. "If the ball sticks together, the soil is too wet and must not be touched. But if it falls apart like this, it is ready."

We took off our shoes and worked barefoot, the mild September sunlight warm on our backs and the damp earth soft between our toes. Soon we fell into a rhythm, pushing our shovels into the ground to turn over the dark clumps of soil, which were teeming with grayish-pink earthworms. Together we raked the soil into raised beds, then carried over buckets of compost to mix in with our hands. Kneeling down, we sank our fingers into the cool, crumbly earth that smelled like rain, sifting it methodically and then smoothing over the surface to make a comfy bed for our seeds. As we worked, we discussed plans for all the things we would grow: lettuce, spinach, peas, carrots, bok choy, radishes, and of course, all sorts of flowers.

Mom was more excited than I'd seen her since we came to El Chorro. She was filled with ideas for the plot, describing how calendula flowers would look beautiful next to the lettuce, how lavender bushes would help attract bees to our plot, and how Abuela Jean told her that cabbages grew better if you lined the bed with chrysanthemums.

"We could put sweet-pea flowers around the trunk of the mimosa tree," she said. "Then, when the tree is bare in winter, the sweet pea vines can climb into the branches. Wouldn't that be pretty?"

She also wanted to plant a wide border of flowers around the plot, starting with red and going through all the colors of the rainbow. "It's like we're artists, Tal!" she exclaimed. "The plot is our canvas, and we can paint any picture we like."

Mom really did look like an artist, I thought to myself, with a smudge of dirt on her cheek, hands crusted in dry clay, the knees of her jeans wet and muddy from kneeling in the paths, and loose strands of hair from her ponytail hanging around her face. Her cheeks were glowing pink, eyes sparkling with excitement, and her movements quick and sprightly as though she were a kid herself.

We squatted across from each other and poked little holes for the peas, then sprinkled tiny lettuce and carrot seeds over the surface and raked them in lightly with our fingertips. Finally we patted down the soil and watered everything, leaving the surface dark and glistening in the rich early evening light.

"Please grow," Mom whispered, and my heart quickened at the thought of all those seeds beginning to sprout underground, pushing down new little roots and sending up stems to become entire plants.

We gathered some fallen leaves and spread them over the surface of our new beds as Masahiro had suggested, to keep the soil wet and the earthworms comfortable. Mom and I worked until it was too dark to see, then finally put away our tools in the shed and headed for the bus stop in the last remnants of daylight, feeling tired and satisfied. I loved returning to the church those evenings after working at the garden, with dirt under my fingernails and images of the little plot beneath the mimosa tree still vivid in my mind.

One day, Mom and I drove all around town with Rowena in her big blue pickup truck, stapling flyers to every telephone pole and cork board we could find, so that people would come to the planning commission meeting on September 14th. If the commissioners saw how many people cared about the garden, surely they would vote to save it!

When the day of the meeting finally arrived, everyone gathered at the picnic tables for a short meeting of our own. There was a chill in the evening air, and people sipped from cups of steaming *ukogi* tea that Masahiro had brought. Many trees in the garden had already begun to lose their leaves and stood half bare against the sky, surrounded by a confetti of yellow and orange.

Masahiro made a short speech about how this was our chance to make our voices heard. "You will each have three minutes to speak, if you so choose," he explained. "But either way, simply your presence in the room will be helpful."

Nacha translated into Spanish, and people nodded their heads and murmured to one another.

"*Sí se puede!*" somebody called out, and then we all took hands in a circle and chanted together. "*Sí se puede! Sí se puede!*"

Even Mrs. Murphey and Bill Mitchell, who usually bickered and couldn't tolerate the sight of each other, stood chanting side by side.

"We're gonna rock this meeting!" Bill Tava yelled. "Nobody can take away our garden!"

"*Qué Dios nos bendiga en esta causa,*" Nacha whispered. "May God bless us in this work."

"*Viva la tierra!*" Felipe sang out with his deep scratchy voice and toothless grin. "*Vámanos, pues!*"

The sky had deepened to purple and the light was rapidly fading as we all headed down the main path of the garden to leave for City Hall.

The meeting chamber was a big, brightly lit room with a high ceiling, tall windows with velvety shades, and rows of cushioned folding chairs like a theater. A soft hum of voices filled the space as people took their seats and waited for the meeting to begin.

We filed in quietly, and Mom and I chose seats near the back of the room beside Antonio and Dominga, who seemed even more shy than usual. Across the aisle, Mr. Furukawa kept folding and unfolding his hands over his wooden cane, frowning in concentration.

I sat up tall in my chair to look around. At the front of the room were a large projector screen, a United States flag, and a long shiny table where men and women in business suits sat in swivel chairs. Beside each person was a name plaque, a microphone, and a pile of papers. I recognized Ms. Patterson and Ms. Dominguez, who had come to speak with us in the garden. In front of the table, two women at a smaller desk were typing on computers and flipping through stacks of paper.

When it was time to begin, the person at the center of the long table tapped a small wooden hammer and asked everyone to stand for the Pledge of Allegiance. Then a woman at the smaller desk called roll, and the meeting began.

Computer keyboards clicked away as the commissioners took turns speaking into their microphones in serious voices, using big words I didn't understand. This went on for such a long time that I wondered if they were ever going to talk about the garden. I swung my feet back and forth and counted the seconds, wishing I'd brought my red notebook.

Finally, a woman at the desk announced "Item number four, public hearing for request by the Richards Development Corporation to consider a General Plan amendment, changing the land-use category from ag-industrial to commercial mixed use, on two adjacent seven-acre and five-acre parcels on Ito St. in West El Chorro."

After more official talk that sounded like another language, two men in crisp white shirts and ties walked up to the desk in front of the commissioners and sat down, spreading out paperwork and adjusting their microphones.

"Good evening, Chairperson Minetti and members of the commission, my name is Andrew Ingersall, staff planner. I will now give an overview of the project proposal."

The screen projector lit up, and Mr. Ingersall spoke on and on about the graphs and diagrams on the screen. One slide showed an aerial photograph of the garden, looking like a strange maze of skinny brown lines through blocks of green. From way up in an airplane, you couldn't see the flowers and fruit trees and hammocks, the hanging wind chimes and little sculptures and colorful vegetables in people's plots. *That's not really how our garden looks!* I wanted to shout.

The next picture showed a view of the garden from the street, similar to how I'd seen it the first time, an unruly jungle stretching out beyond the gate with the faded wooden sign. The row of sunflowers had already begun turning brown, their giant heads hanging heavily over the sidewalk like sad clowns, with tangled masses of bindweed twisting around the stalks and obscuring the rest of the garden from view.

When the next slide appeared, I stifled a gasp at the sight of a computerized image of a shopping mall with condos on top, surrounded by a parking lot filled with cars. *That would be right on top of our garden?* A few people took sudden breaths and shifted in their chairs.

Mr. Ingersall continued with his presentation, moving a laser pointer across more graphs and describing the "economic and social benefits" of the proposed project.

Then the commissioners asked him a lot of questions, using big words like 'mitigation,' 'CEQA,' and 'buffer zones.' What were they *talking* about? I turned around in my chair to look at the people around us, most of whom seemed bored or confused as well. Felipe Sánchez had dozed off with his chin resting on his chest, Bill Tava gazed out the window at the dark sky outside, and Dominga and Antonio were staring ahead with polite, blank expressions. I heaved a sigh and looked imploringly at Mom, who patted my knee and gave a sympathetic smile.

The meeting dragged on, until finally Chairperson Minetti announced that the item would be open for a public hearing.

Those who wished to speak needed to fill out a yellow card, line up at the podium, and keep their comments to three minutes each.

Nacha went first, clearing her throat and adjusting the microphone nervously a few times before beginning. She sounded timid at first, but seemed to gain confidence as she continued. "Good evening to all of you. My name is Ignacia Jiménez, and I live in West El Chorro. As you all know, this land is now a garden for more than sixty people. We are mostly low-income families, and without a place to grow food, many of us would use food stamps. But when we have a way to take care of ourselves, we do not need help from the government! So please, we hope that you understand this is more than a hobby... we are feeding our families. Please do not allow our land to be re-zoned for development!"

I smiled and silently clapped my hands as Nacha walked back to her seat. She'd been practicing the speech for several days, reciting it to me as we pulled bindweed and harvested tomatillos, frowning and asking whether I thought her English was good enough for the commissioners. "*Hooray!*" I mouthed as she took a seat and looked over at me with a satisfied grin.

Next, a person I didn't recognize went up to speak. "Clint Peterson, East El Chorro. I'd just like to point out," he stated in a loud, firm voice, "that most of the property on Ito St. is not even utilized. At least three acres are just sitting idle. I don't think the question is about the value of a community garden, but simply whether that's the best *location* for such a use. The garden benefits only about sixty people, while the applicant's proposed development could benefit hundreds, even thousands, more. I suggest that the garden simply be relocated to a comparable site elsewhere in the city."

Mrs. Matapang was already wheeling herself to the podium in fast, furious movements. I saw Grace and Rowena exchange a nervous glance as somebody handed the microphone to their mother.

"I am María Estrella Matapang," she began in a shrill voice, "and I have lived in El Chorro for a very, very long time. You talk like the garden is something we can roll up like a rug and move elsewhere? Ha! You do not understand anything! We have *fruit* trees! We have worms! Do you see these wrinkles on my face? Yes, that's right! I'm an old woman! I've been in this town longer than any of you, so I know what I am talking about! I saw that land before it was a garden, and it was hard like a big *brick*. After thirty years, it is now good soil that can produce. This does not happen in one day! Do you know how long I have been growing food? No, you don't! I have been growing food in soil for more than seventy years! Yes, seventy. So you should listen to me. I will tell you, it takes many years to make a place that can grow anything. If we start over, I will be dead in my grave by the time a new garden is good for anything! If you think it is something that can just be moved, you are all crazy in the head!"

A few of the commissioners looked at each other or bent over their papers with hints of a smile. I wondered if they thought Mrs. Matapang was just a silly old woman, or if they actually heard what she'd said.

Next, a teacher from El Chorro City College talked about plant and insect diversity in the garden, with a bunch of stuff about 'carbon footprints' and how important it was to have 'green space' in a city.

Then one of the gardeners I didn't know walked up to the podium and began speaking in timid, halting Spanish. Mr. Minetti interrupted to ask if someone at the smaller desk could please translate. Several of the gardeners around us smiled, and I realized it was the first part of the meeting in a language they understood.

"My name is Teresa Molinero," the woman at the front desk translated. "My husband and I come to El Chorro every year to work in the vineyards. We have seen the charts and numbers showing the dollar value of this proposed project...but can you also place a dollar value on the health and happiness of people who work in your city? We don't have a fancy chart with numbers, but we know that many people are happier and healthier because of the garden."

When she finished, a few more gardeners rose from their seats and joined the line behind the podium. Even Antonio Rivas made a brief, polite comment about how his family's plot allowed them to live better and teach their children about healthy food.

"Our plot saves us hundreds of dollars in food every year," the woman at the desk translated for another person. "My family used to get food from Uvas County Food Bank. But now there's so much extra, we *donate* to the food bank!"

To my surprise, even Mom went up to the microphone and nervously told the commissioners that the garden was a beautiful place, and wasn't it important for the city to consider things like beauty, as well as money?

Rowena gave a polished lecture about how most produce in grocery stores was delivered by trucks and airplanes from thousands of miles away, so it wasn't fresh and healthy like food grown here. She spoke fast, gesturing with sweeping arm movements, explaining the benefit of 'local food systems' and the reasons to preserve some city land for agriculture. "Shouldn't people have the right to grow their own food, in the neighborhood where they live?" she concluded, rushing to finish her sentence as the three-minute timer started beeping.

Then Grace went up and made an equally long speech about the possibilities for the unused space behind the garden. "We could actually be growing a lot more crops there," she said enthusiastically, "for people in El Chorro! We could have a roadside stand to sell produce, and people could take classes and learn about growing food…I'm not kidding, that land could provide all sorts of jobs and money, if the city would give us a little more support. You keep talking about 'development potential,' and I think the garden has lots of potential too, if you'd just work with us, not against us."

Abuela Jean explained that the garden was an excellent learning place for children, and Mrs. Ikeda talked about how some gardeners grew traditional cultural foods that weren't available in grocery stores. Then Bill Tava strode confidently to the microphone.

"My people have been getting kicked off our land for the past four hundred years," he declared in a booming voice. "Forced off by someone wanting to profit from the land, to take something without asking permission. But when my people, the Yaquí—the *Yoeme*, we call ourselves—whenever we took something from nature, we always asked permission from the plants and animals first.

"But the Spanish came and found silver in the Yaquí River Valley and started claiming the land. Then the Mexican army tried to kick us off too. The *Yoeme* fought for a hundred ninety years, to protect that land! A lotta people got killed, or ran for their lives. And you know what? That's why I'm standin' here today. Because my grandparents escaped, and went to work like slaves in the Arizona cotton fields.

"So, you see why Yaquí are known for being warriors? We *had* to fight. We never gave up, and many are still on that land today. But what about the ones of us who were forced to leave? Thousands of people up in Arizona now, on the reservation or in Phoenix…and they got no employment, and the kids are gettin' into drugs, 'cause they got no connection with their ancestors, their roots, the *land*.

"So here's my question. The people who know how to live on land and respect it and produce food—why are we the people always gettin' kicked off? By someone who wants to make a buck?

"I can tell you this. My ancestors were strong people who died fightin' for their ground, and you better believe I'm gonna fight for ours! The city of El Chorro's got a battle on its hands, if you try to take that from us! You think it's okay to take a piece of fertile soil and pour asphalt over it? You don't call that vandalism? A criminal act? How come nobody's askin' what the *land* wants?"

The timer on the podium beeped, and Bill stood glaring at the planning commissioners for a moment, shaking his head and breathing heavily. I could see beads of perspiration on his forehead as he returned and sank into his seat.

After it seemed everyone else had finished, Masahiro rose and walked slowly to the microphone. He stood there for a moment, taking a long breath as he often did before speaking.

"My name is Masahiro Tanaka," he began at last in a calm, steady voice. "And I began this garden... more than thirty years ago."

The room grew quieter, and I marveled at how everyone seemed to listen completely whenever Masahiro spoke.

"I could tell you many stories about all that has happened during those years," he continued quietly. "The people for whom this place has been important. The many illnesses that have been cured with our plants. The places that have great meaning for us." He paused and looked steadily at the commissioners for so long that I was worried his time would run out. Finally, he took a breath and spoke again.

"But will it do any good, to tell those stories? In Japan, where I grew up, we have an expression: *hyakubun wa ikken ni shikazu*. This means 'one hundred listenings do not equal one seeing.' So I would like to invite you to come see our garden. Not simply from the sidewalk, but to come inside. Put your hands in the soil... taste the ripe persimmons... talk with the people who are there. I request that you make no decision tonight, in haste, but allow more time to become acquainted with those whose future you shall decide. Thank you."

With the public hearing over, the commissioners spent more time talking into their microphones in flat, monotone voices. Finally, when I thought I'd probably faint from boredom, Chairperson Minetti announced that the item would move forward to a vote.

"I move to recommend the General Plan Amendment," one of the commissioners declared.

"I second the motion," said the person beside him.

I held my breath, looking around at the confused faces of the other gardeners. Apparently the commissioners were not taking Masahiro's advice of waiting longer to make a decision.

A woman at the desk called each person's name.

"Commissioner Anderson?"

"Yes."

"Commissioner Patterson?"

"Yes."

Down the list she went, every single commissioner with the exception of Ms. Dominguez voting "yes."

"The motion has been approved," Chairperson Minetti concluded. "Thank you, and will the clerk please announce item five on the agenda."

We stared at each other in stunned disbelief. Nobody moved for several minutes, and then finally, one by one, the gardeners began rising from their seats and heading slowly to the door of the meeting room.

On the front steps of City Hall, everyone crowded around Masahiro, talking over each other in anxious voices. He held up his palms and waited for us to listen, then began in his usual gentle voice.

"I understand you are worried. But please remember, this is only a first step. In Japan, we say that "even a journey of a thousand miles must begin with a single step.""

"But what can we do now?" someone called out.

"Well," Masahiro replied, "the planning commission can only *recommend* this change, but the city council will make a final decision."

"Don't they usually do whatever the commission recommends?" asked Abuela Jean.

Masahiro waited a moment so that Nacha could translate. "Most of the time, yes," he replied. "But not always. We will have a chance to speak to the city council members before they make a decision... so there is still hope."

Nacha translated again, and a hum of quiet murmurs in Mixteco and Spanish rippled through the group.

Grace suggested another meeting in the garden on Saturday to plan our next steps, and everyone gradually drifted away in small groups to head for home.

ॐ

Mom and I walked down the sidewalk with Bill Tava, who strode heavily and kept his eyes to the ground. After a few blocks, he heaved a sigh and jammed his hands into his jeans pockets, shaking his head.

"Those people just don't get it. Man, I get so *angry*. Just wanna shove some sense into their brains!"

He shook his head a few more times and spat on the curb. "Man, my grandparents would roll over in their graves if they heard me talkin' like that, to those government people."

"How come?" I asked.

He let out another sigh. "It's just not our way, ya know? *Yoeme* might be great warriors, but the older people know how to stay cool, never raise their voice. That's what we grew up learnin.' But I was a bad one. *Corajudo*, they call it, short tempered. My grandma would roll right outta her grave if she heard me talkin' like that."

"Both your grandparents died?" I asked.

He nodded. "Yeah, back when I was in prison. I never got to say sorry for rejectin' what they tried to teach me. My grandpa was a *pahkolam*, a deer dancer... one of the most respected people in our tribe. They dance at ceremonies, to keep the traditions, to remind us how we're connected to everything on earth. The deer songs are kinda like our stories, and our prayers. Real important."

He looked over at me and Mom for a moment, shaking his head again. "My grandpa wanted to teach me, so I could be a deer dancer too after he was gone... but I hated all that stuff. I didn't wanna wear a silly lookin' mask with antlers on my head, and dance around at ceremonies. So I didn't listen. Stopped going to the rez when I turned eighteen, got into a bad crowd in Phoenix. Wasn't til I sat in prison all those years that I finally saw... and by that time, he was gone."

"So you never learned the deer dances?" I asked, disappointed. I remembered Masahiro's story about how *Obaachan* passed her knowledge to him before dying, and I felt sad for Bill Tava and his grandpa not getting a chance to do that.

Bill smiled broadly. "I *did* learn it."

"But I thought—"

"Yeah, grandpa was gone. But when I got outta prison, I went back to the Pascua Yaquí Rez in Arizona and learned every single thing I could, from the elders there. I wanted it all—our ceremonies, our stories, the knowledge for growin' food in the desert. I finally wanted to *be* one of my people."

"Why did you leave again?" Mom asked.

Bill was quiet for a moment. "Well… it's a hard place to be, out there. My buddies on the rez got problems with drugs, alcohol, no jobs… I just had to split. That's when I started workin' with that garden project up in San Francisco, makin' a new life for myself. But I do go back there for ceremonies, holidays, stuff like that. Maybe someday I'll go back to stay."

"Maybe you could start a garden on the reservation," I suggested, "and grow food with teenagers, like you do here!"

Bill smiled again. "Yeah, that's sorta my dream. Go back, teach those kids how to grow our traditional crops, how to learn things from our ancestors, how to stay outta trouble. Yeah. Maybe someday."

He smiled even wider, seeming to have forgotten temporarily about the planning commission meeting and how his grandparents would react to the speech he'd given.

Bill walked us to the transit center, where Mom and I caught the final bus of the day. We'd be arriving at the church late, but hopefully Lorna had secretly saved some dinner for us. Pressing my face against the tinted window as we rolled away, I watched Bill Tava continuing along the sidewalk by himself. His steps seemed lighter than before, his head held high. In that split second as the bus passed by, I thought he might even have been singing.

19

LATER THAT WEEK, I arrived at the downtown bus stop after school to find Mom waiting on a bench, shoulders slumped and face buried in her hands. I ran over, worried. She'd handled the disappointment of the planning commission meeting so well... what could be wrong now?

"I got fired from one of my cleaning jobs," she muttered into her palms. "Kristin said I'm not consistent enough. She says it's always different, depending on my mood."

She slumped down farther and heaved a giant sigh. "It just seems like no matter how hard I try, Tal... I just can't..."

I dropped my backpack and sat on the bench, putting one arm around her shoulder. A few other kids gave us strange looks, but I didn't care.

"It's okay, Mom," I said, desperate to cheer her up again. "You still have all your other jobs, right?"

She gave a small shrug. "For now. But what if she talks to those people? Maybe I'll lose them all."

You will if you start acting like this! I wanted to shout. Why did Mom get discouraged so easily? Why couldn't she be the confident one for once, reassuring *me* that everything would be okay? I kicked at a stone in the pavement, trying to figure out what to do. She had been doing well for such a long time!

She couldn't get sad now and lose all of her jobs!

"Hey," I said, suddenly getting a new idea. "I think those seeds in our plot need some water. Can we go check on them?"

Mom gave an almost imperceptible nod. "Yeah, I guess… if we need to."

I dug around in her purse for bus fare, and we rode to the *Nihonmachi* District and walked to the garden. I led the way down the main path, Mom trailing behind with her eyes toward the ground. But then, opening the little gate of our plot and stepping inside, we got a surprise.

"Look!" I gasped, dropping to my hands and knees beside the first bed. "They're sprouting!"

There in the furrows of soil were tiny greenish-purple seedlings just barely poking up out of the ground, each with two miniature heart-shaped leaves.

"Our radishes!" I exclaimed. "And look, the lettuce is also coming up!"

Mom knelt beside me and ran a finger gently across the row of tiny seedlings. I moved over to the fence where we'd planted peas, poked a finger into the soil, and dug around.

"Hey, look at this too!" I lifted up a swollen pea with an emerging white root. Mom came over to look, turning the seed over a few times and carefully touching the small, tender root.

"Gosh… isn't that something, how you just add water and it does that all by itself?" She bent over and re-buried the seed where I had pulled it out.

Little shoots of bindweed were poking up around the edges of the bed and in the pathways, and Mom began plucking them carefully.

"Wait," I said, running to grab the two rusty forks we had been using to dig up bindweed before. I knelt beside her and started digging too, thinking about something Masahiro once told me. *This is a good time to ask yourself,* he'd said as we hoed young thistles from the herb garden, *what are the weeds you would like to clear from your own life*? I looked over at Mom working beside me and imagined her life as a beautiful garden, wondering if she could somehow weed out all the sadness.

Rowena came over and offered us some extra kale seedlings that she and Grace didn't have enough space to plant, so we decided to clear out the back of the plot to make one final bed. Mom and I knelt side by side, breaking up clumps of clay between our fingers and smoothing over the surface to prepare a comfortable home for the little seedlings. Mom worked without speaking and seemed almost hypnotized by the process, her hands moving rhythmically and head bent low over the ground. When the bed was all ready, we both scooped out little holes and carefully transplanted the fragile seedlings.

"Isn't that amazing," Mom said softly, as she tucked in the last tiny kale plant.

"What?"

"How you can just pick up a whole plant and move it, and say 'grow *here*,' and the roots start going down… and later you can't ever move it again."

We gathered fallen leaves and spread them over the bed like a blanket, as Masahiro had instructed, then scooped up armloads of weeds to carry to the compost. Mom was still more quiet than usual, but I noticed that her movements had become quicker than before, the color gradually returning to her cheeks. On our way back to the plot, she crouched down to examine a large white Calla Lily with its stalk of fine pollen rising from the center.

"I know," she said suddenly. "Let's make a bouquet for Christina and baby Skye. Wouldn't they love that?"

She ran to the shed for scissors and began searching along the paths and the edges of people's plots. Carefully avoiding

Mrs. Murphey's area, she snipped long stalks of Shasta daisies, multicolored zinnias, and pastel yellow celosia, beginning to arrange the stems in one hand.

While Mom worked, absorbed in the array of shapes and colors, I started making my own arrangement for *her*. I decided to try weaving together a crown she could wear, as Abuela Jean had taught me. I gathered bunches of lavender and sage stems to braid together, the air filling with a sweet, slightly pungent fragrance from their leaves. Into this braided wreath, I poked short stems of purple and blue statice, multicolored strawflowers, and tiny white sprigs of baby's breath.

When we both finished, I set the colorful adornment on Mom's head and she surprised me by laughing aloud, saying she felt like a fairy from one of my stories. As we left the garden that evening with our flowers and headed for the bus stop, I could tell Mom was going to be okay.

That night after dinner, she helped with my homework and didn't say another word about losing her cleaning job or needing to save more money. Lorna came and joined us after putting T.J. to bed, spreading out stacks of paper to study for the high school equivalency exam. At a nearby table, Cathy rested her head in her arms and dozed off periodically while reading a paperback romance novel from the lounge. Everyone else was downstairs, and the dining room was so quiet you could hear the hum of fluorescent lights and ticking of a clock on the far wall. On nights like this, I thought to myself, staying at the church was almost peaceful.

I could tell from the expression on Mom's face that she was enjoying the evening too. And at bedtime, when she bent down over the army cot for a goodnight kiss, I caught the faint scent of lavender still in her hair.

20

THE NEXT DAY WAS SATURDAY, and to my relief, Mom got up as usual and went to her jobs. I spent the whole day in the garden, helping with the corn harvest.

By now, the plants had dried into crisp, beige towers that rustled like old paper bags in the breeze. Swollen bean pods hung on the stalks like rattles, and the sprawling vines had shriveled to reveal an array of cream-colored squash on the ground beneath.

Bill must have told everyone about the harvest, because more than twenty high schoolers—including Blade, who was still doing her community service hours—showed up to help. We tramped through the rows of crunchy, withered squash leaves, pulling large ears of corn off the stalks and making a pile at the end of each row. Bill demonstrated how to pull back the papery husks to expose the tidy rows of hard, bright kernels underneath. Most of his corn was large and yellowish white, the type he said Yaquí women ground into flour for *taskari* bread.

After harvesting all the corn, we carried baskets between the rows and picked pods of little white tepary beans we'd planted earlier in the summer. Díaz looked especially pleased, somehow collecting more tepary beans than anyone else.

Bill made a fire in the barbecue pit and cooked a giant pot of stew called *Wakavaki*, made from tepary beans, meat, squash, and vegetables from the garden. He also made a thick porridge-drink from mesquite beans, a desert food that he said was even more important to the Yaquí people than corn.

"This is what my people ate until the corn was ready to harvest," he explained, passing out little pieces of mesquite bean pods from Arizona for us all to try. "My grandma used to go out into the desert and harvest the pods, just like our ancestors. No garden necessary, just go get 'em."

I skipped around from plot to plot all afternoon, helping Nacha and Victor with their corn first, then Felipe, then the Molinero and Rivas families. Although everyone's corn patches looked the same from the outside, I was surprised to discover when we pulled back the husks that almost everyone had different types of corn! There were cobs with deep maroon kernels, others speckled blue and white, some striped orange and yellow like flames, even a shiny metallic-looking green. Every corncob was like a piece of artwork, different from all the rest.

Nacha explained to me how everyone had worked together in spring, making a schedule to plant their corn at different times so the varieties wouldn't cross-pollinate with each another. "This way, we can save our seeds for planting the next year," she said with a smile. "Every family has a corn that is special for us, from where we were born. So it should not receive pollen from other kinds, you see?"

Some people had even tied bags over their corncobs and sprinkled the pollen by hand, to prevent them from getting mixed up with other people's varieties. "But you see what happens, still?" Nacha asked me, holding up a mostly red cob with a few pale yellow kernels mixed in. "We cannot remain separate forever, I think."

"Maybe the combination of everybody's corn will be the prettiest and tastiest of all!" I suggested.

Nacha laughed and patted my head. "We will leave that in the hands of God."

She and Victor had brought a hand-cranked mill from home, and Nacha let all the kids take turns grinding fresh cornmeal. Then she built a small fire and rolled out dough for tortillas, just like her mother used to do in Mexico when she was a girl. The air filled with the scent of wood smoke and toasting flour, as tortillas cooked on the griddle and Nacha passed them out for everyone to sample.

After lunch, we all gathered around the picnic tables for another meeting about saving the garden. A group of college students from a club called "Sustainable El Chorro" even came to help. The corn harvest seemed to have given everybody new energy, and people had lots of ideas. We could put up more flyers, write letters to the newspaper, and even have a float in the environmental parade that the students were organizing. Masahiro would contact the city council members and invite them to come visit. One student even suggested having a free concert in the garden, and another offered to set up a *Nihonmachi* Garden website. Alex, the club president, said he would contact local TV news stations, and somebody else suggested "occupying the land" by setting up tents and camping in the garden so it couldn't be bulldozed. Alex stood beside a whiteboard easel and took notes as people shouted out their ideas.

Some of the students seemed angry, saying we needed to "fight back against white oppression" and stop "corporate empire" from taking over the world. Most of the gardeners looked confused by this, but they applauded politely when Nacha thanked the college students for coming to help us.

"What if we just talked to Mr. Richards ourselves?" I asked Masahiro later that same afternoon as we sat under the fig tree, eating a snack of rice balls and *umeboshi*. "I mean, if he saw how special the garden is to us, maybe he wouldn't even want to buy it anymore."

Masahiro took a small bite of *umeboshi*, gazed up at the yellowing fig leaves, and smiled a bit sadly.

"Tali-chan, I wish that could be."

"Why couldn't it?" I insisted. "My mom says every single person has a heart, even if it's buried way down, so everyone deserves a second chance."

But Masahiro shook his head. "I have already written letters to Mr. Richards' company, along with photographs of our garden. But he refuses to respond or to answer phone calls. I wish I did not have to say this, Tali-chan, but there are some people whose hearts have hardened to stone and cannot seem to be softened."

I hung my head and poked at a crevice in the dry soil. "Okay."

Masahiro sighed. "Mr. Richards is like the unkind neighbor, in the story of 'The Old Man who Made the Cherry Trees Bloom.' Do you remember?"

I did. In the old Japanese folktale, a cold-hearted man killed his neighbor's little dog Shiro, because the dog had helped the neighbors find buried treasure. But even after he was dead, Shiro's spirit continued to help his owners by bringing them good fortune. He even gave them the magical power to make cherry trees bloom in the middle of winter. Of all the stories Masahiro had told, I didn't like that one much, because the dog died and the mean neighbor never even apologized for what he did.

"Sadly, it seems that Mr. Richards is that way," Masahiro concluded. "It is not his fault...perhaps many painful things have happened to him. Perhaps people have not treated *him* with kindness. But somehow, his heart has become like a rock, and he only cares about money. I hope the city council members will have greater softness and understanding toward us than Mr. Richards has had, and will refuse to sell the land to him."

I nodded with a sigh. "Yeah, we *have* to convince them!"

Later that month was the environmental parade organized by Students for a Sustainable El Chorro, and we rode in the back of Rowena's pick-up truck with a bunch of potted plants, flowers, and posters about saving the garden. When the parade was over, we marched across town with a group of students, yelling *"Sí se puede!"* and "Power to the people!" all the way to City Hall. A small crowd had gathered around the front steps, where a woman in a navy-blue suit stood talking into a microphone. She paused for a moment, and everyone applauded.

"That's the mayor," Bill Tava told me. "She's one of the people who'll vote about our land."

The mayor continued her speech in a clear, strong voice, describing all the things El Chorro was doing to become an "environmentally sustainable city." Every few minutes, she paused and people clapped their hands.

Suddenly one of the college students yelled out, "Then why are you destroying gardens?!"

People around us turned their heads.

"Save El Chorro's green space!" another student shouted. "Power to the people!"

More students began chanting, beating pots and drums and marching closer to the front steps of the building. I could barely hear the mayor's speech anymore, over all the noise.

Before I knew what was happening, more people came running toward us from every direction, wearing cardboard vegetable costumes and pushing wheelbarrows of soil, which they began dumping in piles onto the sidewalk. Some threw handfuls of seeds into the air and shouted things like "Reclaim our city!" and "Food not lawns!"

The mayor tried to continue her speech, but the students yelled even louder. One girl stood on a trash can and chanted into a megaphone, while others ran around wrapping light poles and tree trunks with green plastic tape. In the midst of this hubbub, a group of students ran up the steps of City Hall and formed a line across the entrance, locking themselves to the railings and to one another with heavy chains.

I looked up at Bill, whose face was a mixture of shock and adrenalin. He tilted back his head, let out a holler, and joined in the chanting. Most of the other gardeners just stood silently, looking at each other in confusion. It hadn't been their idea to disrupt the mayor's speech... but what now?

Suddenly, there came a symphony of sirens and revving engines, and a line of police encircled us, gripping long poles and telling everyone to quiet down.

Nacha pushed her way through the crowd toward me and laid a protective hand on my shoulder. "Do not worry, *mija*," she said into my ear over all the noise. "I am here with you."

Most of the other gardeners had disappeared when the police showed up, and those who remained were now backing cautiously away from the steps of City Hall. The mayor had given up trying to finish her speech and stood watching as the police took over, commanding into their megaphones that the protesters "disperse immediately."

But the students refused, chanting even louder and lying across the front steps with their signs held high in the air. I stood beside Nacha and watched, alarmed, as police officers began removing students one by one and leading them away in plastic handcuffs.

"The people, united, will never be defeated!" Alex yelled as an officer gripped him by the arm and led him down the sidewalk. The other students applauded and cheered.

It wasn't until several more students had been arrested and taken away that I spotted Masahiro. He was sitting cross-legged on the sidewalk in the middle of all that commotion, legs folded on top of each other and hands resting lightly on knees, just like he did at the meditation pond each morning. But now his eyes were open, calmly watching everything that was happening. Costumed students and onlookers moved frantically about, many yelling or chanting, others watching with frightened faces, but Masahiro simply sat in the middle of it all. He wasn't trying to get away, or protect himself, or anything…just *sitting*, like the little Buddha statue on the altar at his apartment. For some reason, when I spotted him perfectly still in the midst of such chaos, my own pounding heart began to settle down. It was almost as if I could hear Masahiro telling me that everything was okay. I took a deep breath and held tight to Nacha's hand as she led us away from the crowd and down the sidewalk, back toward the garden.

∾

That evening, lying on my cot in the church basement, I wrote my own version of 'The Old Man Who Made the Cherry Trees Bloom.' In this new story, the unkind neighbor realized what he'd done and had a change of heart, vowing to help his neighbors however he could for the rest of his life. Together, they planted thousands of special cherry trees that bloomed during winter, filling everyone in the country with happiness.

Even if Masahiro was right—if some people's hearts *were* like stone and couldn't ever be changed—anything could still happen in a story.

21

ALICIA EVENTUALLY HELPED Mom to find a new job, working at the cash register for a department store at the far end of town. No buses went there, so Mom bought a used car with the money she'd saved cleaning houses.

"Don't worry," she told me. "With holiday overtime and housekeeping jobs on my days off, I'll be able to make car payments and *still* keep saving!"

Lately, she had so much energy I could hardly believe it. The new Mom was always moving, always doing something: laughing and joking with people at the Day Center, helping move cots, talking on her new cell phone, excitedly describing our plans for the future.

After a breakfast of cold cereal at the church each morning, she would drive me to school before heading across town to her new job. When school was over, I stayed in the library with the "homework club" until she picked me up and we went back to the church for dinner.

Mom kept cleaning houses on weekends too, so she no longer had time to spend in the garden. But at least she still let me go by myself on Saturdays and Sundays, to see my friends and take care of our plot. The seedlings we'd planted were growing fast, speckled lettuce leaves glistening with dew and scarlet radish tops peeking up out of the soil. I gave Mom full reports but wished she could be there to see for herself.

One day in early November, many of the gardeners celebrated a holiday called *Día de los Muertos* to remember people who had died, like the Mexican version of *Obon*. Back home, Nacha told me, everybody gathered at town cemetaries to decorate their family graves and have a big picnic. But hardly anyone had graves to visit in El Chorro, so they celebrated *Día de los Muertos* at the garden instead. Some people planted trees or rose bushes to honor deceased family members, and Nacha said this was second-best to having actual graves to visit.

Most people had also set up *ofrendas* in their plots: tables covered with photographs, jewelry, toys, candles, and favorite foods of the people who had died, as well as little rolls and sugar candies the shape of skulls. The Rivas family had three *ofrendas*, one for Dominga and Antonio's first child who had died as a baby, one for Lina's grandpa, and one for a cousin who died trying to cross the border to the United States. The edges of the plot were decorated with intricate tissue paper flags, and Dominga sprinkled bright orange marigold petals along the paths to guide their loved ones to the right spot.

Every family seemed to be having its own little private party. Felipe Sánchez sat on a folding chair beside his *ofrenda*, strumming the guitar and singing for hours, and many other people had boomboxes or radios playing softly as they sat around the little tables talking in Spanish or Mixteco.

I spent most of the day playing with Pablo and Lina, using the skull candy as prizes for our button tournaments. I knew it was probably the last time we'd play together before they left for Coachella, and I felt quietly sad, wondering if we'd all be together in the garden ever again.

∾

The next week, Mom emerged from the back office of the Day Center after her regular meeting with Alicia, knelt to look me in the eyes with a huge smile, and announced that we were going to move into our own apartment.

I was stunned. "You mean here in El Chorro?"

She nodded. "Can you believe that, Sweetheart?"

"But—but then how will you save money? For a house, I mean? Aren't we still going to Washington where houses are cheaper?"

Mom stroked my hair and sighed. "Tal...I know you're excited about having a real house of our own someday. But we need to take it step by step. This kind of thing takes time."

She paused and struggled to find the right words. "See, in our situation right now, since I haven't always been able to pay bills on time, there's no landlord who would rent us a house. Even if we had the money. It's too complicated to explain, Sweetheart. But basically Alicia knows a special program to help people like us...just to get back on our feet, so we'll have better options later."

She looked into my eyes pleadingly. "And think about it. Winter's just about here, and wouldn't it be nice to have somewhere of our own for Christmas?"

I thought about it for a moment and gave a small nod. "Yeah, I guess that's true. And if we save the garden—"

"Exactly," Mom broke in, smiling. "Then you and I can keep our plot a bit longer and enjoy the delicious vegetables you've been growing! Right?"

She looked happy, and that was the most important thing, so I gave her a hug and said it was good news. But secretly I crossed my fingers that things would actually turn out as well as she'd said.

∽

The weekend before we moved into our new apartment, there was a big Thanksgiving Dinner at the church for all the homeless people of El Chorro. Mom and I spent the whole day in the church kitchen, chopping vegetables with the other volunteers. Farmers' market was over for the year, so I had decided to ask Grace and Rowena and the other gardeners for donations of extra food from their plots. Almost everyone contributed, and we had to make five trips to Grace's truck to carry it all inside! The old ladies in the kitchen kept saying, "Well aren't those the nicest vegetables you've ever seen?" I beamed and told them proudly that it's because they were homegrown and *we* helped grow them.

Almost everyone from the Day Center came to the feast, as well as many people I'd never seen before. The room was filled with long tables of steaming food, little kids running around, and the echoing din of voices and laughter.

Mom and I sat at the end of a table across from Lorna and T.J., and beside Jared and Kim. Lorna made jokes all the way through dinner, and we laughed until our sides ached. Even Kim, who seemed to become ever quieter as her belly grew larger, couldn't help but laugh when Lorna was around. Halfway through dinner, Blade came over and squeezed onto the bench beside me, whispering something about her mom driving her crazy and Sun Dragon being a total jerk. Cathy threw a warning look across the table and told Blade to watch her mouth around the children, or *else*.

When dinner was over, Mom disappeared into the kitchen for a moment and surprised everyone by returning with a large pink-frosted cake glowing with eleven candles. My birthday was still a week away, and neither Mom nor I had brought up the topic at all. I knew she was busy trying to keep two jobs and make arrangements for our new apartment, so I'd decided it would be okay if we skipped my birthday for one year.

But she *had* remembered, after all! Everyone came crowding around us: Christina with baby Skye, Sun Dragon, Blade and her mom, Cathy, even Peco, peering at us through the plastic mosquito-eye with his usual lopsided grin. Someone turned down the lights in the big room and everyone started singing, with Sun Dragon joining in on his flute and T.J. and Alyssa and the other little kids drumming their hands on the metal tabletops.

"Make a wish!" Cathy called over the applause.

That was easy. I squeezed my eyes shut, wished with all my might for a real true home of our own, then took a huge breath and blew out all the candles at once.

"You go, girl!" Lorna hollered, and Lance let out a shrill whistle and strummed a riff on his guitar.

Cathy wrapped a newly knitted scarf around my shoulders, Blade reached into her pocket and took out a little wooden sunflower she'd carved for me, and Lorna presented a potted plant for our new apartment. Mom gave me some books and magazines about gardening, filled with colorful photographs. Then Peco walked over, took my wrist in his rough, disfigured fingers, and pressed something into the palm of my hand.

"Lookey," he said with a raspy laugh.

It was a plastic mosquito eye just like his own, but with the initials TT written sloppily across it in black marker.

"Wow, you got *me* one?" I grinned and held the little toy up to my eye, and there were a million Pecos staring through their own pink plastic mosquito eyes, grinning back at me.

Looking around the table at the smiling faces of our friends, I suddenly realized how much I was going to miss them.

☙

The next weekend, Mom and I emptied our locker in the church basement and moved into the new apartment. It looked a bit like the farmworker housing where Pablo and Lina lived, just a few long buildings surrounded by asphalt parking lots, with cars and trucks parked everywhere and not a blade of grass in sight.

Our apartment was small, dimly lit, and smelled of mildew and cigarette smoke. The front door opened into a living room with stained orange carpet and one bare window, a cubbyhole kitchen even smaller than Masahiro's, a bathroom with a leaky faucet and no shower door, and one small bedroom we were planning to share.

"It'll be nicer once we get some furniture," Mom said optimistically, opening the cupboard doors and peering in at the torn, yellowing contact-paper. "Just think, Tal, we can fix this place up however *we* want!"

Just to prove it, she took the next day off from house-keeping and we drove downtown to pick out a second-hand sofa, a bed frame and mattress and chest of drawers, a small kitchen table, and even a television set with a shiny wooden stand. I worried that it would be too expensive, but Mom said she could make it up soon with overtime hours.

"Relax, Tal!" she told me. "This is a time to celebrate! Let's fix this place up as nice as we can, okay?"

Our new furniture was delivered to the apartment, and we spent the whole afternoon arranging things: re-lining the cupboards with fresh contact paper, filling them with dishes and silverware and cooking pots, scrubbing the bathroom clean, and making our bed with its brand-new sheets and pillows. I taped a few drawings and photographs on the wall beside the closet, and Mom hung the potted plant from Lorna by the living room window. She was right; the place *did* look a lot better.

But after that first day, Mom and I hardly spent any more time at the apartment together. She was always working, and

I'd arrive on the bus after school and do my homework alone at the kitchen table, watch TV or write stories for a while, make dinner, and wait impatiently for her to come home. When she finally did, we'd sit in the kitchen for a little while and talk about our days, or I'd massage her shoulders and read a new story from my notebook. But soon it would be time for bed, time to start the whole thing over again. I counted down the days until Saturday, when I could return to the garden.

The weather had grown colder, and the garden looked strangely bare and flat with the tall jungles of corn gone. The temperature reached freezing one night, leaving the tomato and pepper plants all shriveled and brown, the remains of un-ripe fruit rotting on the ground underneath. The farmworkers' plots were all empty now, covered in leaves or dry cornstalks, and the hammocks and wind chimes had all been taken down for winter.

Even in the cold, Masahiro still went to the garden every day, bundled in thick sweaters, rubber boots, and a knitted beanie. He would sit by the meditation pond in the morning and then set to work pruning the bare bushes and fruit trees, weeding paths, and planting clover to feed the soil for next season. Grace and Rowena kept on working in their plot too, and one day I helped them to plant rows of onions and garlic, which would grow through the winter and be ready to harvest in summertime.

"But what if the garden's not here anymore next summer?" I asked. They shrugged and said it would just feel too weird to skip planting onions and garlic in November, after doing it for so many years.

The sun was setting early now, so on Saturday evenings I usually went back to Masahiro's apartment for miso soup, and we would sit at the kitchen table drinking green tea together by lamplight until Mom arrived to pick me up after work.

He told me lots of stories about growing up in Takamura village with his cousins, about traveling to America to reunite with his parents and brothers, and about how he met his wife Kiyo at Gila River Relocation Camp. Sometimes I shared my own made-up stories from my red notebook, and Masahiro would tell me old Japanese folktales about the adventures of Momotaro—"Peach Boy"—and his three companions, the dog, the monkey, and the pheasant.

Sometimes we also looked through seed catalogs together, scanning the glossy photographs of a million different vegetables and fruits, reading the descriptions and circling ones that sounded good to try planting.

If Masahiro was feeling tired, we sometimes spent the evening in silence. I would sit on the couch writing stories as he napped in his rocking chair or knelt before the little Buddha statue to light small sticks of incense for his family members.

Some evenings, Mr. Goto, Mr. Furukawa, and Mr. and Mrs. Ikeda all came over for dinner too. Masahiro and I would arrive early from the garden with lots of vegetables, cutting them into delicate strips and filling platters with green onion, cabbage, *shiitake* mushrooms, and tofu. Masahiro would set up a hot-plate on the kitchen table and prepare a broth of soy sauce, sugar, and rice wine called *sake*; then everyone would choose their own vegetables to put into the broth for a few minutes before scooping it into their own bowls.

"Do you know the reason we call this meal *shabu-shabu*?" Mrs. Ikeda asked me one evening with a smile. "Because that's the sound when you swish the vegetables around in the broth, with your chopsticks. This is what our parents always served at parties, when we were growing up…so whenever I smell *shabu-shabu*, it feels like a party to me!"

She was right; those nights *did* feel like parties. Masahiro's tiny apartment would fill with laughter and delicious aromas as he and his friends reminisced about the old days, telling stories full of names and Japanese expressions I'd never heard. Sometimes the men played a long game of *goh* after dinner, and Mrs. Ikeda would make green tea with roasted brown rice and teach me songs that her mother taught her long ago. During those evenings at the apartment, it felt almost like I'd been here all along, part of the El Chorro *Nihonmachi* for my entire life.

In December, we learned that the city council's vote about the garden was postponed until January. It would be similar to the Planning Commission meeting, where anybody could stand up and speak for three minutes. Many people from El Chorro would probably attend, and we would also present our petition with its hundreds of signatures. Masahiro had already given tours of the garden to two council members, and he seemed to be feeling hopeful.

Mom seemed more hopeful than usual too, and not just about the garden. She'd been taking every hour of overtime she could get, sitting at the kitchen table adding numbers on pieces of scratch paper and counting down how much she still owed Uncle Jim. Sometimes she left before I woke up in the morning, posting little notes with smiley faces on the refrigerator door. Even during her time off, she was always on the move: cleaning, doing laundry, making phone calls, cooking, paying bills, running errands, going to the library to look up real estate ads in Washington. At the apartment, she would set the television to an oldies music station and sing along while bustling from room to room doing chores. Even in the middle of the night, I sometimes awoke and heard her whistling to herself in the kitchen, putting dishes away, or rearranging the furniture to try out a new look. In spite of working such long hours and hardly sleeping, Mom seemed full of energy. She would often show me our monthly bank statements, explaining what the different numbers meant and pointing out how much she had already saved.

Mom never took the little pill with breakfast anymore, and when I asked why, she said they made her feel sick and weren't worth the trouble. "Who wants to have a headache every day?" she said. "But don't tell Alicia, she thinks I'm still taking them. It's silly. I'm just fine."

And Mom did seem fine. She had Christmas Day off work, and we did a small gift exchange with just the two of us in our new apartment. I kept thinking about Blade and her mom, Jared and Kim, Lorna, T.J., and everyone else hanging out all day in the crowded Day Center downtown, and I knew we should be grateful to have a place to spend Christmas. But at the same time, I couldn't stop imagining that maybe next year we'd be settled for real, in a place we were going to *stay*, a place we could truly call home.

22

ON NEW YEAR'S EVE, we had a candlelight vigil in the garden. It was a clear, pitch-black night with no moon, cold enough to see our breath coming out in clouds of mist. But everyone still came: Masahiro, Mrs. Murphey, Nacha and Victor, Grace and Rowena and Mrs. Matapang, Bill Tava, Bill Mitchell, even Abuela Jean, bundled in what seemed like a million sweaters and scarves.

A big New Year's festival was happening in downtown El Chorro, and some of the college students (who had apparently been released from jail after just two hours and still wanted to help us) set up a downtown table with flyers, photos of the garden, and our petition for people to sign. Everybody who signed could light one candle to take back to the garden. If we got enough candles, we'd be able to light up the entire place and maybe even get on television for all of El Chorro to see! Most of the gardeners took a shift standing by the table and bringing newly lit candles back to the garden in a golf cart borrowed from the college.

Mom and Mrs. Murphey and I collected more than fifty signatures during our shift, returning triumphantly to the garden to add our candles to the others. The little flickering lights were everywhere: lining the sidewalk and main paths, casting long shadows through the vine trellises, and making the few remaining cornstalks glow and sway like ghost dancers. Even in winter, with so many of the trees bare and plots untended, I thought it was the most beautiful I'd ever seen the garden.

Later that evening, the local news station really did come to film us, putting up a tall antenna and filling the area with floodlights. A reporter interviewed Masahiro and Rowena about why the garden might be torn down and how we were trying to protect it, and the cameraman filmed a group of students arriving from downtown with a new batch of candles.

After they left, we all sat around a bonfire near the fig tree, sipping from mugs of steaming Mexican cocoa as Bill Tava told Yaquí stories and Felipe Sánchez strummed lightly on his guitar. Bill loved telling stories about the *Surem*, a tiny people who inhabited the world long ago and lived in perfect harmony with each other and nature. One day, a talking tree warned everyone about white men coming with weapons and bringing a time of great noise, confusion, and suffering. The *Surem* were frightened by this message, so they grew into taller, stronger people called the Yaquí, who could fight back. But the *Surem* disliked violence, so the ones who couldn't bear such a future went into the ocean and mountains to continue living as before. These spirits of his ancestors were still there, Bill told us, living as magical tiny people in the wilderness and helping anyone who was in trouble.

Bill's stories continued late into the night, and as the air got colder, I wrapped myself in one of Abuela Jean's crocheted blankets and crawled into Mom's lap like when I was small, leaning my head against her shoulder and gazing sleepily at the glowing faces around the circle. Masahiro and Mrs. Ikeda sat on folding lawn chairs, sipping from tiny glasses of *sake*, and Bill Mitchell lay on a plaid blanket by the fire with four

of his cats, sitting up occasionally to poke the coals and add
another log. Mrs. Matapang had fallen asleep in her wheelchair, mouth hanging open, and Rowena leaned against one
big wheel, staring into the fire as though hypnotized. Even
Mrs. Murphey, sitting not too far from Bill and his cats, was
busy chatting with Mom and seemed to be enjoying herself.

When it was almost midnight, Mrs. Ikeda passed out little
paper bowls of buckwheat noodles called *toshi-koshi*, or, as
Masahiro explained, "Passing-of-the-Year Noodles."

"*Toshi-koshi* is a symbol of hope and a long life," he told us.
"This is how people in Japan bring in the new year."

Just then, we heard a roar of cheering from downtown
as fireworks filled the sky, and suddenly everyone was standing and raising their cups of *sake* or *tequila* or hot cocoa and
shouting "Happy New Year! *Feliz Año Nuevo! Ake mashite
omedeto! Manigong Bagong Taon!* Here's to the garden! Here's
to all of us!" And we were all clicking our glasses together
and hugging and cheering, turning our faces upward to watch
the fireworks blossoming in the sky over downtown.

Our bonfire illuminated everyone's smiles with a warm
orange glow, and in that moment, the world seemed perfect.
Maybe everything *would* be okay, I thought. Maybe the garden
would be saved. Maybe Mom would earn enough money to
get our own place, and then she wouldn't have to work so hard
all the time, and we could plant a garden together. Maybe Tío
Raúl and Tía Yolanda would return safely from Mexico and
the whole family would be here again next summer, planting
corn and grilling *nopal* cactus on the barbecue, just like always.

Maybe all the prayers rising up from our garden, to the
Virgin Mary and Jesus and Buddha and the spirits of the
ancient Yaquí ancestors, would actually be heard, and we
would all somehow be okay.

23

THE WEEK AFTER NEW YEAR'S, everyone gathered at City Hall for the big meeting. All the gardeners who hadn't left for winter were there, as well as a bunch of college students and other people from El Chorro. The room was so crowded that many had to stand in the doorway and along the walls.

Mom was working at the department store that night, so we had arranged for me to go back to Masahiro's apartment until she could pick me up later. He sat beside me in a folding chair near the front of the room with a serene expression on his face, as if this were a church service instead of a meeting about the survival of our garden. *How come he always seemed so relaxed?*

The evening began just like last time, with lots of boring and confusing talk that droned on forever, but now I was too nervous to do anything but clutch my red notebook and wait.

When it finally came time for the public hearing, Mr. Ingersall gave another slideshow presentation. He showed the same diagrams and aerial photographs of the garden, the computer images of a mall and condominium complex, and the graphs explaining why this project would benefit the city.

The council members asked a bunch of questions about things like "environmental review" and "zoning ordinances," which Mr. Ingersall answered with more words I couldn't understand. Then Mr. Richards' staff person went up to the podium and answered another batch of confusing questions.

Finally, when I'd resorted to playing tic-tac-toe with myself on the back of my notebook, the mayor announced that the public comment period would begin.

People lined up behind the podium to speak and mostly repeated the same arguments as before, explaining how much food people were growing for their families, how the garden was an historic site, and how the proposed new location was noisy and right next to the freeway, with poor soil.

Grace told a story about the "victory gardens" that were planted all over the country during World War II, when people dug up every bit of available space for growing food: not just backyards but also public places like schoolyards, city parks, vacant lots, and strips of grass around office buildings. "Did you know that almost half the fresh vegetables eaten in this country in 1944 were grown in those gardens?" she asked. "Imagine if that happened again today, how much pressure it would take off our farmland and freeways!"

Several people used the words "environmental racism," asking why the city council was voting during a time when so many of the migrant workers were away from El Chorro and couldn't even attend.

Manuel González, an older man with a hunched back and gray stubble beard, shuffled stiffly to the microphone. Lifting his big calloused hands in the air to show the council members, he spoke in heavily accented English. "I worked in the fields my whole life with these hands. Picking thousands of pounds of food for other people, for you. I worked very hard, my entire life... Now I am old, and I just want a little space with good soil to provide some food for myself. Is that too much to ask?"

Bill Tava was less polite, gripping the podium firmly and speaking in a booming voice. "Hey, my name's Bill, I live in El Chorro and I'm a member of the *Yoeme*, the Pascua Yaquí tribe. Listen, my ancestors would *not* understand what's goin' down in this room today. What does it even mean, to own land? Do you just own a square on the map, or also the air above it and the creatures in the soil? Do you own the insects, even though they go freely wherever they want?"

He took a breath and lowered his voice a notch. "Look. We built up that soil, so all those living things could come back. If you sell the land, can we just pack them in a suitcase when we go? Or is all that yours too? Did you ever ask all the animals in the soil how *their land* should be zoned? What about them? Who says it's even up to us?!"

Bill's face was deep red, the veins in his neck popping out as he returned to his seat. I remembered what he had told us about being *corajudo*, short tempered, and how his grandparents would roll over in their graves if they heard him speak that way. I silently hoped they could understand why Bill was so upset, if they were actually listening right now. After all, hadn't they too been forced to leave their land years ago?

Masahiro went up to the microphone last, calmly stating that his own views had already been spoken by others, and that he hoped the council members would truly listen to us. "Please remember," he concluded, "it is quick to destroy something that takes a long time to form. A building can be erected in a single year, but it takes many years to build good soil. Would it not be easier to move your development, which does not yet exist, than to move a garden that has existed for more than thirty years?"

Then he thanked the council members for listening and slowly returned to his seat beside me.

The mayor asked if there were any more comments from the public, then announced that it was time for "council discussion and action." The council members droned on as I let my mind wander, imagining a perfect ending in which they *gave* us the land so we'd own it forever. I was startled back to reality when the clerk finally began calling a vote.

I held my breath. Even Masahiro seemed to stiffen, clasping his hands together and watching intently. But except for one council member, who had come to visit the garden twice and promised us full support, the rest all voted "yes."

A heavy silence fell over the room as the mayor announced that the motion had passed, for a general plan amendment changing the zoning of lots 478 and 467B in West El Chorro from "ag-industrial" to "commercial mixed use."

Then, as if nothing had happened, the meeting moved on. We sat there looking at each other in stunned, deflated silence. *That was it?* All our hard work over the past months, our petitions and articles and letters to the editor... none of it made any difference? The land would now be re-zoned, so the city could easily sell it to Mr. Richards for his mall and condominiums.

I craned my neck back to look at Grace and Rowena, who were staring silently at each other, and at Manuel González, who had buried his face in his big calloused hands. In front of us, Abuela Jean kept shaking her head slowly from side to side, and Nacha stared blankly ahead like a statue. Masahiro sat still with his eyes closed and head bent slightly forward, as if meditating.

My mind flooded with images of monstrous bulldozers crashing through the garden, tearing down the little fences and vine-covered trellises, smashing our tender young lettuce plants, packing the soil into tire tracks, uprooting fruit trees, even knocking down the bamboo forest and the fig tree, then shoving everything into heaps of rubble. It was more than I could bear.

The land hadn't actually been *sold* yet, I reminded myself. But I knew it was almost the same thing. Why would they change the zoning, if they weren't going to sell the land? I could tell by the expressions on everyone's faces that we had lost our battle.

Gradually, without speaking, the gardeners and other audience members began leaving the room. Masahiro waited for a long time, until everyone else was gone, before slowly rising from his chair and motioning for me to follow. We walked through the quiet lobby, out the double doors, and down the deserted front steps of the building. It was cold outside, and we stopped to put on coats and scarves before heading down the sidewalk to the bus stop.

"So I guess that's all?" I mumbled, wanting to somehow fill the silence.

Masahiro looked tired, his face drawn and pale under the faint glow of the streetlamps. He gave a slight nod, coughed, and silently pulled the scarf closer around his neck. It wasn't until we reached the bus stop a block from his apartment that he finally spoke.

"*Shikata ga nai…*" he began, almost too quietly for me to tell if he was speaking Japanese or English. "That is what *Obaachan* used to say. 'It cannot be helped.' We have tried our best, Tali-chan, and now we must accept it as best we can."

"But isn't there *anything* else we can try?"

Masahiro shook his head slowly. "I do not think so."

"But we can't just give up," I persisted, "after all that work! We can't let them just tear it down!"

"There comes a time to stop resisting, Tali-chan," he answered quietly, "and to let go of our desired outcomes. Holding too tightly is the source of great sorrow."

"But if we let go, then the garden will be destroyed!"

Masahiro coughed again and gave a long, tired sigh that seemed to come all the way up from his feet and out into the cold night air.

"I know you are sad, Tali-chan. I am too…I feel a heavy sense of loss, tonight. My only comfort is to remember the teaching of the Buddha, who said that nothing in this world ever remains the same for long. If we accept that, we will find great peace."

I folded my arms across my chest in protest. "But if you just accept whatever, then people can take away everything you love!"

Masahiro looked down at me with a soft tenderness in his eyes, letting those words echo down the empty street without trying to argue or convince me otherwise. When we reached the TIENDA MEXICANA, he led the way up the rickety wooden staircase and into his warm, quiet apartment. We peeled off layers of clothing and hung them on the coat rack by the door.

"Would you like some tea?"

I shrugged halfheartedly, and he went to the kitchen to prepare some anyway. When he returned, we sat on the sofa holding the little ceramic cups of green tea and warming our faces over the steam, just as we'd done so many evenings in the past few months.

After a while, Masahiro looked up and spoke softly. "May I tell you a story?"

I stared down at my teacup and nodded.

"Once, long ago," he began, drawing out the words, "there was a Chinese man whose horse ran away. His neighbors expressed sympathy, and the man simply said, 'Who knows if it is bad or good?' Later, the horse returned home, bringing along a beautiful wild stallion. The neighbors congratulated him on this good luck, but the man said, 'Who knows if it is

good or bad?' Then one day, the man's son was thrown off the
wild stallion and broke his leg. The neighbors expressed pity,
and the man said, 'Who knows?' Soon a war began, and all
the young men in the village were forced to join the army, but
the son was spared because of his crippled leg. Still, his father
would only say, 'Who knows whether it is good or bad?'

"You see, Tali-chan, we never know. As *Obaachan* used to
say, *ningen banji saio no uma.* What seems at first a tragedy may
be a blessing in disguise."

"But how could losing the garden be a *blessing!*" I asked,
hardly able to believe Masahiro could say such a thing.

"Who knows?" he replied. "Perhaps we will find a new
place to begin, and by building this new garden we will—"

"No!" I broke in, setting my teacup down on the table
and rising to my feet. "We can't just start over!! Don't you
get it? The garden's not just a place to grow vegetables! It's
like... like... our *home*. It's like losing a home!"

I heard a car pull up outside and realized it was probably
Mom, but I was too upset to stop. "It's not just about plants,
it's about *us*! We're growing there too! They can't just cut off
our roots and say 'live somewhere else.' What if we're like
carrots, or something else you can't transplant? Maybe we'll
just wither up and *die* with no home!"

Masahiro gazed at me silently for a moment, then rose to
his feet and went to the door to greet Mom. They stood out on
the landing and talked quietly for a few minutes while I sank
back onto the sofa, arms folded across my chest.

I was angry at Masahiro. Angry at him for giving up and
seeming so calm. How could he say that stuff about peace and
acceptance, when they were going to bulldoze his meditation
pond and herbs and everyone's plots?

"I wish I'd never even *had* a plot!" I told him later that
evening, as we were finally leaving. "I wish I never even saw

the garden in the first place!" Swallowing back tears, I followed Mom out the door and down the apartment stairs without
looking at Masahiro or even saying goodbye.

∾

I didn't go to the garden that weekend, or the following
week. It was going to be destroyed, so what difference did it
make? I didn't want to see Masahiro either. Every day after
school I took the bus straight home, let myself into the quiet
apartment and did homework on the couch, then turned on
the television without really watching. Before Mom arrived
from work, I would make macaroni or heat up a frozen pizza
in the microwave, but the food tasted plain and boring without
vegetables from the garden. We were out of miso, and I didn't
care. I didn't want anything to make me think of the garden or
Masahiro. I tried to pretend none of it ever existed.

"Tal, I know you're sad about the garden," Mom said one
night, coming into our room after I'd already pulled the covers
over my head. "But someday we'll have our own place, and
you and I can plant a big vegetable garden there, 'kay?"

"I don't care," I said, turning toward the wall. "That's not
the same."

She sat on the edge of the bed and gently stroked my hair.
"I know... but we have to do the best we can, right? Isn't that
what you always tell me?"

I shrugged and didn't say anything. It was like Mom and
I had switched places!

She bent down and kissed the top of my head. "I know it's
hard, Sweetheart. But I'm sure you'll start feeling better with
time."

∾

I didn't believe her at first, but to my surprise, Mom was right. I did start to feel a tiny bit better, at least on the surface. We'd be leaving El Chorro soon, I remembered, so who cared? Instead of thinking about the garden, I started thinking once again about Washington, about moving up there and getting our very own place. Not a lonely apartment surrounded by parking lots, but a real house in a real neighborhood, with a yard and space to grow our own garden. The more I imagined this, the easier it became to distract myself from thinking about the *Nihonmachi* and everyone there. I knew Mom was saving up money as fast as she could, and maybe soon we'd have enough to go and have a real fresh start, like we'd been planning all along. We could go somewhere brand-new and just be a normal mom and a normal daughter, who had never been homeless, or "clients," or gardeners who tried to save their garden and failed. I couldn't wait to get to our new lives and never look back again.

24

B UT WHEN I ARRIVED HOME from school one day the next week, I realized something had gone horribly wrong. I opened the door to find the apartment in disarray and all of our nice new furniture gone. The blinds were closed, piles of laundry lay haphazardly around the dim room, and stacks of paper and receipts were scattered on the floor where Mom's desk used to be. But worst of all, there was Mom, sitting wrapped in a blanket in the corner, eyes red and puffy.

"What happened?!" I cried out, forgetting to shut the door and running across the room to her.

She could hardly speak through her tears. "Your uncle Jim called today. He was angry... because... I owe him money..."

"Did he come here?" I asked, alarmed. "And take everything away?"

Mom shook her head and wiped her eyes with the back of one sleeve, but more tears kept coming.

"No, I sold it," she managed between sobs.

"You sold our stuff?"

"The furniture," she choked, staring into her lap. "And the car... and with the money I'd saved, it was almost enough..." Her voice cracked again and came out angrier this time. "But I *paid* him, the bastard."

I was stunned. Everything Mom had been saving up for Washington, for our own place? All those hours of overtime, those bank statements with their neat columns of numbers—now back to nothing?

Mom took a shaky breath and sat up straighter, but when she looked at me, her eyes welled up again. She buried her face in her hands. "I'm so sorry Tal... I'm so, so sorry...this isn't fair to you."

I gave her a long hug and rubbed her back, feeling the tears fill my own eyes too. But I blinked them back hard and tried to act okay.

"It's alright, Mom. You can save up again."

She was too sad to talk anymore, so we sat there in the corner for what seemed like a hundred years, until the draft from the open door became too cold and I eventually went to shut it.

Mom didn't go to work the next day, and when I arrived home from school, she was still sitting in the corner of the living room. I opened the blinds and tried to straighten up a bit, folding laundry and making neat stacks of papers along the bare walls.

"It's really okay," I told her, making a bed of folded blankets for myself on the floor across from hers. "Don't worry. It's not that bad. We still have a place to live, and you have a job! And you can save up money again..."

But it didn't matter what I said. The whistling, energetic, hard-working, hopeful Mom was suddenly gone, replaced by a smaller, sadder version of herself I hadn't seen in ages.

The next few days, I hardly had time to think about the garden *or* Washington anymore. Mom only got worse, saying she didn't feel well and couldn't eat, lying under the blankets asleep all day or scribbling unfinished letters to Uncle Jim. I worried what would happen if she used all her sick-days at work, and how she would pay rent by the end of the month. And even if Mom *did* feel better, how would she get to work without a car? There were no bus stops near the apartment, so she would have to leave before sunrise and walk down the highway to the nearest shopping center to catch a bus downtown, then transfer to another bus after that.

I worried about these things in class, on the school bus, while trying to do homework, and staring up at the ceiling from my pillow at night. I tried to cheer Mom by making her favorite foods and turning the TV to the oldies station, but nothing helped. She only got worse, face pale and eyes sunken, the old sparkle completely gone. The days dragged on, and I started to wonder if maybe she really *was* sick. But she didn't have a cough or fever or bellyache, or anything like that—just a terrible case of sadness.

One day I arrived home from school to find her in worse condition than ever, new piles of crumpled tissues around the makeshift bed.

"Alicia came today," she said in a small, thin voice. "We had an appointment scheduled...I forgot..."

My heart started racing. "Alicia was here?! She saw the apartment?"

Mom gave a weary sigh and an almost imperceptible nod. She squeezed her eyes shut for a long moment, and I thought she might start crying. But then she spoke again, almost in a whisper. "She says I need to start taking those awful pills again...and pull it together...and if things don't change—" Her voice caught in her throat, and two tears slid down her cheeks. "Then she may have to call somebody from Child Protective Services."

With those words, she broke down completely, sobbing too hard for me to understand what she was saying. I suddenly remembered something Uncle Jim once said, about calling "CPS" to take me away to another family, just like when I was four. Child Protective Services, isn't that what Mom had said? The people who took kids away from their parents?

"They *can't* do that!" I blurted. "They can't take us away from each other!"

Mom shook her head and buried her face in her arms.

"I'm sure things will get better," I said. "They just need to give you a chance!"

But even as the words came out, I wasn't sure. What if Mom really *didn't* get better this time? What if she actually needed those pills, in order to stay happy? What if even the pills weren't enough?

I knew only one thing for certain. If I went to live with someone else, Mom would definitely not be okay, ever. She needed me! We needed each other. I sat there beside her for a long time, wishing I could somehow explain this to Alicia. I knew she would be returning next week for another meeting with Mom—maybe even sooner, now that she was concerned about us. Something had to change, and fast.

It wasn't until later that night, lying beneath my blankets on the floor and listening to Mom's soft, shallow breathing across the room, that I finally had an idea.

25

THE NEXT DAY WAS SATURDAY, and I got up early and announced that I was going to the garden. Nacha would be picking me up at our apartment and bringing me back later, I lied to Mom, who nodded blankly and didn't ask questions.

I gathered everything I needed and put it in my backpack, including the entire $7.63 from the spare-change jar on top of the fridge. It was a cold, drizzly day, so I took my warmest jacket and pulled the hood low over my eyes, hoping nobody would notice I was too young to be walking along a highway by myself. Eager to start as soon as possible, I set off through the apartment parking lot to the street, where I took a deep breath and began in the direction of town. The backpack already felt heavy underneath my raincoat. Stepping through dry weeds along the roadside, with cars and semi trucks whizzing by so close I could feel gusts of wind as they passed, I kept my eyes glued straight ahead and moved steadily onward, reminding myself that I had to do this for Mom.

I didn't want to see the garden again. I didn't want to see everyone's plots dismantled, or a sign saying it all belonged to somebody else, or even worse, to find that bulldozers had already torn everything down. I didn't want to see Masahiro either. *How could he say that stuff about acceptance, after all our hard work?* I didn't want to see anyone. But probably no one would be around on a cloudy day like this, I thought, when the garden was going to be destroyed anyway. I would just get a few things, then head back to the apartment and probably never return to the *Nihonmachi* Garden ever again.

After what seemed like hours of walking through a misty drizzle, I finally reached the shopping center where I'd seen a bus stop. I planned to come back here later and buy as many groceries as I could get for $7.63, so that if Alicia came back, she would see that Mom and I had more food in the house than just oatmeal and instant noodle soup. But for now, I sank onto a bench and crossed my fingers that the bus even came on Saturdays.

Just when I'd almost given up the entire plan, one finally arrived. The driver looked at me with raised eyebrows and asked if my parents knew where I was going. I reassured him that yes, of course, they were meeting me downtown, and he waved his hand not to worry about putting any quarters into the slot.

The bus was mostly empty, and I sat on a seat in the very back, mentally rehearsing what to do in the garden. When we reached downtown, I asked the driver what time he would return to the shopping center, and he gave me a schedule and said the last bus of the day was at three o'clock. I nodded with relief. It was almost noon, so I had plenty of time to walk, get what I needed, and return downtown.

༄

The garden seemed quieter than I'd ever seen it. Many of the plots were now covered in fresh weeds, the painted signs and colorful flags all gone. Grace and Rowena had removed their tools and metal sink, leaving only a few scattered rows of vegetables that hadn't died yet from the frost. The fig tree was completely bare and looked half its original size, just a tangled mass of sticks with wet logs and benches scattered haphazardly underneath. With no leaves on the trees or dense vines growing up the fences, the whole garden looked even flatter than I remembered, nothing but a maze of wire, crates, and shipping pallets half-buried in grass. *No wonder the city council thought it looked like a junk heap,* I thought.

Determined to stay no longer than necessary, I walked down the main path to the tool shed, knelt on the cold cement, and reached under the bottom shelf to retrieve a round tin box Masahiro had given me. I cracked open the lid and peeked inside, relieved to find everything still there. All the little paper envelopes and bags of seeds, carefully labeled by variety and date, that I'd saved all year long for the garden Mom and I would start together up in Washington. Of course we could buy seed packets from a store up there, but I was worried it wouldn't be the same. It had to be *these* seeds, from *this* garden, because this was the place where I'd seen Mom rise up overnight from her sadness like a flower bulb rising from the soil in spring.

Maybe other gardens could do the same magic, but maybe they couldn't. And I needed that magic right *now*, to take it back to the apartment and plant it in pots and jars and yogurt containers all over the counters and window sills, wherever Mom could see it and start to feel better again. This had to work, before Alicia came back! It was the last bit of hope I could think of.

I clutched the tin to my chest and headed tentatively over to Masahiro's herb garden. He didn't seem to be around, and I wondered if he even came to the garden anymore. Would I be able to remember all the different plants in those special teas, without him here to show me? I pulled scissors and a plastic shopping bag from my backpack, found the *ukogi* bushes along the back fence, and began cutting leaves.

Next I would get *ikarisu* and St. John's Wort, then check to see if there were any *kuko* berries left...

"Talia! That you, child?"

I jumped and turned around. It was Mrs. Murphey, coming toward me with a trowel in one hand and a bucket full of muddy flower bulbs in the other.

"Well, Lord have mercy, what became of you? I haven't seen you and your mama in a million years."

Part of me wanted to tell Mrs. Murphey everything, and another part wanted to turn and run away before she found out. But I just stood there holding my plastic bag, scissors poised in midair.

"We been lookin' for you high and low," she said, setting down her bucket and walking toward me through the knee-high grass. "Now, don't get alarmed, but Masahiro got sick last week, and he's in the hospital right now. Boy, does he ever want to see *you*."

My heart fluttered. "Masahiro's in the hospital?"

She reached forward and gave my shoulder a gentle pat. "Don't you worry, child, they're takin' real good care of him. That head cold was lookin' a lot like pneumonia, so he finally let us take him in."

I thought about the dried herbs neatly lined up on a shelf in Masahiro's apartment, the *hatugomi* and *karin* and *hasucha* for curing a cold, and how *Obaachan* used all those plants to cure Masahiro's lungs when he was a boy.

"But what about his plant medicines?" I asked, confused. "Didn't he use them?"

Mrs. Murphey sighed. "Those herbs got their place, child. He's cured every one of us from *somethin*.' But they got their limit... especially at the ripe old age of ninety-four."

"Masahiro's ninety-four?" I asked incredulously. I always knew he was old, but I never realized he was *that* old.

She nodded. "Wouldn't know it, huh. He's just about the youngest old person I ever seen! But even he could use more help this time, you see? We're all prayin' he's gonna pull right through this."

It felt like the ground was dissolving beneath my feet. "But... he *will* be okay, right?"

She gave my shoulder another pat. "That's what we're prayin.' But it's God's hands."

For a moment, there was no sound but the tip-tip-tap of rainwater dripping from tree limbs onto the carpet of wet leaves. Then Mrs. Murphey spoke up again. "He sure is hankering to see you, child! Your mama around? They got visitor time at three o'clock today."

I thought fast. "Oh, my mom has a cleaning job today... she's picking me up later. But maybe I can go with *you*!"

"Well," Mrs. Murphey hesitated. "I dunno. You think your mama wouldn't mind?"

I shook my head emphatically. "She won't."

"Well, if you say so, we'll go this afternoon."

She picked up the bucket and shuffled back to her plot, leaving me to finish cutting herbs. I snipped slowly at the *ukogi*, thinking about Masahiro. Were they letting him drink his special tea in the hospital? Was anyone taking care of his potted plants back home?

A few of the herbs had lost their leaves for winter, but I harvested what I could, putting the plastic bags carefully in my backpack and hoping the plants would stay fresh until I could hang them up at the apartment. Then I went over to Mrs. Murphey's plot and watched silently as she dug up bulbs from the muddy soil. Where would she plant all those bulbs next spring, when the garden was gone?

I'd been planning to avoid Mom's and my plot, but now, stuck waiting until three o'clock, my curiosity won out. Trying not to think about it being destroyed, I walked down the leaf-covered path to our little spot by the mimosa tree. Everything had grown bigger in the past few weeks, ruby-veined chard leaves curling around bright stems, carrot tops beginning to protrude slightly from the soil. Even if the whole garden was going to be destroyed, I couldn't bear the thought of leaving all those beautiful vegetables behind. *Besides,* I thought, *we do need more food in the apartment.*

I took out the scissors and remaining plastic bags, began clipping lettuce leaves, and then unearthed some small purple carrots, radishes, and a few green onions. It wasn't until all the bags were full and I was leaving the plot that I suddenly remembered Lina's box—all her special treasures, under the *agave* plant where her umbilical cord was buried!

I ran down the path, past the fig tree to the Rivas family's plot. Squeezing between the fence and the *agave's* giant blue-gray leaves, I knelt down and dug around with a stick to unearth the old metal lunchbox. It was caked in mud, with a more rust than I remembered, but the contents inside were unharmed. I crammed the box into the last bit of space in my backpack and returned slowly to Mrs. Murphey's plot, filled with sadness. What would Lina say when came back and learned that her special spot, where she was supposed to return all her life, was gone?

∽

Just before three o'clock, Mrs. Murphey and I walked to her car and drove to the hospital. I silently crossed my fingers that she would give me a ride home later, since I'd be missing the last bus.

The woman at the front desk pointed the way to Masahiro's room, number 136-B, and we walked side by side down the brightly lit, disinfectant-smelling hallways. I knew we'd found it before I even saw the number. Felipe was strumming his guitar in the doorway, Rowena's laughter echoed out into the hall, and I could hear Nacha speaking in Spanish with one of the nurses. And there were plants everywhere! Small pots of geraniums and bright yellow narcissus filled the windowsill, a collection of bonsai trees stood on a table in the corner, and even the Everlasting Tomato Plant was there in its large bucket beneath the window. It almost seemed like a whole garden had been transplanted into that tiny hospital room!

Rowena looked surprised to see me, rushing over to the doorway and exclaiming how glad Masahiro would be that I'd finally come. A nurse came over too, asking if we could please limit the number of visitors in the room so that Mr. Tanaka could keep resting. Rowena said she was going back to work anyway, and Nacha whispered something to Felipe, who rose from his chair and followed her to the door.

"We'll just stay in the lobby for a while, *mija*," she said, giving me a wink and a light pat on the back. "He wants very much to see you."

I followed Mrs. Murphey into the room, past a light blue curtain separating the area nearest the window. On the other side of the curtain was Masahiro, half sitting and half lying on a bed with beeping machines around him, looking small and frail under the thin blanket. He had a clear plastic mask over his nose and mouth, attached by a thin tube to a tank beside the bed, but his face lit up with the usual gentle smile as we approached. Reaching slowly with both hands, he carefully removed the mask from his face to speak.

"Tali-chan." His voice was even quieter than usual. "I am very happy you are here."

"Are—are you okay?" I asked, a tiny bit scared to see him like that.

Mrs. Murphey went over to the windowsill to replace an older vase of flowers with a new bouquet she'd brought, and Masahiro watched with a slight smile.

"Yes... it is okay now. This is helping me to breathe." He returned the plastic mask to his face and closed his eyes for a moment. When he opened them again, he seemed to have more energy than before. He lifted the mask away and laid it down on the blanket beside him. "I have missed you."

I lowered my eyes, remembering how angrily I'd spoken at his apartment the night of the city council meeting.

"I'm sorr—" I began, but he shook his head and spoke before I could finish.

"No need to apologize; you have done nothing wrong. I only wanted to know if you and your mother are alright."

I hesitated, not wanting to worry him while he was sick, but found myself unable to hold it in any longer. It felt like a big wall I'd been building up suddenly began to crumble, and before I knew it, the entire story came pouring out: how Mom was too sad to get out of bed, how she wasn't going to work anymore, how I might have to live somewhere else if she didn't get better soon.

Masahiro listened until I'd finished, then nodded slowly.

"Aaah... I am afraid she has been away too long from the soil and the sun, Tali-chan. Your mother needs to have life around her: growing plants, living beings. Without this, she is like a fish trying to breathe in the air."

"But everything was fine for a long time," I protested. "Even after she stopped gardening!"

Masahiro thought quietly for a moment, then said, "A plant can live for quite some time without being watered, that is true. But finally, it will begin to wither."

I pictured Mom in the crowded department store across town, working overtime and driving back late at night to sit alone in the quiet kitchen, eating microwave pizza and adding columns of numbers on scratch paper. She seemed okay, all those weeks.... but I pictured her now, lying wearily in the corner of the bare living room like a withered plant, and wondered if Masahiro was right.

I told him my idea to plant seeds all over the apartment, making a temporary garden on the countertops and window-sills and front doorstep. He brightened up at this suggestion, saying he hoped there would be enough sunlight.

"You may take these," he said, glancing toward the plants on the windowsill. "They require only a small amount of sun."

"But don't you need them here in this room, to help *you* get better?" I asked.

"Don't worry," he replied with a smile. "There are many more in the garden. Someone will bring them to me."

I stiffened at mention of the garden, not wanting to think about Masahiro's beautiful herbs being torn up by bulldozers, or how we'd never work there together again. He must have noticed, because he drew in a slow, wheezing breath and his face grew more serious.

"Tali-chan, I have something important to tell you."

I waited as he closed his eyes for a long moment and gathered his thoughts. His face looked even more wrinkled than I remembered, the skin pale and tissue-paper thin.

A nurse arrived at the doorway and peeked in, wrote something on her clipboard, and continued down the hall. Mrs. Murphey had settled herself onto a chair in the corner with and looked like she might begin to doze off. I wondered if Masahiro was falling asleep too, but then he opened his eyes and looked steadily at me.

"I have been lying here all these days, with much time to

think," he said quietly. "I am thinking about something you said a while ago, which I cannot forget. Do you remember when you said every person has a kind heart, even if it is buried deep where we must dig to find it?"

I nodded, remembering our conversation from under the fig tree. "Yeah, and you said that's not always true, like with Mr. Richards. And you were right."

Masahiro shook his head slowly. "No, Tali-chan. I have come to see that *you* were right. It is something I once knew, but had forgotten. You are a young child, but very wise… you reminded me."

I was speechless. He thought I was wise? That I taught *him* something? And besides, if Mr. Richards actually had a kind heart, why did he want to destroy our garden?

Masahiro coughed weakly and seemed to be having difficulty breathing again. With shaky fingers, he lifted the oxygen mask to his face and took several longer breaths. I waited until he finally removed it and spoke again.

"A few days ago," he began, "a woman came here to visit. She is a daughter of Mr. Richards, and she wants to help us."

I raised my eyebrows in surprise. "His *daughter* wants to help? Why?"

"She has a young nephew, a teenager, who has been having problems. Like your mother, he becomes very sad… too sad to keep going. He is now staying at a home far away, for young people with troubles of the mind and heart. But he dislikes it there, and wants desperately to leave. They have a small garden, and it is the only place he likes to be."

I stood at the edge of the bed, eyes glued to Masahiro's tired face, leaning in to catch every word. He spoke more slowly than ever, pausing for breath between sentences.

"So, you see, this boy is soon coming to live in El Chorro with his aunt. She heard about our garden, and the students who work with Bill Tava. She would like her nephew to join them. She believes this may be his only hope for healing."

"But the garden won't even be here anymore," I pointed out miserably.

Masahiro made a great effort to pull himself up straighter against the pillow, fixing his eyes on mine. "The zoning has changed, yes, but the land has not been sold. There is still a tiny chance—very tiny—that the city council might decide not to sell it. Or perhaps, Mr. Richards might decide not to buy the property."

"Why?" I asked doubtfully. "Just so another kid can garden with Bill?"

"Ah, but not just *any* kid," Masahiro said, smiling. "The grandson of the developer himself... a boy who is in great need of help. Even someone like Mr. Richards, who seems to care only about money, surely cares about his own *family*. If he has a heart, then perhaps this is a way to reach down to it."

I thought for a moment. "So what can his daughter do? Why did she come talk with you?"

"She has tried to persuade her father," Masahiro replied, "and he will not listen. 'There is plenty of dirt in the world,' he says. 'They can garden elsewhere.' But she says that would take too long to begin, and her nephew needs help right away."

"So if he won't even listen to *her*, what can *we* do?" I asked, getting frustrated.

Masahiro drew in a long, uneven breath and nodded. "Yes... that is what I wish to talk about, Tali-chan. On Tuesday, the city council will vote about selling the land. This is our final chance to speak, before a decision is made."

"But we already know what they decided!" I interrupted. "That's the whole reason they changed the zoning, right? To sell it? Isn't that what you said?"

Masahiro nodded slowly. "Yes, it is true... there is only a

very tiny chance. But now I see you were right, we mustn't give up until the last bit of hope is gone."

"*You said* there was nothing left to do." I fixed my eyes stubbornly on the floor. "You said to just accept it."

"Tali-chan…" Masahiro's voice was almost a whisper. I looked back up at him, the creases seeming to grow deeper than ever around his soft, gentle eyes.

"I know it was hard for you, when I said that… and it is true that we may still not succeed. This door may close, and another will open. Like the Chinese man who lost his horse, remember? We never know what is good or bad, so we must simply accept what comes."

"Then what's the point in trying?" I asked, memories of our defeat at the last city council meeting flooding back into my mind.

He closed his eyes and thought for a moment. "*Obaachan* used to tell me, '*jinji wo tsukushite temmei wo mate.*' This means 'do the best you can, then wait for the ruling of heaven.' Even if there is the tiniest hope, we must try as hard as possible. That way, if we do not succeed, we know it was simply the ruling of heaven."

"But if we keep trying and it doesn't work, we'll just be sadder!" I protested.

Masahiro looked down and nodded. "Yes… we might be sad. But if we have both love and wisdom, we will be okay."

I frowned, trying to make sense of this. Masahiro gazed at me for a long moment, then finally tried to explain. "With love, we continue trying to save what we love. And with wisdom, we will accept whatever happens. Can you understand this, Tali-chan?"

I nodded my head uncertainly.

Masahiro looked exhausted. He closed his eyes, lifted the mask to his face, and breathed weakly into it for a few minutes.

I glanced over at Mrs. Murphey, who had indeed fallen asleep, mouth open and chin pressed into the folds of her neck.

"So you're saying we should go to the meeting?" I finally asked, when Masahiro removed the mask.

He coughed again and nodded weakly. "I would like *you* to go, Tali-chan. I believe you are the person to whom they might listen."

I was startled. "Me? Why would they listen to *me*?"

Masahiro smiled softly. "At my apartment, after the meeting, you said something very special. Do you remember? You said the garden is not only to grow food, but for *us* to grow. That it is like our home."

I nodded, remembering.

"Well… everyone has spoken many times, but nobody has said that. Perhaps we could not find the words, or were afraid they would laugh at us, or afraid they could not understand. So we have been arguing from our heads. But you are brave, Tali-chan. You speak what is in your *heart*. This is why I would like them to hear you too."

I stood completely still at the side of the bed, not feeling brave at all.

"So you—you want me to go to the meeting? And talk?"

He nodded. "This is our final piece of hope. It is small, but it is still hope."

I tried to imagine what I would possibly say, up at the microphone, with the city council members in their suits and ties all watching me. *Why would they listen to an eleven-year-old kid?* But when I looked back at Masahiro's earnest face, all I could think about was how hard he'd worked to save the garden, and how he couldn't do anything more while here in the hospital. I remembered how he'd helped me and Mom start our own plot, even though we might leave El Chorro at any time.

"M-maybe..." I stammered.

"It's okay," Masahiro said gently. "You do not need to de-cide yet. The meeting is not until Tuesday. But you will think about it?

I nodded.

"Remember," he said, "with love and wisdom, you will be okay, no matter what happens. And you have both." He coughed again and winced, lifting the breathing mask back to his face for a long time.

"Are you going to be okay?" I asked hesitantly when he finally removed it again. "Do they let you use your herbs here?"

Masahiro was quiet for a while, then answered in a voice so quiet I had to lean even closer to hear him. "Those herbs have their place and time, Tali-chan. They can help to give us a long and prosperous life. But *Obaachan* was right. We must also accept what comes. Even the old tomato, which may sur-vive many years, will finally go back into the circle."

"The circle?" A strange knot formed in my stomach.

Masahiro closed his eyes and nodded. "In the garden, every plant seems to begin and end... from a seed to an old dry straw. But if you look closer, you will see there are no beginnings or endings."

I stared hard at him, trying to understand.

"When you put a seed in the ground," Masahiro began again patiently, "the plant seems to appear from nowhere, yes? It forms out of water, air, sun, and soil. And later, when that plant dies and returns to the ground, the same materials rise up from it to become a new plant. So, this new plant is not separate from the other, you see, because they are part of the same circle that has been spinning forever."

"But *people* don't grow out of the soil," I protested through the lump in my throat, afraid of what Masahiro might be saying.

He took another raspy breath and nodded. "Yes...with us, it is not so simple. We are made of the same material as plants—water, air, light—but we are also made of wisdom and stories. These move through us, into other people. We cannot hold onto them forever, just as a stone in a streambed cannot hold the water that passes over it. If we learn this, it will be easy to accept what comes."

"But you won't—I mean, you're not—" I couldn't finish the sentence.

Masahiro reached out a thin, calloused hand and placed it gently on top of mine. "Tali-chan, this is not something we can know. Perhaps we have many days ahead of us, or years...but nobody knows this. Our time will come when it comes, and that is only part of the circle."

He squeezed my hand, and I was surprised by his strong grip. We stayed like that for a while, not talking. I suddenly wanted to wrap my arms around Masahiro's shoulders and cry, for everyone and everything— for him and the other gardeners, for the Rivas family, for Mom, and for all the beautiful things that couldn't last forever. But I just stood there, looking at my small hand in his wrinkled, leathery one.

Then the nurse came to tell us that visiting hours were over and Mr. Tanaka needed his rest.

Masahiro did look tired. He had closed his eyes, the lids so thin I could see small blue veins running through them.

"I'll go to the meeting," I said, suddenly making up my mind. "For you."

He cracked his eyes open and smiled, giving my hand another squeeze but seeming too exhausted to say more.

"And I'll come visit again, to tell you what happens."

Masahiro nodded and released my hand. "I would love that very much, Tali-chan. And please... remember what I told you."

I promised him I would remember, then turned to wake up Mrs. Murphey and return with her to the lobby.

∾

It was drizzling as we walked outside through the parking lot. To my relief, Mrs. Murphey offered to drive me back to the apartment, where I reassured her that I'd call Mom at work right away to say I'd gotten a ride home early. I was becoming a fantastic liar.

Climbing up the stairs to our front door, I felt both heavy and light-headed at the same time. It seemed like days since I'd left for the bus stop that morning, and I had completely forgotten about buying groceries. But at least we had vegetables from the garden... and maybe if I cooked a nice dinner, Mom would get up and eat with me.

But when I opened the door, I found that the blinds were still drawn, and she was lying fast asleep under her blankets in the corner of the dim living room. She stirred and squinted her eyes open as I came in.

"Tal... is that you?"

"Yeah, I'm back. Nacha dropped me off."

I wanted to tell her about my conversation with Masahiro and how scary it was to see him sick in the hospital, about the developer's daughter going to visit, and how there might still be a tiny chance to save the garden. But when I walked across the room and saw Mom's sad and sunken eyes, I decided not to say anything. She was having a hard enough time already, without worrying about all that.

I went over to the window, opened the blinds, and set up the small potted plant I'd brought from the hospital room.

"It's from the garden," I told her. "I thought you might like having it here."

For a second, I thought I saw a faint hint of a smile cross her face. I dug around in my backpack for the bags of herbs. "I brought you some stuff for tea, too."

"Oh, Tal," she murmured, pulling herself up a bit against the wall. "That's so nice of you. I've let you down terribly..."

But before she could say anything else, I went into the kitchen to start the kettle. I was getting tired of Mom's sadness, of her lying there not doing anything, not knowing how to make things better. *What was the problem?* Was it really something in her brain, which could be fixed by two pills a day? Or was it like Masahiro said, a condition that could be cured with plants and soil and sun?

I didn't even care anymore. Other people's moms took care of *them*, not the other way around! Standing at the stove waiting for the tea water to boil, I silently wished Mom could be the stronger one, making a plan and telling me not to worry, reassuring me that she'd work everything out.

When the water boiled, I prepared two cups: plain green tea for me, and Masahiro's *ukogi* St. John's Wort for Mom. I carried these into the living room, where we sat together on the floor in silence, sipping our tea in the fading evening light.

26

ON TUESDAY AFTERNOON, I took the bus home from school like any ordinary day, let myself into the quiet apartment, and observed that nothing had changed. Mom still lay under her blankets in the corner of the living room, more pale and dazed-looking than ever, hardly even saying hello. I went immediately to the kitchen and checked on my hanging bundles of drying herbs, then rummaged through the near-empty cupboards looking for something to eat.

"Mom, have you had any lunch?" I called out into the next room. "Do you want me to make you a salad from the garden?"

"No. I can't eat right now," she said in a low, dull voice.

I sighed. "Then would you like a cup of tea? You know, the special—"

"Tal, please. I don't want anything."

I could hear her turn over, voice becoming muffled under the blankets. "I don't feel well."

The digital clock on the stove read 4:08. Less than one hour to go... I crossed my fingers that Mom would fall asleep before then.

To my relief, at about 4:40, she finally did. I leaned close and whispered her name a couple times, cautiously, just to make sure she was completely out. No response.

Moving swiftly around the small apartment, I gathered a few things and shoved them into my backpack: flashlight, red notebook, coins from the jar above the fridge. Then, keeping a watchful eye on Mom's heap of blankets across the room, I cracked open the door as quietly as possible and slipped out into the cold evening air.

It was almost dark by now, and a thin mist drifted down in front of the street lamps. Taking a deep breath and hugging both arms tightly around myself, I set off through the parking lot toward the street.

At first, I'd worried about what Mom would think if she woke up and couldn't hear me in the apartment, but then I decided she was probably too immersed in her own problems to notice.

I was sick of the whole thing. Why was I always the one worrying about *her*? Why didn't Mom pay attention to these things, making sure we had plenty of food, or that I did my homework and was safely home after dark... isn't that what other moms did?

I trudged along the highway, picturing her in the empty apartment, curled beneath her blankets and trying to escape from the world, from all her sadness... maybe even from me.

She doesn't care what I do, I told myself, striding down the gravel shoulder of the road. *She's too sad to care about me.*

At night, the shopping center seemed even farther than before, and the trucks whizzing past with their bright headlights seemed much closer. I tried hard to be invisible or look like a grownup so nobody would stop. At one point, when it seemed like a car slowed down while passing, I scrambled down into the ditch beside the highway and began pushing my way through the tall weeds, tingling with adrenaline. It felt as though I were watching a movie of myself, not actually doing this in real life.

When I finally reached the shopping center, I ran quickly to the bus stop and sank onto a bench, silently praying that I hadn't missed the final bus of the day. I reached into my jacket pocket and pulled out the wrinkled schedule, checking for the millionth time to make sure it really came at 5:30.

After what seemed like an eternity, the bus arrived. Behind the wheel was that same driver as before, and he raised his eyebrows suspiciously as I began dropping quarters into the slot. "Are your parents with you, little girl?"

"They're meeting me at the transit center downtown," I replied, trying to look innocent and hoping he'd believe me a second time.

"Alright then…" The driver sounded unsure. "You know, it's safer to ride with an adult, especially at night."

I nodded. "'Kay, I'll tell them."

"Why don't you sit right up here by me?" he suggested, motioning to the seat nearest the front. I sat down and played along as he asked me a thousand questions, all the way into town. I made up a whole story about how my aunt worked in that shopping center, and how I was hanging out with her this evening while my parents went to a meeting. They were both professional landscapers, I told him, and were helping design a plan for more community gardens in El Chorro. *It's a good thing I write so many stories,* I thought proudly to myself.

When we arrived at the station downtown, I thanked the driver and got off the bus quickly, trying to disappear into the crowd so he wouldn't notice that nobody was waiting to pick me up. By this time, the mist had turned into a steady drizzle, and I pulled the raincoat over my backpack, thrust my hands deep into the pockets, and began walking. The rain came down harder, beginning to soak through my pants and socks, but at least City Hall was only a few blocks away. I retraced the map in my head, rehearsing which streets to turn on.

I'm doing it, Masahiro, I said silently in my mind. *Here I am.*

In the warm foyer of the building, I peeled off my wet raincoat and jacket, took a deep breath, and cautiously pushed open the glass door of the meeting chamber.

The room was almost empty this time. Sitting in the front row with their laptops and briefcases were Mr. Richards and his two staff people. On the other side of the aisle, in the same row where I'd sat beside Masahiro just a few weeks before, were Bill Tava, Abuela Jean, and another woman who looked vaguely familiar. Most of the gardeners hadn't come this time, probably because they'd given up hope after we lost before.

I walked quietly down the aisle along the wall. Then suddenly, getting closer, I realized who that woman beside Bill was.

Could it be? *Hattie?* Mom's old friend, who'd been mean to us the first day in El Chorro! What was *she* doing here?

Hattie turned around and saw me, squinting as though trying to place who I was. Then her eyes grew wide, and she smiled thinly and gave a little wave. She seemed nervous: sitting up straight, clutching her purse, turning around a few times toward the double doors at the back of the room.

Bill Tava noticed me too, waved in surprise, and motioned for me to come over.

"Hey, you made it!" he whispered.

I took a seat next to Abuela Jean, who gave me a little squeeze and talcum-powder-scented kiss on the cheek. "Hello Sweetie! We've missed you so much!" She turned to look around the room. "Is your mother here?"

I thought fast. "No, um, she had to do some errands. So she's picking me up afterward."

Abuela raised her eyebrows slightly, but to my relief, let it go. "They are going to vote about the garden soon," she whispered. "Do you think you'll say a little something this time, Sweetie?"

I pumped my head up and down resolutely, even though I was feeling more nervous by the minute.

"What a brave girl!" she said, patting me on the shoulder. "We're so proud of you."

Up at the front of the room, the council members were droning on in their usual confusing way. The digital clock on the wall showed a large red 6:22, and I wondered for a split second if Mom had noticed I was gone. I hoped the part of the meeting about the garden would come soon, but I also hoped it would never come.

I leaned forward to peek at Hattie, who was still gripping her purse and staring straight ahead. *Why in the world was she here?*

When the mayor finally announced that it was time for public comment regarding the sale of two properties on Ito Street, Hattie was the first to stand up and walk over to the microphone. She cleared her throat and spoke.

"My name is Hattie Johnson, I live in El Chorro, and I'm here to ask that you please reconsider the sale of this property. You may not realize that the community garden on Ito St. is also the site of a program for troubled teens, and I'd like to enroll my nephew in that program. As far as I can tell, nobody in this city offers horticultural therapy for at-risk youth, and my nephew cannot wait months for a new program to be created! I am appalled that the city would deny him this opportunity, which others have had. Where are your priorities? Please ask yourselves that, before voting to sell this land."

My head was in a whirl. Hattie had a nephew who needed help, who wanted to come to the garden? But Masahiro had said... Could it be that Mr. Richards' daughter, who wanted to help us save the garden, was *Hattie*? It seemed too crazy a coincidence to possibly be true.

I watched in startled amazement as she returned to her seat, jaw clenched. Mr. Richards leaned forward in his seat across the aisle and glared at her, but she kept her eyes ahead and refused to look at him.

Then Bill Tava went to the microphone. "You've already heard everything I have to say," he said in a low, angry voice. "The garden is a place where folks are learnin' skills. It's a place where kids headed for trouble are findin' somethin' better to do, gettin' their hands in the soil instead of gettin' into drugs. People are healin' their lives, alright? You can't get that from no condominium complex."

"Besides," he continued, voice growing louder, "that land has been there a helluva lot longer than us, and it's *gonna* be there a helluva lot longer too. Who do we think we are, with all this buying and selling? The way my ancestors woulda seen it, the land can't belong to anyone. *We* belong to the land. Whoever's been takin' care of it, that's who belongs to it. And you can't take that relationship away by signin' some piece of paper. I'm warning you, it isn't gonna be easy to remove us! I'm pitchin' my tent tonight! You can *bury* me there before you'll separate me from that sacred ground!!"

He returned to his seat, red faced and breathing hard.

Abuela Jean spoke next, her speech short and polite. "I am asking you again to please reconsider. We have already demonstrated what an important place the garden is for the health and wellbeing of our migrant families, especially the young people. Those kids need a place for outdoor activity and social interaction, and they need the nutrition that their families could otherwise not afford. If you care about the wellbeing of children in our community, please think again before tearing down our garden."

She came and sat back down with a small sigh, and the mayor asked if there were any final comments from the public.

Abuela Jean nudged me gently and said, "Go on, Sweetie. You can do it." But my heart was pounding in my ears, and I couldn't seem to move.

"In that case," the mayor said, "having concluded the public comment—"

But then suddenly my hand shot up in the air, waving back and forth like I knew the answer to a question in school. The mayor paused and looked straight at me.

"I—I have a public comment," I blurted out, and with another nudge from Abuela Jean, slid off my chair and moved down the aisle to the podium.

Mr. Richards and his staff people turned and stared at me, looking surprised. A couple of the council members smiled. The room was quiet, everyone waiting.

I swallowed hard, hands balled into fists at my sides to keep them from trembling. Someone came over to the podium and adjusted the microphone for me.

"My—my name—is Talia Trevino," I said in a voice that came out smaller and higher pitched than I expected. "I live in El Chorro, and I work in the garden, with... with my mom. And what I wanted to say—" I paused and took a big breath, thinking of Masahiro— "is that it's not just somewhere we grow food."

The blood started rushing in my ears, and everything I'd rehearsed to say at the meeting suddenly became tangled in my mind. What had Masahiro said the council members needed to hear? What was I supposed to tell them? My heart pounded, and the silence stretched on.

You are brave, Tali-chan; you speak what is in your heart. That's what he'd said. *We've all been arguing from our heads... but you speak what is in your heart.* What did Masahiro mean? What was in my heart? I squeezed my eyes shut for a moment, trying to think, but all I could see was Mom huddled in the corner of the living room, sinking deeper into her sadness every day, farther and farther away from me. Then I closed my eyes even tighter and saw another image of Mom, with her hands in the soil, magically rising up from her sadness as she had so many times when we tended our plot or arranged flowers with Mrs. Murphey. Before I knew what was happening, the words came flowing out.

"There's something amazing about that garden. I don't know why, but some people who have really hard problems go there and it's like medicine for us. I don't mean like plant-medicines, even though they help too... I mean just *being* there.

"Maybe people are afraid to talk about this, so they haven't told you. Maybe they're worried you won't understand... but something happens when you're in the garden, with your hands in the soil, touching everything and seeing all that life just coming out of nowhere. It's like everything changes. The whole world seems different... and you can't tell if you're taking care of the garden, or it's taking care of you.

"And it's like that for lots of people, not just me! There's one guy who might be in prison now, if he didn't have the garden. And some kids who were doing crimes and stuff that hurt themselves and other people, now they come and grow plants instead! And there's also a woman who's son died, and she thought she'd never be happy or have a reason to live anymore, until she made a flower plot there. And some of us... some of us don't have a place of our own, to come back to... so even though it looks like we're just growing vegetables, really it's like we're growing a *home*."

I swallowed hard. "When my mom and I used to be h-homeless... I thought my biggest dream in the whole wide world was to have a place of our own, to live in. But now we have an apartment, and it's not like I expected. I mean, it's somewhere we can sleep and cook food and keep our stuff, which is good...but it doesn't feel like home, the way the garden does."

I paused to catch my breath. Now that the river of words had begun, I couldn't make them stop. I'd never even thought about most of these things before, but suddenly they were all just streaming out of my mouth from nowhere. "And the city pays money to have places like the Linden Day Center, for helping people who need help, right? Well, our garden is that kind of place too! Like for my mom, she had lots of appointments to get medication and stuff like that, 'cause..."

My voice caught in my throat, and my eyes began to burn. I blinked hard and tried to keep on going. "'Cause...she has something wrong. I don't know what it is...but she gets really, really sad sometimes. Like, too sad to keep going, too sad to do *anything*."

I struggled to keep my voice steady. For some reason, I had to say this. "And the psychiatrist said maybe it's a sickness in her brain...and I don't know if that's true or not. She got medicine, and I think maybe it helped...But it makes her feel sick and get headaches, and she just doesn't want to take pills every day. But the garden always helped her too, every time."

The thought of me and Mom working in our plot together, which might never happen again, was more than I could bear. Hot tears brimmed over and slid in two long tracks down my cheeks, but the words just kept pouring out, as if they were never going to stop. "S-somehow it always helped her get better. She could still get up in the morning...and take care of us...and go to work...and keep getting us back on our feet. But when she stopped going there, everything changed. And now it's worse than ever. And I'm really scared."

My voice was quavering uncontrollably, but I kept going. "I'm scared, because if the garden is destroyed.... will my mom ever be okay again?"

The timer on the podium flashed red, but nobody moved. It was dead quiet in the room, everyone's eyes glued on me.

And the words just kept coming. It was as if someone poked a tiny hole in the bottom of the ocean, and all those miles and miles of water were just flooding out, no way to patch it up anymore.

"I don't know if it's that exact piece of land," I went on, "or if it could happen other places too... but I just know we need our garden. 'Cause it helps us to be okay, and to get better from all kinds of things. It's sort of like—"

My voice caught and the tears began again. "The garden's kind of like a *mom*. Someone who knows what you need, and takes care of you... and no matter how upside down or hurt everything gets, she's always there, just the same. And you can go sit with her until you feel stronger again... it's like that.

"I know you could give us some other place," I went on, wiping my eyes with the back of one sleeve and trying to regain my composure. "And maybe it could be like that too. But that's sort of like saying 'Don't worry, you could have a new Mom!' or 'Just find a new home!' I mean, how would you feel if somebody took away your house and gave you a new one and said 'Look, it's just the same! A bed, a kitchen table, a stove... ' And you had to start over and leave behind the place you're part of, where all your memories are... where you really feel like you're *home*?"

I stopped and took a long breath. I knew it had been more than three minutes, but nobody said anything. I stood for a moment with those last words echoing in my ears, and then, as if in a dream, turned and walked back to my seat.

The room was completely quiet. Abuela Jean was dabbing her eyes with a handkerchief, and two of the council members had taken out tissues as well. Hattie sat completely still, eyes fixed on the podium as if in a trance.

Finally, the mayor cleared her throat and said "Thank you. Are there… any other comments from the public?"

Nobody moved or spoke.

"In that case, having concluded the public comment—"

"Yes, I'd like to say something else."

It was Mr. Richards himself, rising from his chair and beginning to move toward the podium.

I held my breath. *Would he change his mind, and tell the city council he didn't want the land after all?*

"I simply wish to state," he declared, adjusting the microphone, "that I maintain my offer to purchase both the 7-acre and 5-acre lots on Ito St., as I see their potential to benefit a larger segment of your constituency than the small group currently served."

My heart sank. Mr. Richards still wanted to buy the land! So Masahiro had been right all along… some people just didn't care. Some people had a heart made of stone.

"However," he continued, straightening his necktie and speaking a bit louder, "I do intend to revise my plans, before approaching the council for final approval of the project. I will maintain my proposal for a mixed-use shopping and condominium complex on the east side of the street, but I would like to propose a *different* kind of development for the 5-acre lot where the garden currently stands, one that preserves this unique asset and broadens its offerings to the city of El Chorro."

I looked over at Bill and Abuela, who both seemed as confused as I was.

Mr. Richards cleared his throat. "Until tonight, I was misinformed as to the true value of the garden for members of our community. Personally, I… know a young man… whom I believe might benefit greatly from such a program."

Hattie stifled a gasp and shifted in her chair.

"And who knows how many others there are, like him? I'd like to see how such programs could be incorporated as *part* of this urban redevelopment plan, and I intend to revise my company's proposal in order to enhance the benefits of the current land-use, rather than replacing it. In short, my offer stands to purchase both properties at their current development value, with the intention that the 5-acre lot remains—in perpetuity—a community space and garden."

I couldn't believe my ears. Bill and Abuela Jean stared at each other, then at me. Could it be true, that Mr. Richards actually wanted to buy the land and *protect* our garden?

I leaned forward to peek at Hattie, whose face had gone even paler than usual. She was fumbling in her purse for another tissue, her makeup smudged with tears.

"Thank you, Mr. Richards," the mayor was saying. "Are there any further statements from the public?" She paused and waited. "In that case, we will now bring this item to council discussion and action. Would any council members like to comment?"

One of the council members cleared his throat to speak, but at that moment the doors of the meeting room swung open and two police officers strode into the room. People turned in their seats to see what was happening. I turned to look too, and there behind the officers, face ashen and frantic with worry, was *Mom*! I froze, unable to believe my eyes. Abuela Jean turned to me with a concerned expression.

"I apologize for the interruption," one of the officers said, "but we're looking for a missing child by the name of Talia Trevino."

Suddenly everything became a blur of confusion, and the next thing I knew, I was in the City Hall lobby with Mom wrapping her arms around me, burying her face in my hair and sobbing. "Tal... oh Tal... I was so worried about you..."

We knelt on the cold linoleum, holding onto each other like life rafts for a long, long time. From the corner of my eye, I could see the police officers standing by the door waiting. *What would they do? What if I'd gotten Mom in terrible trouble?*

"I'm sorry..." I whimpered, beginning to cry again.

But Mom just kept her arms wrapped around me and whispered, "Thank God you're okay," over and over again.

"Tal, why didn't you tell me?" she asked at last, letting go and brushing a strand of hair from my face. "Why didn't you ask me to bring you here?"

"I thought you were too upset to do anything," I mumbled, looking at the floor. "I didn't want to worry you."

"You didn't want to *worry* me, so you snuck out of the apartment alone at night?!" she asked incredulously.

"I didn't think you'd notice," I whispered, "when you were so sad."

Mom shook her head slowly, tears filling her eyes. "Oh Sweetheart, oh Sweetheart... I know I've been so out of it. I've been... I've just been really... depressed." She bit her lip and shook her head some more. "And I haven't been taking care of you like a mother should."

She buried her face in her hands for a long moment, then looked up again into my eyes.

"Tal, I know you were trying to take care of me... to protect me from getting more upset... but it's not supposed to be that way. I'm your mom, and you're my daughter. And no matter what happens, I care about you and want to make sure you're alright. Oh, Tal... I promise to try to change things and get better, so I can be there to take care of you when you need me... and so you'll never, ever think you need to do something like this again. Okay?"

I nodded, and she pulled me into her arms and held me close again for a long time. We both looked up, startled, when the double doors swung open and Bill and Abuela Jean came rushing into the lobby from the council meeting room, looking dumbstruck.

"Is it actually saved?" I asked, pulling away from Mom's arms and wiping my face with one sleeve.

Bill and Abuela nodded, their faces breaking into grins a mile wide, and suddenly they were both hugging me too, all of us laughing through our tears and exclaiming and talking at once.

Mom looked bewildered. "You saved the garden?"

"*Talia* did," Bill told her proudly. "Your daughter has to be the bravest, most amazing kid I've ever known."

Abuela Jean nodded in agreement. "I can't believe what you did, Sweetie. It's a miracle!"

Mom stared at me open-mouthed. "But—you mean—Talia, you convinced them to—"

"Not the city council! Mr. Richards!" I jumped in. "He changed his mind! He wants to buy the garden to *protect* it!"

I laughed again. Abuela was right; it was a miracle. The whole thing seemed too amazing to possibly be true.

"Do you think he'll keep his promise, though?" I asked, suddenly feeling concerned. "What if he was just saying it?"

As I spoke, the double doors of the meeting room swung open again, and out into the lobby walked Mr. Richards, followed by Mr. Ingersall and his staff.

"Yes," he was saying. "As the future property owner, I am committed to preserving that garden in a way that serves *all* of our interests."

Before we could say anything to him, one of the police officers came over and asked Mom to please follow him outside. I knew we were probably in for it, but I was too happy to care. The garden was saved, and that was all that mattered in the whole world. *The garden was saved!*

Luckily, as it turned out, we weren't in too much trouble after all. The officer gave me a firm lecture about not running away from home, then said if we wanted a ride back to the apartment we needed to leave *now*.

Mom nodded, and we followed him down the steps of City Hall to the police car waiting by the curb. I glanced back toward the building, wanting to run in and say goodbye to my friends, but Mom touched my shoulder firmly and shook her head.

As we climbed into the backseat of the police car, the door of City Hall opened and I saw Bill and Abuela stepping outside, followed by Mr. Richards and Hattie. I pressed my face to the window and watched them standing in a small group on the front steps, staring at us as the car pulled away from the curb and down the quiet street.

Mom had been watching too. "Was that *Hattie*?" she asked in astonishment.

I nodded. There was too much to explain. "It's a really long story, Mom."

∾

When we arrived back at the apartment, I was surprised to find Mrs. Murphey there. "Thank the Lord you're both okay," she breathed, rushing over to envelop us in an enormous hug.

"She was waiting in case you came back here while the police and I were out looking for you," Mom explained.

I hung my head, embarrassed that Mrs. Murphey knew I'd run away and that she'd seen our messy apartment. But then the news of the garden came flooding back, and it was all I could think about.

"We *saved* it!" I exclaimed. "We saved the garden! It's safe forever and ever!"

Mrs. Murphey looked flabbergasted. "What are you sayin' child? Lord, you can't mean that."

"She does mean it," Mom said. "Apparently, Talia worked some sort of miracle at the council meeting tonight."

"Is *that* where you been?" Mrs. Murphey exclaimed, eyes growing even wider. "Well, Lord have mercy..."

We all sat down right there on the floor in the empty, chairless living room as the story gradually began to unfold, from Hattie going to see Masahiro in the hospital, to my visit with him a few days before, to Mr. Richards' decision to protect the garden instead of destroying it.

Mom and Mrs. Murphey shook their heads in amazement.

"And that man didn't care about nothin' but money..." breathed Mrs. Murphey. "He was the most cold, heartless—"

"No," I interrupted, grinning. "That's the thing! He *does* have a caring heart, just like everyone. We just needed a way to reach down to it."

I was almost too excited to sleep that night. What would Masahiro say when he heard the news? And what about all the other gardeners? Lina and her family would return in spring to find everything still there... the fig tree, their plot with the giant *nopal* cacti, Lina's special *agave* with her umbilical cord and box of treasures buried underneath... and they'd all start digging and preparing beds for a whole new crop of corn and beans, just like last year. I lay in the darkness, smiling up at the ceiling and imagining it.

But most important of all, Mom was okay. At least for now. I prayed that it would last, that she could return to work and be able to pay our rent. If the garden could be saved in just one night, then perhaps there could be a miracle for us too.

27

MOM DECIDED TO LET me skip school the next day, so we could "take a breath" after all that had happened. It was another gray and overcast morning, and Mrs. Murphey came over to the apartment to pick us up early and drive to the garden.

She'd prepared a picnic lunch, including freshly baked gingerbread muffins with Abuela Jean's spiced applesauce, to celebrate our victory. We had considered calling the other gardeners and making it an official party, but then decided we didn't want anybody else to know until we first shared the news with Masahiro during visitor hours that afternoon.

As soon as we arrived, I bolted from the car and went running down the main path toward the fig tree. I hardly knew where to look first. The bamboo forest and meditation pond... Masahiro's herbs... Abuela Jean's tidy plot, tucked under its blanket of straw for the winter... Mrs. Murphey's flowers. Everything seemed to be glowing with a peculiar brightness that hadn't been there a few days before. I could practically see the young seedlings that would sprout in just a few months, and could almost hear the shrieks and laughter of the migrant children and smell the aromas of sweet corn and *carne asada* barbecuing on grills. *The garden was here to stay.*

Mrs. Murphey shuffled off to prepare a new bouquet of flowers for Masahiro, and I grabbed Mom's hand and led her excitedly over to our plot to show how big the vegetables had grown. We squatted down in the muddy path beside a row of radishes and carrots, and Mom reached out to touch the dew-covered leaves.

A carpet of weeds had sprouted in the past few weeks, and we began pulling them from the cold, muddy soil. As we worked, I could see hints of the old sparkle slowly returning to Mom's face, as if the life of the garden were gradually seeping right through her skin.

"I want to tell you something, Tal," she said after a while. "But don't worry, okay? Everything's going to be alright."

She took a deep breath and gazed up over the trellis of snap pea vines at the cloudy sky. "A couple days ago, I got laid off from my job at the department store."

I gasped.

"It's partly because I stayed home a few days without calling in sick... but also the holidays are over, so they were ready to let some people go—"

"Then how are we going to pay rent?" I asked, alarmed. I'd been afraid she might lose her job, but I didn't think it had *already* happened.

"That's what I wanted to talk about, Sweetheart. I just don't think we can... After paying Jim back and missing work, there's no way I'll have enough by the end of the month to pay rent, so—"

"Then what are we going to do?" I asked, feeling the old desperation rising in my chest.

"It's okay, Tal," Mom replied. "You know... I was thinking, maybe this is like a sign. Maybe it's the perfect time for us to head up north and have that brand new fresh start we've always talked about, somewhere more affordable."

She rolled a small handful of soil thoughtfully between her hands. "Especially with Uncle Jim finally paid off, we could just have a completely new start somewhere... get our very own place..."

I stared at Mom. Less than a week ago, this would have seemed like the best news in the world, but now her words sank heavily in my chest. I knew that if we stayed in El Chorro, we would probably be homeless again soon, right back where we started... but *still*. Now that I had stood up in front of the whole city council and realized the garden was like our true home, everything felt different. I no longer wanted to leave. Even if we had no house, no apartment, nowhere to live at all, I still wanted to stay here.

Seeing my crestfallen face, Mom shook her head and spoke again. "Never mind Sweetheart, who knows what will happen. This is a time to celebrate. We can think about all that stuff later, 'kay?"

I nodded, wanting to push away all thoughts of leaving El Chorro. After pulling the remaining weeds, we went to find Mrs. Murphey and sat down together for a picnic. Mom dried the tabletop and benches with her jacket, and Mrs. Murphey spread out food in front of us, along with a new bouquet of calendula and narcissus for Masahiro. I could hardly sit still, wishing time would go faster so we could visit the hospital and tell him everything.

While we were eating, the sun peeked out from behind the clouds for a few minutes, illuminating a million water droplets like jewels all over the bare tree branches. Listening carefully, I could practically hear the worms, bugs, gophers and other creatures down in the soil, stirring from their sleep and beginning to move under the layer of wet leaves. In the empty, dripping skeleton of the fig tree, a little bird began to chirp, and I remembered that Mom and Mrs. Murphey and I were not the only ones for whom the garden was a home. It was now preserved for its many other residents as well. I tilted my head back toward the bright sky and took a deep breath that smelled of rain and wet leaves, sweet decaying straw, and soil. It felt as though the whole world of the garden had been washed clean and was now re-awakening.

∾

After lunch, Mrs. Murphey drove us all to the hospital to see Masahiro and tell him the exciting news. She and Mom went up to the receptionist's desk and said we were there to visit Mr. Tanaka, room 136-B, but I was impatient and hurried down the hallway ahead of them. There was a hum of voices, and I was surprised to find the room crowded with so many people visiting all at once.

Bill Tava was heading through the open door with a large potted plant in his arms, but he set it down immediately and dropped to his knees, arms outstretched, when he saw me. I grinned at him and ran over for a big hug. Standing enveloped in Bill's muscular arms, I noticed over his shoulder that the bed by the window was empty and freshly made with crisp white sheets.

"Did they move him to another—" I started to ask, but as Bill pulled back from the hug, I saw that his dark eyes were brimming with tears. The room began to spin, and my entire body went weak.

Bill shook his head and whispered, "He's gone now, honey."

Everything froze, and that one moment stretched on and on, as though time would never move again.

Then suddenly everyone was gathering around us, and it was too much to take in. I felt as though my whole body had gone numb and was sinking down to the bottom of the ocean, watching everything get farther and farther away.

Mom appeared, and for the second time in two days, she pulled me close against her chest, stroking my hair and sobbing, rocking back and forth forever and ever. *It couldn't be true. He couldn't possibly be gone!*

When we finally let go of each other and rose shakily to our feet, we saw people from the garden moving solemnly around us, carrying buckets, vases, jars, and potted plants from the hospital room to the parking lot outside. A nurse stood on the opposite side of the room, talking quietly with a man and woman I'd never seen before. When she left the room, they walked over to us and the man extended a hand to Mom.

"Hey," he said. "I'm David. You must be Nora?"

Mom nodded, looking confused.

"I'm pleased to meet you...but so very sorry it's under these circumstances. I'm the grandson of Masahiro's older brother Kazuo. And this is my wife, Gina."

Mom shook their hands, still too stunned to speak.

"Kazuo?" I repeated, my voice coming out hoarse. *This man was Kazuo's grandson?*

"Yeah...we live up in Seattle, but we used to come down here a lot when I was a kid, to visit *Oji* Tanaka." He took off his glasses, wiping them on his shirtsleeve and letting out a long sigh. "I so regret that we didn't stay in touch over the years, especially after Grandpa Kaz died..."

"We flew down here last night," his wife said, "as soon as we heard he was sick and there was no other family around. I just wish we'd known earlier."

"When did he—" Mom began, but she was unable to finish the sentence.

"Early this morning," Kazuo's grandson replied softly. "But we waited, because the nurses told us you'd all be coming... to take care of his plants and things. We wanted to be here when his friends arrived."

He cleared his throat and looked out the window at the stark white sky, blinked a few times, then returned his gaze to us. "I'm so sorry...I can see how much you all loved him."

Another nurse appeared in the doorway with a clipboard. "Mr. and Mrs. Tanaka-Hughes?"

"Yes," the woman replied, stepping toward the door, "that's us." They went over to speak with the nurse, leaving me and Mom standing beside the bed in the now almost-empty room. I stared at the smooth white sheets.

"He'll never know we saved the garden," I said, my voice barely a whisper.

Mom came closer and put one arm around me, saying that maybe he somehow knew.

We were startled by a raspy voice behind us. "He knew," Mrs. Murphey interjected. "'Cause he *believed* in you, child. He knew he could go on up to heaven ,and you were gonna do it."

I thought about this and shook my head slowly, the words coming out careful and unhurried, as if Masahiro himself had been speaking. "No... he didn't know for sure. But it actually didn't matter."

Mom and Mrs. Murphey both turned to me, puzzled. I wanted to tell them it didn't matter to him whether the garden was saved, because Masahiro knew it would sprout up and keep growing *somewhere*... just like plants that didn't really die but passed their energy on to new plants, through seeds. I wanted to explain how Masahiro believed *we* were the seeds who would keep the garden living, no matter what. But my throat closed up and no more words would come out. We all stood there for what seemed like a hundred years, until at last the numbness inside me began to dissolve.

"I just wanted to be there again... with him."

Then everything went blurry, and I turned away from the bed and saw Masahiro's Everlasting Tomato Bush sitting beneath the windowsill, still waiting to be carried outside. Collapsing to the floor and bending into the dense foliage that still smelled sharply of the garden and summertime and Masahiro himself, a giant storm finally broke loose inside my chest. Wrapping both arms around the bucket that held his beloved tomato plant, I pressed my face to the dark, damp soil, and watered it with my tears.

28

WE HAD A MEMORIAL SERVICE for Masahiro at the Buddhist Church the following week. Everyone from the garden and the Japanese community was there, including many people I'd never seen before.

There was a lot of chanting and incense burning, and then a priest stood up and gave a speech, which Nacha translated into Spanish. After so many meetings to save the garden, she had eventually become a skilled translator, no longer nervous about her English but now speaking with poise and confidence, her clear voice filling the room. Then the priest chanted again for a long time while each person walked up to the altar to light their own little stick of incense for Masahiro. Finally, we all went to the altar together and bowed, those who knew the words chanted some more, and the service was over.

While everyone stood around in small groups afterward, eating *manju* pastries and sipping green tea, Kazuo's grandson made his way through the crowd toward me and Mom. He motioned to the door, asking if we could speak privately for a moment. We glanced at each other with curiosity and followed.

It was another cold, drizzly afternoon, and the three of us stood under the eaves of the old building, bundled in sweaters and wrapping our arms tightly around ourselves to stay warm.

Kazuo's grandson shifted his weight from foot to foot, looking slightly uncomfortable.

"There's something I wanted to tell you," he began. "It's something that *Oji* Tanaka told us, the night we arrived at the hospital... the night before he died."

We waited, eyes fixed on him.

"As you probably know," he went on, clearing his throat a little, "my great-uncle had no kids, and it's a very small family. So he basically left everything to us— me and my wife."

Mom leaned forward, a puzzled expression on her face.

"Well," he continued, "*Oji* could barely speak anymore, that night... he was so weak. But he told us if anything happened, he wanted you and your daughter to have that property. You know, the old grocery store with the apartment on top."

He paused, and Mom and I stood there speechless, staring in disbelief. "He—he wanted—?"

Kazuo's grandson smiled softly and nodded, bearing a faint resemblance to Masahiro's own gentle smile. "Yeah. You two were obviously quite important to him... like family. He said it plain and clear, he wanted that place to be for you."

Mom was too stunned to speak, her lower jaw suspended as though detached from the rest of her face.

"I don't know if that's even something you're interested in. I mean, it's an old building, with maintenance issues and—"

But Mom was already shaking her head, half laughing and half crying, trying to tell him it was the most miraculous thing that could possibly happen to us.

David Tanaka-Hughes didn't know how much we needed a miracle. But looking from Mom's incredulous face to mine, I think he began to understand. We stood there under the eaves crying and laughing and hugging each other for a long time, trying to find the words to thank him. But it was all too strange and impossible to even fit into words.

"There's nothing in writing," he told us at last," but I wanted to honor *Oji* Tanaka's wishes. So maybe we can make arrangements to sign the papers soon, so I can transfer the property to your name?"

∾

Later, back inside the church, as I climbed a step-ladder to help Mr. Furukawa hang a photo of Masahiro on the wall, I caught a glimpse of Mom standing across the room with a tall blond woman and lanky teenage boy. The woman turned to the side for a moment, and I recognized her as Hattie. The boy, I realized, must be the nephew who suffered from sadness.

It was too noisy to hear their conversation, but I climbed one step higher and peered over the sea of heads, fixing my eyes on Mom and Hattie. *What were they saying?* Would Hattie mention the way she'd spoken to Mom that day at the hotel? Would they talk about the city council meeting... the garden... the cures for sadness? Whatever it was, I could see they were both smiling, and then to my amazement, leaning forward to embrace. Hattie turned to the teenage boy, who reached out to shake Mom's hand.

"You gonna hammer that nail?" Mr. Furukawa asked, tapping his cane against the wood floor impatiently.

I jumped, suddenly remembering the task at hand. The photograph I was holding had been taken by Mrs. Ikeda the previous summer. In it, Masahiro stood straight and tall at the entrance of the garden beside the wall of sunflowers, his straw hat in one hand and a basket of freshly cut herbs in the other. His eyes were closed in the bright sunlight, but on his face was the same peaceful, contented smile I'd come to know so well.

Masahiro "Ojiisan" Tanaka, the caption read. *1917-2012. Master gardener and herbalist, community member, and beloved friend.*

I hammered in two nails and carefully hung the frame, checking to see if it was straight.

"How's that?"

Mr. Furukawa said nothing, just nodded solemnly and lifted his cane off the floor, pressed both palms together, and bent forward at the waist in a long, quiet bow to his old friend.

29

WHEN SPRING FINALLY CAME, we gathered in the garden to have a ceremony of our own and to spread Masahiro's ashes. It was a chilly morning, but the sun shone warmly over everything. Just a week before, the fig tree had sprouted a million tiny hand-shaped leaves reaching into the sky, and the apricot trees were covered in pale pink buds.

The farmworkers had just arrived in El Chorro for the beginning of another grape season, and everyone had quickly gotten busy clearing weeds from their plots and digging into the cold soil, raking furrows to plant corn once again.

The entire Rivas family came to the memorial, looking formal and somber in their fancy church clothes, including Raúl and Yolanda, who had managed to return safely across the border a few weeks before. Lina cried a little when she found out about Masahiro, and Pablo stood very still with his hands jammed in his pockets, not saying anything. He seemed older than when they'd left in November, more serious and quiet, like Toño. But Lina was the same as ever, giving a squeal of delight and throwing her arms around me when she arrived at the garden and discovered that Mom and I were still there.

Earlier that morning, we'd cleared an area in the weeds just beyond Masahiro's herb plot and planted a small *ume* plum tree—the real kind, from Japan—which Mr. Furukawa had ordered from a special nursery. At its base, he placed a small clay urn holding the ashes that were now all that remained of Masahiro's body. We gathered in a circle around the tree and stood in silence for a while.

Then Mrs. Matapang and Mrs. Ikeda told the story of how Masahiro started the garden, and Nacha translated as people spoke about his kindness in helping them to start a plot or providing herbs when they were ill or injured. It seemed that everyone had a story about some time when Masahiro helped with something, healed them, or taught a valuable lesson.

"He didn't talk a heckuva lot, that's for sure," Mrs. Murphey chuckled, "but when he did, Lord almighty, those were some words o' wisdom."

Nacha made her own short, teary speech about how Masahiro was like a guardian angel who had always been there for her family over the years. "I know he was not a Christian," she concluded, "but he lived like one. I am saying a prayer to *La Virgen* that his soul may rest in peace." There were murmurs and nods of agreement all around the circle.

I waited until after everyone else had spoken, just like Masahiro always did, then took a long, slow breath and looked around the circle from person to person.

"Masahiro taught me a lot about life," I began softly. "He taught me that it's a big circle that never stops. I think when he said that, he wanted us to know he'd still be here, sort of. In the plants and soil… and in us. Because we have all his stories. He said that people are made of the same stuff as plants, except with stories and wisdom too. And none of that stuff really goes away… it just passes on."

I wasn't sure if this was making any sense, even to myself, but I wanted to say it anyway. "I don't know if that means he's up in heaven, watching us," I went on, "or coming back as an earthworm or a tree or a brand-new baby... or maybe he's just some sort of invisible thing that's everywhere, like sunlight... I don't know. But he always said there are lots of paths up the same mountain, so I guess he wouldn't mind, whichever one it is."

I paused and thought for a moment. "I didn't always understand, when he said that stuff... but I think I'm starting to get it, a little. Maybe by the time I'm ninety-four, I'll have it all figured out," I added with a small laugh.

But then the laugh hardened in my throat and rose up as a sob. "I miss him. Really, really bad."

Mom and Nacha, who were standing on either side of me, both came closer and put an arm around my shoulders. We stood for a while without saying anything, just looking at the newly planted *ume* tree and little clay jar.

I wiped my eyes and nose with the back of one sleeve. "But at least... at least whatever part of him is left can be here, in the garden."

Bill Tava went over to the young tree, picked up the clay urn and carried it solemnly to where I was standing. I looked up at him in surprise.

"Wanna help give his body back to the land, with me?" he asked softly.

I glanced around the circle in hesitation, not sure I should be the one to do it, but everyone seemed to be nodding gently and smiling through their tears.

"Go ahead," Nacha whispered, giving me a gentle push. "If you want to."

I stepped forward into the circle with Bill, and everyone gathered closer as we carefully opened up the little jar and sprinkled its contents onto the soil around the base of the *ume* plum. Then Mrs. Murphey gave a handful of wildflower seeds to each person to scatter on top, and Bill chanted a Yaqui prayer

to each of the four directions while we all hugged and finally
made our way slowly back to the main part of the garden.

Everyone stayed late at their plots that day, working until
dusk. Mom and I cleared the weeds to prepare a new bed for
planting squash, peppers, green beans, and shiso, then knelt to
tuck our seeds into the moist earth. Finally, when the sun had
sunk low behind the trees, I transplanted Masahiro's special
Everlasting Tomato plant into the corner of our plot, where
it would get lots of winter sunlight and be sheltered by the
mimosa tree and lavender bushes. I knew this was the year
Masahiro had planned to do his experiment, transplanting
the tomato bush to see if it could survive a winter outdoors.
It would grow all summer long and put down deep roots, to
get even stronger and have a better chance of surviving the
frost. Even if everything was just one big circle, like Masahiro
said, I still hoped his experiment would work. He had been so
curious to see if it would.

The light in the garden was deepening from the pale peach
of sunset to a thick dusky blue as I patted the final scoops of
soil around the tomato plant. The air was chilly, the trees dark
silhouettes against the sky, and the first few stars had already
appeared. Mom returned from putting away the tools we had
been using and watched as I tied the tomato plant carefully to
a trellis made of stalks of bamboo.

"You think it'll really survive out here next winter?" she
asked, brushing soil off her hands.

I shrugged, stroking the leaves of the tomato plant that
had lived three years longer than any other tomato plant in the
history of the garden. I knew it would eventually go back into
the soil like everything else, but for now, it was here.

"I don't know," I told her. "I guess we'll find out."

We stood there for a moment, looking at the hairy leaves
and tough, twisted stem of the perennial tomato, finally in the

ground. Then Mom laid a gentle hand on my shoulder and said, "Are you ready to go home, Sweetheart?"

I looked around our plot, at the freshly planted furrows where little seedlings would begin emerging in the next few days, and then around the whole garden that would soon be filled with new jungles of corn, heavy-laden fruit trees, and the sounds of radio and little kids yelling to each other in Mixteco. I thought about the old apartment above the grocery store, where Mom and I had recently moved in and set up our new furniture. We'd decided to keep Masahiro's *butsudan* right where it was, in the living room, adding a framed photograph of him beside the one of his wife. Every morning before school, I knelt before the little altar and lit a stick of incense for both of them, hoping that somehow, wherever he was, he'd know we were saying thank-you.

Mom held her dirt-stained hand out to mine, and I felt the faint trace of a smile begin to creep across my face, the way sunlight gradually warms the soil after a night of frost. I reached out, took her hand, and nodded.

"Okay. Let's go home."

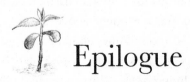 Epilogue

IT'S BEEN A WHOLE YEAR now since we gathered in the garden for Masahiro's ceremony, and the young *ume* tree is once again covered in pale pink blossoms. Sometimes, when nobody's around, I go sit there by myself and look for him in the branches and grass and sprouting weeds. I try to imagine that he's there with me, staring out at the world from inside of everything, or wherever he is. I still miss him.

To everybody's delight, the perennial tomato plant survived last winter, sheltered by the mimosa tree and a thick blanket of straw mulch. Some of its outer leaves and branches died from frostbite, and the plant looked droopy and brown for a while, but in spring it recovered and began growing a set of new leaves.

It's hard to believe that Mom and I have been living in the apartment above the grocery store for more than an entire year. We felt like visitors there at first, hesitant to move things around or change anything, but then it finally started to seem like our own place. Jared and Kim and their baby, Hollyhock, have been living with us for a while too, staying in the other bedroom until they save enough to move back to Kentucky near Kim's family. Sometimes I help take care of the baby or prepare dinner for everyone, and it almost feels like we're a family, the five of us together. Masahiro's small, crowded apartment isn't the house-of-our-own with a yard and porch and white picket fence that I always dreamed about, but that doesn't matter, because the garden and all our friends in the *Nihonmachi* neighborhood are what make it truly home.

Mom still cleans houses, but she doesn't need a second job anymore, because we have a place to live and the TIENDA MEXICANA pays rent to us. So now she can work in the garden almost every single day, planting and weeding in our plot or arranging flowers with Mrs. Murphey.

She still gets sad sometimes, but instead of staying in bed, she usually goes to the garden and spends more time there. It doesn't magically fix everything, like in the story I once wrote, but her sadness seems to pass more quickly than before. Mom says the garden helps just as much as that little pill she takes every day. She's been having smaller and smaller doses, and the new prescription is only half of what she started with. It seems to be okay for now, but Mom hopes someday she won't need it at all.

Hattie still brings her nephew to the garden almost every weekend too, and Bill's helping him make a plot beside Blade's. Mom and Hattie aren't exactly best friends again, but at least they're on good terms, waving to each other across the garden and sometimes even trading some extra vegetables.

We expanded our plot last summer and planted our very own "three sisters" jungle of corn, beans, and squash, along with many rows of tomatoes. There was so much extra food that we had three canning parties with Abuela Jean and made lots of trips to the Day Center and food bank with donations.

These days, Mom is busy helping Grace and Rowena turn the field behind the garden into an actual farm, where they're going to grow vegetables to sell to lots of people. They want to have a table at farmers' markets in cities near El Chorro, and to get people in town signed up for weekly produce baskets. The Rivas and Molinero families are helping too, and they've been having meetings to plan their new farm. If it goes well, Mom might not even have to clean houses anymore, but could become a full-time food grower and florist! Even better, Pablo and Lina's family might not have to work in the vineyards and spend winters in Coachella, but could stay in El Chorro year-round and work on their *own* farm instead.

Mr. Richards has been helping them make a business plan, as well as meeting with Bill to talk about an official gardening program for "at-risk youth." The shopping mall and condos across the street are almost finished, and Mr. Richards even has ideas about how we could sell vegetables and rent plots to people there, to help raise money for our other projects.

Last week, the owners of the TIENDA MEXICANA announced that they're moving away to a larger building soon. At first I was worried, but then Mom had an idea to create our very own store downstairs. We could sell vegetables and flowers and teas from the garden, as well as stuff from other farms around El Chorro, just like Masahiro's family used to do. There's still a bunch of complicated paperwork and planning, but Mr. Richards says he sees "a great potential market" and wants to help. We decided to call our new business the *Tanaka Gardeners' Cooperative*, in honor of Masahiro.

A few days after the city council meeting last February, Mr. Richards surprised us by showing up at the garden one Saturday and asking to speak with the "girl who made the speech." We sat across from each other at a picnic table, and he thanked me for my bravery in helping to show him things he hadn't seen before. As we talked, I saw for myself that Mr. Richards really doesn't have a heart of stone, like we used to think. He just hadn't seen how things looked in our eyes, and we hadn't seen through his. Everybody thought we were in a war that needed to have winners and losers, but it turned out that all our hopes could actually come true at once.

I'm in seventh grade now at El Chorro Junior High, and a few weeks ago, everyone in my English class had to write a creative story about a topic that's important to us. I put off the assignment for weeks, pretending it didn't exist. I hadn't written any stories in the whole year since Masahiro died, and I didn't want to start again. "That's just a little-kid thing I used to do," I told Mom, when she asked why I never wrote in my red notebook anymore. *Who would ever believe those silly tales,* I thought, *with their picture-perfect characters and happily-ever-after endings?*

One afternoon at the garden with Mom, pulling weeds from a bed of tomato plants, I wrestled aloud with the assignment. "I don't even like writing anymore," I complained. "There's nothing to say."

"What about how we saved the garden?" she suggested.

I gave a shrug. "Who would care about that, except us? It's not even a story... just real life."

But then, suddenly, I remembered something Masahiro once told me, the day we were harvesting herbs together and he told me about returning to Japan as a child.

Sometimes the best stories are your own life, he'd said.

I pulled weeds in silence for a while, thinking about this. Maybe saving the garden would make a good story after all... I tried to imagine where I would begin, how I'd describe the *Nihonmachi* Community Garden to someone who had never seen it.

But I realized that I couldn't tell the story of the garden without telling mine and Mom's own story about coming to

El Chorro on our way to Washington, and how we wound up staying. And I couldn't tell our story without the stories of the Rivas family, and Bill Tava, and Mrs. Murphey, and Blade and Abuela Jean and everyone else. And of course, I couldn't tell any of our stories without telling the story of Masahiro Tanaka.

I stood up and brushed the dirt off my hands, went to get my tattered red notebook from under the mimosa tree, and headed away from our plot, down the narrow footpath into the bamboo forest. Settling down cross-legged on a flat rock beside the little meditation pond, with late afternoon sunlight filtering through the bright green stalks and rustling leaves, I opened my notebook, turned to a fresh new page, and began to write.

Glossary

abuela	grandma
Ake mashite omedeto	Happy New Year (Japanese)
bebecito	little baby
bueno	good
Buenos días	Good morning
butsudan	Buddhist altar
carne asada	grilled / roasted meat
claro	of course
contratista	labor contractor
Dios mío	Oh my goodness / my God
Feliz Año Nuevo	Happy New Year (Spanish)
hecho a mano	homemade / made by hand
hierbas	herbs
hola	hello
las uvas	the grapes
maíz / elote	corn
Manigong Bagong Taon	Happy New Year (Tagalog)
manju	a type of Japanese pastry
mija	a short form of "mi hija," my daughter (term of endearment)

Mixteco	an indigenous people from southern Mexico, and their language
muchas gracias	thank you very much
Nihonmachi	Japan-town
obaachan	grandma
paletas	popsicles
qi	energy, life force
Qué preciosa	How precious
Sí se puede!	Yes it's possible / Yes we can!
tatami	a Japanese mat of woven straw
tía, tío	aunt, uncle
tienda	store
ume	an Asian tree related to apricot and plum, with sour fruit
umeboshi	pickled ume fruits
Vámanos, pues!	Let's go!
Viva la huerta!	Long live the garden!
Viva la tierra!	Long live the earth!
Yoeme	Yaquí name for their own tribe